THE ANIMAL

The Animal

RACHILDE

Translated by Lauren Fischer

Foreword by Eleanor Keane

RACHILDE & CO. | SEATTLE

Rachilde & Co., Seattle
© 2024 by Rachilde & Co.

For more information, contact Rachilde & Co.
rachildeandcompany.com
Originally published in France in 1893 as *L'animale*
Published 2024

1st Printing

ISBN-13: 979-8-9916634-0-3 (paperback)
ISBN 979-8-9916634-1-0 (ebook)

Names: Rachilde, 1860–1953, author. Fischer, Lauren, translator.
Title: The Animal /
Rachilde; translated by Lauren Fischer; foreword by Eleanor Keane.
Other titles: *L'animale*. French.
Description: First American edition | Seattle: Rachilde & Co., 2024
Identifiers: ISBN 979-8-9916634-0-3 (paperback) |
ISBN 979-8-9916634-1-0 (ebook)

Cover description: Crosshatch drawing of two figures facing the viewer: a light-skinned young woman with light eyes and black hair, braids twining around her neck, and a kitten near the woman's right shoulder. A red filter overlays the drawing except for their eyes, which are black and white. The author's name, Rachilde, is styled in capital letters, and the title, The Animal, is styled in upper and lowercase letters. With a foreword by Eleanor Keane is beneath.

Foreword

The literary work of Rachilde (Marguerite Eymery, 1860–1953) caused a sensation in fin-de-siècle Paris. By the time *The Animal* (*L'animale*, 1893) was published, Rachilde was a prominent and provocative figure at the heart of the decadent literary tradition. Born Marguerite Eymery in the rural Périgord region of France to an aristocratic mother and a military father, in 1881 she moved to Paris, where she reinvented herself as "Rachilde, *Homme de Lettres*" ("man of letters"), cut her hair short, wore trousers in public, and entered decadent society. She established her own literary salon and fostered friendships with some of the most influential literary figures of the time—notable examples include Aubrey Beardsley, Jean Lorrain, Colette, and the socialite and *salonnière* Natalie Clifford-Barney.

Decadent culture offered Rachilde a valuable outlet for her creative potential and subversive imagination. At a time when modern concepts of sexuality and queerness were nascent, decadent literature reveled in dismantling traditional gender roles, and offered new and challenging perspectives on concepts of sexual dissidence, transgression, and pleasure. Rachilde's work, with its innovative treatment of gender identity, female desire, and monstrosity, marked a pivotal moment in the development of the decadent tradition. We can see this in *The Animal*, which reworks decadent tropes, such as the animalistic "wild woman" and the femme fatale, in order to grant subjectivity to the female protagonist.

However, Rachilde's interest in themes of sexual transgression and gender subversion can also be traced back to her earliest beginnings as a writer, and even detected in her own childhood. From an early age Rachilde was aware that her father had wanted a son instead of a daughter, and in an effort to appease this disappointment she pursued traditionally "masculine" hobbies, such as riding and fencing.

Rachilde's formative years were also marked by an interest in the occult and supernatural. As a child she became fascinated with the family legend of a werewolf ancestor, to the extent that she self-identified as a werewolf even as an adult. Her androgynous pseudonym of "Rachilde"—the name of a fictitious Swedish nobleman—resulted from a séance, and enabled her to assume a masculine literary persona. In these examples we see the seeds of occultism and supernatural metamorphosis that take root in *The Animal*.

Today, Rachilde is arguably most well known for her early novel *Monsieur Vénus* (1884). The work's unflinching consideration of sexual dissidence, horror, and gender subversion caused a *succès de scandale,* and its publication in Belgium led to Rachilde's prosecution in absentia on charges of obscenity. Rachilde capitalized on the notoriety of *Monsieur Vénus* with a prolific range of novels, plays, and short fiction that fused the erotic with the macabre, and established Rachilde as one of the leading fin-de-siècle literary pioneers.

Yet despite this remarkable success, Rachilde's work largely fell out of prominence by the mid-twentieth century. Despite the sexual emancipation exhibited by many of her female protagonists, Rachilde adopted a more conservative feminine appearance after her marriage to Alfred Vallette in 1889, and publicly disavowed feminism in her work *Pourquoi je ne suis pas féministe* (*Why I Am Not a Feminist*, 1928).

However, Lauren Fischer's new translation of *The Animal* offers an exciting opportunity to see how Rachilde grapples with themes of taboo desire, female sexual agency, and the supernatural at the height of her literary career. An exhilarating and experimental work, the transgressive relationships at work in *The Animal* anticipate our modern understanding of sexuality and gender fluidity, and showcase Rachilde's deft alignment of female desire with the feral.

Readers will find much to savor in *The Animal*'s protagonist, Laure Lordès, a sexually hedonistic young woman determined to live on her own terms and act upon her desires. Laure's uninhibited appetite for indulgence—both sexual and gastronomic—is a celebration of female appetite and a refreshing alternative to restrictive nineteenth-century ideals of femininity.

Despite Rachilde's rejection of feminism, Laure's embrace of her own difference and desires holds an undeniably proto-feminist charge. Furthermore, Rachilde's childhood fascination with the hybrid otherness of the werewolf resurfaces in the magnetic otherness of Lion, Laure's adopted stray kitten, which arguably reflects Rachilde's early awareness of her own non-conformity. Instead, such otherness is reframed as both a challenge to reductive fin-de-siècle perceptions of physical normativity, and the boundaries between human and animal. Laure's defiance of patriarchal bourgeois society and her desire to harness her own wildness will no doubt hold resonance for readers seeking a bold, decadent, and wholly memorable heroine.

ELEANOR KEANE

ELEANOR KEANE is a PhD researcher in the Department of English and Creative Writing at Goldsmiths, University of London. Her thesis examines fin-de-siècle fairy tales as examples of queer decadent narratives, and her research interests focus on the decadent fairy tale, literary decadence and the visual arts, and expressions of gender, decadence, and sexuality within the late nineteenth century. Eleanor is a member of Goldsmiths's Decadence Research Centre and the British Association of Decadence Studies (BADS) Executive Committee. She holds an MA in Literary Studies from Goldsmiths and an MSc from City University. Her article "Baudelaire's Celestial Vision of Jeanne Duval" was included in *Volupté: Interdisciplinary Journal of Decadence Studies*, 4.1 (2021). Eleanor co-organized Decadence and the Fairy Tale, a symposium hosted by the Decadence Research Centre at Goldsmiths in March 2023.

THE ANIMAL

1

That night, the young woman wandered around her room for a long time, trying to calm herself. Decidedly, her nerves were rebelling, and she could no longer find the reason for the painful insomnia that had persecuted her for months. At first, she had thought that an illness was threatening her and that she would soon die, as punishment for her sins. Then, thinking that she was relatively good, she dismissed this idea of special punishment. But why did she always fall asleep last, at dawn, when the windows of their bedroom lit up and put her in a daze, as though struck by tragedy? Why was the man beside her sleeping so soundly, without the nervous jolts that tormented her? She contemplated him for hours on end, searching for the secret of his bliss. He would lie there, his mouth slightly open, with the air of rocking himself to sleep as if on water, letting himself be carried along by gentle waves, finally floating on his back with the sureness of driftwood, while she plunged into abysses of unpleasant reflections, felt cold chills running through her body, or experienced intense heat in the hollow of her chest . . .

She was not a spiteful, anxious woman, and yet she resented his too-peaceful sleep. Under the heavy mass of her hair, it was as though a pointed forefinger settled in the back of her mind, twisting her brain, stirring little vipers that gradually unraveled, began to swarm, to hiss, to tangle abominably. The ordinary actions of the day took on mournful hues. Then she relived her childhood years and realized that she had once been freer, if not happier. There were rays of sunshine in her past life, and her memories brought her a scent of woodland lily of the valley that saddened and softened her. Everything she had thought forgotten, insignificant, day and night, took on desperate proportions. The usual misfortunes were accompanied by a feeling of irremediability, of things one could no longer get rid of. A circle was shrinking around her; to break it, it was necessary to live an active life, and she was presently organizing a reform program, intent on submitting it to her lover. She would even bump into him, as if by accident. He would not flinch, his nerves not at all taut in the way of her own, and, discouraged, she would leave him alone, with one more grievance against him.—Darkness breeds in a woman a spirit of opposition, a spirit of sadness that will not let her understand that a man can sleep at the very moment that she is awake, and the melancholy spirit, the worst of demons, for it pities her while leading her astray in a mirage, makes her see normal things in the guise of grave wrongs.—She would get up, step over him gently and start gliding across the parquet floor, touching every object to get used to seeing it through the tips of her fingernails, coming and going like a ghost, her nightgown falling over her bare feet.

That night, a greater tension of nerves brought her to tears. She cried to please herself, but the explosion of this intimate storm gave her terrible theories. One does not cry when one is very happy. She suspected that she was unhappy without knowing it. So there was a presentiment. If she became reasonable during the day, did that prove that she was mad at night? Besides, reason was something manufactured by several generations of men. Learned men had crafted philosophies to suit themselves, while women emerged spontaneously into being with instincts that had to be naive concepts of truth. These revelations were coming from above and below, at the hour of calm and mystery, around midnight, and there was nothing to say that the ideas of the day were the best. The young woman, more particularly, without a doubt, was splitting herself into two existences: the daytime and the nighttime; and she came to the conclusion that, perhaps, for her, it would be necessary to sleep during the day and be active at night. If this was the only way to get rest, she would change her routine, that was that.

Sitting on a swaying bamboo armchair, she tapped the carpet with her toe to speed up the movement and wondered if there were many creatures like she, awake among the sleepers. Evoking feminine silhouettes, she grouped them around her armchair, in meditative poses, some sly, elbows buried in the folds of the bolsters, looking at the husband with a mocking eye that scrutinized even in the shadows; others, swaggering, leg tensed, ready to pounce, to flee from her meeting with the incubus; moreover all of them honest lovers, like she, not dreaming of a new love—simply dreaming of the impossible. How many worried men, at this midnight hour, for how many women wandering barefoot through the bedrooms? Oh! Of course, there were the workers and the revelers, the latter yawning, the former doing naughty things; but of this heap of vulgarly busy individuals, she was not concerned, she was thinking of the men who watched with a sharp eye over the fantastic *ideas* illuminated by the moon, or who wander, without any avowed goal, in the inky blackness of nights hermetically closed to all of the rays of the sky, who wander around looking for the end of torment without complaining aloud, without exclaiming, with the untimely brusqueness that characterizes them. "But, sacrebleu . . . ! What time is it . . . ?"

Yes, for men, there are hours. Time is subdivided into reasons for being . . . time, eternity, that which has no reason for being . . . "At such and such an hour," says this gentleman, "I get up and I am respectable." "At such and such an hour," says the second gentleman, "I go to bed and I am not respectable." Is it not extremely ridiculous to go from good deeds to less good deeds on the swing of a pendulum? This anxious woman felt that there was no man, at this moment of supreme nervousness, who was in communion of thought with her. They all had a reason to be up and about, and when the reason went, they quickly fell back into nothingness, into the blackness of sleep. This was her superiority over them, even if she suffered for it—this funereal vigil over nothing—and she spread out, enthroned, swaying silently like a sick queen in the midst of a motionless court of chimeras.

The faint sound of an animal's paws made her brow furrow. Above her, from the ceiling, came the trotting of velvet feet. Their bedroom, a former photographer's studio, was glazed on the east side and had a ceiling of frosted glass set in lead rhombuses. Very thick, this glass let in only a dubious amount of light during the day, but on moonlit nights in summer, a sort of phosphorescence radiated from these rhombuses, seeming to cut into a green snow, or a hail cloud ready to burst over the earth in streams of strange opaline liquor. At midday, this ceiling was nothing out of the ordinary, and the east-facing window, concealed by yellow silk curtains, immediately brought to mind the traditional pose of a bride for an album card; but at midnight, when the curtains were lowered, the lamps extinguished, and the room was felted in a fabric of darkness, this ceiling took on a somewhat fearsome allure.

This small photographer's apartment on the sixth floor had no attic, the ceiling was the roof, and they had refrained from putting up any grating. On this plain roof, one could hear sparrows and swallows hopping about in season. The slightest rainstorm would wreak havoc, and the last few drops would give off harmonica notes that would fill one's brain with exquisite melancholy.

The young woman listened to the sound of the footsteps; it broke the dangerous spell of her reveries and dispelled her fevers. She reached the end of the room facing the bed, and slowly climbed an iron ladder attached to a skylight opening in the ceiling. She groped for the rungs. Her head soon touched the skylight, she removed the bolt, then listened again. From a distance, the sleeper's breathing was quiet; nothing had awakened him. She knew that the lead-encased rhombus was difficult to lift, and she took terrible pains to push it without making it screech on its hinges. She mustered all of the strength of her back and shoulders, and opened it. When she arrived at the highest rung, she put her arms through the opening, smelled the fresh air, and felt a child's joy. To raise this skylight and satisfy a vague curiosity, she had put as much persistence into it as escaping from a prison. The next day she would laugh about her escapade, but in that moment of nervous crisis, she found herself with all of the audacity and perversity of a criminal. The young woman, her feet clinging to the ladder, her head in the wind, leaned with both arms crossed, as if on the balcony. She saw nothing out of the ordinary, just a cat running away to the next chimney.

It was a lovely night, one of the first warm nights of spring. At this height, a wayward breeze was blowing, and a few clouds reflecting the gold of the moon seemed to be rising from the streets, along with the muffled rumblings—which one could not quite explain—of late-night carriages. This glass roof dominating the house was bordered by a tiny wall of glazed brick, isolating it from the neighboring attics. The surrounding chimneys, like the trees of a forest, crowded around the flat surface, so plain, so milky, always so swept clean by the winds, washed by every shower, that it looked like a mirror of that mother-of-pearl white stuccowork with which the Chinese have the secret, and with which they adorn certain pagodas. And, to complete the chinoiserie, the peacock-blue sky was iridescent with nebulae, imitating the shimmer of lacquer, and adorned with an enormous moon the color of fresh gold, of an absolutely artificial kind. The young woman, distracted, breathed and blinked her eyelids; her tears, already forgotten, dried along her cheeks, and she became ecstatic. For a moment, the chimneys amused her, for there were all sorts of them. Chimneys topped with mushroom caps held in place by thin straps, with tall top hats, with halos working during the day, drawing pious images on the pure air; good old chimneys, in country straw hats, in piped bonnets; grande-dame chimneys, a silver arrow in an ebony bun; jester chimneys, ending in a weasel's snout, with a sort of three-decker cap on one ear; religious chimneys, haloed by a cap with flapping wings; then all of the big bourgeois chimneys of brick and stone, outlining enormous bodies, waistless and armless, bodies of decapitated men, their arms tied to their backs; all of the working chimneys, the army of the thin, the distant, the indecisive, barely outlined in tremendous depths, whose squadrons are commanded by the giant factory chimneys.

The young woman heard scratching on the frosted glass, and the velvety trotting began again; a whitish object, barely detaching itself from the surface of the roof, began to glide stealthily; two brilliant points, leaping like shooting stars, jumped across the sky, tracing elongated orbs around the woman's head. The cat was both frightened and delighted by this head lying flush with the roof like a ball ready for play. Covered in hair, the ball intrigued him above all by its superb tail. The breeze blew the long strands of the young woman's black hair in all directions, veiling her face where her eyes no longer shone, but looked like two holes. The cat approached, one of its front paws bent, ready to flee if the ball turned hostile, but it did not move; and then it stared at her, whiskers bristling, plunging its two brilliant points into the two black holes, wondering if through these holes one might not catch a glimpse of human mysteries, the key to the world's riddle! And then, suddenly, the cat would bounce away, its tail in a hoop, its spine rounded, its ears lying back. The young woman was childlike enough to mew softly. Suddenly, furious mewing resounded behind the chimneys, a brown object falling from the sky. This second, bolder cat came straight for her head, swore in her face, and in succession three other cats flew out of the tin pipes, falling on the pale lacquer lake where their claws produced scratching sounds that set one's teeth on edge. She was careful not to frighten them. With all kinds of winks and gestures, she invited them to play with the big silky ball she seemed to represent to them, not even noticing that her feet were going numb and the ladder rung was bruising her soles. On the wind of freedom that buffeted her hair, the woman was inspired by the strange inhabitants of the rooftops. Ah! The dear animals, beggars of the impossible, and making themselves at home in the springtime! They also summon chimeras. She could hear them, in the electric hours, uttering their feverish cries above the bedroom, imagining them prowling around like little lions seeking prey; and when love was finished, unhappy, disappointed, scolding, they wept their anguish, sometimes with the cries of children whose throats are being cut, sometimes with the scraping of broken violins!

Not quite sure what she wanted with them, the herd of beasts lined up in front of the woman. It was a very clear night, and they could understand one another in the light of the festive moon. The white cat curled up closest, acting as a link; the black cat sat on his backside, grave, tail curled with dignity; and the gray cat, and the fawn cat, and the pale cat—a sickly youngster, this one, who'd come late to the Sabbath—posed interrogatively. The woman laughed softly. They all mewed in unison, stretching their necks and waving their plumes; then the white cat began to creep forward in fits and starts, shivering with mischievous pleasure, ducking under the chin of the disheveled head that no longer frightened him. A gust of wind lifted the black hair, gathered it into a single sheaf and spread it over the cat. Then it was all over. Caught in this trap as if in a skein of silk, he rolled and twisted, squealing with glee. All imitated him. The seduction of the thread had worked. What cat could ever resist something that serpentines on the ground? When the devil, wrapped around the trees of paradise, was making his speeches, Eve's cat was undoubtedly watching from her corner for Satan's slender tail lost under the turf: and her descendants, the tomcats, will never tire of watching for the wriggling bait, the funny little bit of tail! It is their folly, their ideal; they see it on every side, in every rug, in every rut, on furniture and on rooftops. True poets that they are, they would abandon their pâté to follow, through the air, the trail of a virgin's thread.

The young woman fished them out one by one from among the fragrant casting net. The black cat rubbed against her breasts, the gray cat frolicked with the longest strand, while the fawn cat rolled over the pale cat, one on top of the other, frenzied spools, spinning in opposite directions and tangling the skein most horribly. She suffered a little from all of this tugging and pulling, but for a crown she would not have given up the game. She was indeed the joyful companion they'd been longing for; under the veil of her hair, her face attentive, she appeared to them the most adorable of females. Who knows the secret hopes of certain gutter paladins? Who can tell the ardor and audacity of their desires? Did the black cat not dream, on a carnival night, of meeting a living star, a dark comet with a trailing train of tufted silk? Who knows if the big black cat did not dream, on evenings when female cats were scarce, of leaping fantastically with all four paws onto a moon with Persian eyes, or an angora star? Do cats not imagine the winter sky as a pelt from which sparks would fly, and, melancholy as they stroll in the shade of chimneys, do they not think that thunder is the great purr of a goddess?

The gray cat, having performed a series of artistic weaves, found himself almost strangled, and the woman had to rescue him with patient dexterity. To thank her, he gave the signal of a hellish dance. All of the beasts, leaping together from dizzying heights, looked as if they were tumbling down from the clouds. Sometimes, silhouetted against the roundness of the moon, the blackest became immense, ears erect like diabolical horns, paws splayed across the span of this golden globe, crushing this world between his steely muscles. The white cat, leaping in turn, in an extraordinary pose of a skinny nude girl, darted through a nebula, glittering with silver dust, and the others, pirouetting, rising on their sharp claws, like ballet dancers on their toes, waving their tails, at the ends of which twinkled stars, crystal flowers blooming on fabulous furry stems or jets of fire ending in whips. The woman, delighted, flicked her tongue at them, hardly feeling the cramp in her ankles. Following the rhythm of a wild quadrille learned from who knows where, the four large ones danced around the youngest. They rushed at him, tumbling over each other, mingling their limbs to form an octopus bristling with fangs and claws.

They hissed, imitating the sound of a blade placed on the grindstone, then stopped to creep back with the faces of furious panthers, and suddenly, braving the precipice of the street, they suspended themselves from the edge of the roof, climbed back up, glided toward the woman on invisible wheels, suddenly opening heraldic maws and spitting musk, their tongues curling at the tips, like red sabers.

The young woman finally laughed out loud; fearing she'd wake the neighbors, she hid her face in her arms, for the surrounding roofs were full of attics, and a few dormer windows might well be open on this fine April night.

When she straightened up, the whole gang had vanished: a trick of enchantment could not have been quicker. Only that big black devil of a cat remained, obscuring the moon. He approached, counting his steps, sniffing the frosted glass. Close to her, an inch from her face, he let out a long, fierce mew, puffed himself up, laid his ears back; then he examined the entry to the room and gave a nudge to the corner of the skylight. The woman stroked him. His face was fierce, yet she was so enamored that she had no reluctance to clasp him close to her again; so he sniffed the scent of her hair, which he mistakenly took more and more for fur . . .

Back at home, very disheveled, the young woman had to light a candle and recomb her hair.

"Where did you come from?" murmured the man, who only awoke upon feeling her shivering beside him. "Come on, Laure, you are not being sensible."

A little bewildered by her adventure, she did not dare answer her lover, who went back to sleep.

And the young woman, her eyes dilated in shadow, vainly seeking rest, plunged back into the abyss of her memories.

2

Laure Lordès was born in Estérac. In Estérac, the little southern town, there was a big house as silent as the bottom of a well. Two copper ovals of the *notaire* emblazoned the house above its moss-green door.[1] The stone stoop was green, the same green as the door, and the walls were adorned with fines herbes, and the signs were verdigris, and the window panes had emerald tints.[2] Inside the dwelling, the notaire's offices were lined with green cardboard boxes, tinged with blue. A well-worn carpet, which must have once been green, absorbed one's footsteps.

Behind the house, a grassy courtyard between the cobblestones was engulfed by vines whose thick leaves were so dark in color as to be frightening; they were neither crazy vines nor Virginia creepers,[3] and they mockingly produced a few grains of verjuice that never ripened.[4] In one corner of the courtyard, a

1. French *notaires,* who draw up contracts and are more like American lawyers than notary publics, use signs with two oval emblems.

2. Walls illustrated with fines herbes were called herbarium wallpaper, which was popular in the nineteenth century.

3. Crazy vines refer to corkscrew vines or Liana plants.

4. Verjuice, the juice of sour grapes or crabapples, is used in French cuisine to make sauces.

plant of angelica blossomed to phenomenal height. The soil in the enclosed courtyards is full of vagaries: parsley is sown there, and it comes from hemlock. They secrete poisonous juices near humans, and the most harmless plants often distill poisons, which they hide under a rare sumptuousness of vegetation. The notaire of Estérac had first sown fuchsias in this corner of the courtyard; on his side, an unknown breeze had brought a seed of angelica; the fuchsias, well cared for, smoked, weeded, watered, potted in winter, had all died one after the other; but, on the other hand, the chance seed made a stem, the stem a beautiful plant, and the beautiful plant soon became a shrub.

Since the angelica were so successful, the notaire decided on a bed of angelica. It was the sweetest pleasure of his life. Oh! The huge green angelicas, like fairy parasols! Oh! The angelicas with leaves drooping like curtains, the angelicas mixing the flavors of the sacristy with the flavors of jam, the perverse angelicas whose sweet ribs are eaten by children and kill rats, so say the old women! Oh! The perfidious angelicas who love the corners of walls where it is dark, the oven-like heat, and gloom, who amplify odors and turn them into aphrodisiacs for the animal senses! Monsieur Lordès, the notaire, had a tender respect for these plants, which had come here like gypsies and had embedded themselves in the bad soil as if they were at home. He pruned them himself and offered the stems sacrificed by his pruning shears to the few clients of his firm. In season, Madame Lordès candied the thick stalks, carefully blanched in boiling water, and crystallized them in a sugar syrup that constituted the most important secret of her household.

Angelicas made all dreams come true; they took the place of gardens, baskets, vegetables, trees, arbors, vistas, and skies. They distinguished the law firm and the notaire. One would say, "Monsieur Lordès's angelicas," or "our notaire's angelicas," quite simply. For the past fifteen years, they had astonished clients. Priests came to see them with puzzled nods. Strong-minded people would say they were "as tall as Lordès's angelica." Women smiled at the perfumed plants and, removing their gloves, touched the singular satin-finish of the greenery. Monsieur Lordès would then indulge in an easy joke: "Back in the days when we dressed in leaves, I would have had enough to cut beautiful skirts for these ladies." If anyone raised an eyebrow, Madame Lordès, a thick creature, bared her breast and triumphantly made herself an apron from the glossy material. They stood before the angelica trees in thoughtful poses, chatting in the low tones of devotees in church, calculating the limited number of surprises that nature spares for good people. Often, through the broad leaves, behind a branch, shone two eyes, two carbuncles.

"It is Laure who is there," Monsieur Lordès would say.

"The girl," Madame Lordès would add, "is always stuffed in there like a saint in her alcove."

Her mother had brought her into the world past the age of forty, having already despaired of her birth, and little *Dieudonnée* could ransack their favorite plants: she was spoiled.[5] When she took her first steps on her own, she was led before the miniature forest and dazzled by the marvel; reliable witnesses saw her clap her hands and heard her exclaim with delight. From the age of reason, she penetrated the dark canopy formed by their dwarf grove and became accustomed to the strong scents exhaled by the broad leaves. Saturated with this perfume, nourished by the candied stems, shaded by their umbels and flowered from time to time with a cluster of their modest white flowers called

5. Dieudonnée is a French name meaning "Gift of God."

"nun's flowers," it seemed as if the child was, too, a kind of angel destined to astonish the city. Besides, it is worth mentioning that she wouldn't hurt a fly. She was reserved, corolla-pale, grew immense hair, black hair, and her breath embalmed those who, by chance, kissed her on the mouth.

The child's mood was unusually singular.

Innocent, yet troubled by ridiculous ideas, her fear of evil was so intense that it could have been mistaken for remorse. Had she lived too long in her parents' womb . . . before living, to know that one can be guilty without committing a crime? All frail, all pale, with her dark eyes rimmed, her hair rolling in a single braid down her back like an enormous snake, she would walk on tiptoe, peer through the holes in the locks, and slip, coughing, into the kitchen when a man was chatting with the maid, and she would magnetize you with cold caresses until she got what she wanted. Well brought up, far too well brought up for her size, she knew there were some stories she shouldn't try to unravel, and instinctively averted her eyes when a nurse unswaddled a male infant. She was pretty and appreciated her advantages from the age of seven; the first compliment she received surprised her less than her first punishment. Once, she asked her parents a strange question. She wanted to know why the Jesus on the cross was wearing a belt . . . if he was dead? And if there were naked Jesuses in churches. Her mother told the story to the whole town, finding it so delicious. Her father laughed about it in the café among the old gentlemen and let slip, on this scabrous subject, a few aphorisms for the occasion. "We are foolish when we are little." "Girls, in spite of everything, are more advanced than boys." "Children should be told the truth, even if they were not born under angelic skies." He ended his speech on how to bring up children with a sentence from a work by Victor Hugo, whose bewildering concision appealed to him.

Madame Lordès, believing her daughter to be chaste, inclined toward the precociousness of her virtue; Monsieur Lordès, a Republican since the 1870 war, opted for a natural curiosity that denoted uncommon intelligence.

The child was not only advanced, she was rotten—a lovely rot of white mushrooms and embellishment. She was *naturally* decomposed, like bubbles that form on stagnant water, on ponds where hemp begins to ret, whose bubbles, being very pretty, are iridescent with all of the shades of the rainbow and have nonetheless risen from infection. Born under the angelica, perhaps in the flash of passion that the fabulous height, the unexpected, almost unhealthy beauty of these plants had aroused in her parents, conceived on a proud day, she carried in her veins (green on her white skin) terrible ferments. Preserved, she would be a delicacy of love; barely blooming, she had the contradictions of flowers growing sadly and deteriorating walls stronger than rocks. No other innocence could match hers, since she was born with the germ of evil. She was sin itself, and it was not for her sins. This vegetating notaire and his wife combined all of their sins into a single branch, which sprang up suddenly in the middle of their autumn after ferocious fertilization. All of a sudden, their backyard garden, moldy with peelings, animal entrails, and dishwater, sent up angelica, and, imitating it, they conceived an angel of darkness. Does one know what it takes for the naive bourgeois to go about the shameful goal of procreating a being who insists on not being born? There must be such a thing as cold lust. And Laure Lordès, the suave angelica, had undoubtedly emerged from that kind of lust. Seemingly insignificant details make monsters. All it takes is the combination of all of these details to possess the secret of the magic formula that creates appalling femininity. This notaire, always seated, counting and writing, concealed troubling things. What can be born of a man who is always seated? A man whose brain does not travel, whose eyes are only busy under a green lampshade, looking for ways to increase a sum? Mechanics for money invent mechanics for love, and can healthy beings be born from mechanics?

Nothing could be more honest than the sight of this courageous man going to consult doctors on his case. Madame Lordès, abandoning the poetry of burning candles to the Mother of Christ to obtain a child, had ingenuously submitted to all of the tortures, the result being to sanctify her. Ah! They, each of them, had put much courage into it! Succeeding with angelica was not *as* difficult as succeeding with a child. If only they had tried wholeheartedly at the beginning of their marriage (which was already a loveless marriage), but after fifteen years of union, they felt horrible disgust. Imagine a man spitting into his hands and saying, "Let's go!" and a woman reciting litanies in libertine poses, to judge what they must have suffered, then forgive each other when they finally became proficient in their routines. Behind the emerald windows, the moon no longer dared to contemplate them . . .

All this will melt away, be mitigated, thought the husband, *as soon as a conception is announced.* To activate the angelica cuttings, had they not bought a batch of pig manure, the filthiest manure after human manure! And never would foliage spread a sweeter odor than this privileged foliage . . . The child born of their little infamies would be of a precious species: they both vouched for it by the purity of their intentions, if not their deeds. Unfortunately, neither love nor nature blessed the fruit of their efforts. No pleasure made their hearts so tender as to conceive a generous heart, no renewal made their flesh blaze so as to emit human flesh. They made an angelic child, a plant; but, in addition to its negative virtue as an ornamental plant, it had the gift of acting as an aphrodisiac. They poured into this graceful little mold all of the spices they had eaten, drunk, or breathed, all of the equivocal sweets, all of the witchy liqueurs, all of the aromas of musky decomposition. In a latent state, they infused into these blue veins, green by dint of being blue, all of the sensual poisons with the miraculous science of caresses and the appetite of all lovers.

After the birth of their daughter, their kitchen continued to resemble a chemistry laboratory. As they had turned to the magic of exciting foods to procreate, they continued the feast to give themselves the strength they needed for conscientious breeding. Incessantly, Madame Lordès prowled around the furnace, a large, dark cast-iron machine embedded beneath a monumental fireplace, in a vast room tiled with greenish sandstone, one door of which opened onto the courtyard. Monsieur Lordès was well versed in the kitchen, and the maid, a heavy farm girl drawn to the city by the lure of rich food, did her best to help both spouses, while not forgetting to tithe. Eternally lit, the fire in the dark oven cooked and reduced the infernal stews of the Midi, which gourmets devour blinking their eyes and feigning to conceal their appetites, as if it were a pregnant woman's desire or a libidinous act. Bordelaise dishes spiced up with condiments from the four corners of the world, meats rubbed with garlic and cayenne pepper, red pepper sauces, sprinkled with parsley and fine herbes more or less poisonous, cheeses with shallots, charcuterie with white wine, were the order of the day, and this everyday fare would have made a blasé pleasure-seeker shudder. These good, somewhat sad people, one almost devout, the other almost philosophic, were mixing the meals of decadent Romans, and this diabolical diet no longer disturbed their sleep, they couldn't even find taste for anything anymore.

Everything was bland to the man who sprinkled his eggplants with a light pinch of gunpowder, a fertilizing system once recommended by a wily peasant on his return from a prickly appointment, and everything seemed permissible to the woman who introduced a pinch of sorrel salt into roast mutton to prevent it from spoiling, when the leg, being large, had to *do three times as much*. In summer, watermelons and melons, half emptied of their seeds and then filled with old brandy or kirsch, were placed on the sideboard of this vast kitchen, as cool as a convent refectory. In winter, strings of mushrooms and boletes, sliced into rounds of tawny leather, dried under fumigations of lavender wood, contained, in their tinder-like bitterness, veritable heartburn. Wide-mouthed bottles held gherkins from sunny lands, ears of wheat picked before they were ripe and macerated with nutmeg, and truffles, the royal poisoning of the valued maids. During the month of September, all of the tables were garnished with the remains of angelica. Here they congealed in candy sugar, there they were infused in rum with coriander and aniseed. Everywhere, you could see the enormous stalks stretching out like sections of the same snake, of a beautiful dead green, ready to be reborn light green with the addition of alum and violet flowers. Madame Lordès did not yet use arsenic to obtain a metallic green, but she would one day, the way seasonings were developing in this house.

The couple's conversation ranged from the latest way of candying the plant without altering its firmness, to the need to stimulate digestion. Monsieur Lordès—clients so few and far between—would go into a certain cupboard in a hermetically sealed room with no furniture, study jars, crystal funnels, Joseph paper, and look through old manuscripts borrowed from the *curé* d'Estérac.[6]

Laure watched the many sweetenings, soaked her fingers, sucked a piece of cinnamon that she discarded once the syrup was gone. Gluttony grew on her like a religion. The mystery of the room, the church-like tiles in the kitchen, the notaire's sententious tone, all led her to believe that the liquorists were priests, making hosts in which the divinity was pleasantly replaced by sugar.

There were few guests in the notaire's home, but every visit was a new subject of culinary discussion. On Sundays, after Mass, they sat in the salon, a gloomy room adorned only with a terracotta hanging lamp, pierced with holes that let the green hair of a fat plant fall through, with the transparency of spun glass. The pedestal table, with its solid mahogany legs, was immediately covered with strange bottles. Men were served brandies spiced according to the new formulas, while ladies were passed the box of angelica, cookies, and sweet liqueurs, with the customary exchange of pleasantries.

"It is better to pay the bill of the pâtissier than that of the doctor."

Besides, they couldn't see beyond the end of their nose. All this sugar, attenuating the effects of spices and the fire of spirits, provided them with unctuous intoxications from which politics and love, two hot topics in the provinces, were absolutely excluded.

The captain of the gendarmerie, an intimate friend of the house, with the dumbfounded air of a sentry out in the cold,

6. Joseph paper is a filter paper invented by Joseph Montgolfier (1740–1810).

tasted the green, pink, yellow, and amber liqueurs like an ox that had inadvertently drunk eau de toilette. He had only one response: "It smells like soap, your damn concoction!"

And the notaire fought against this resistance with all of the destructive instruments that can be compressed onto a liquor label. "Let us see, Captain, there is that one again, hand me your glass! Tell me about it! It is my latest creation. I found the recipe in a fashion journal and had my ingredients flown in from Paris."

The captain swallowed and remained dreamy for a moment, wanting to proceed with good will. "Yes, yes," he concluded, "you have capital . . . a mixture of eau de cologne and lemon . . . I do not hate it . . . yet . . . No, here, I will rinse with a little pure rum: do you mind?"

The notaire, vexed, feigned noisy gaiety: he would go out for a moment, then come back with a jar of plums, which set the ladies alight, for plums will always stir the caretaker lying dormant at the heart of every provincial . . .

Laure, seated on a stool, tasted everything in all of the glasses, with no determined preference, then took away a stick of angelica to play tea party. She liked to eat her treats when she was alone and no one was watching. She would often crawl on all fours behind an armchair or into a corner of the courtyard, where she would crunch, chew, sniff, and taste in imitation of the little dogs that devour with shifty eyes and their tails between their legs, not liking to be bothered. This little girl made only crude poetry: her pretty movements or the amusing attitude. Already very much a woman, because without thinking herself, she made one think, and always anxiously fearing evil, like a beast that wants to break free but is afraid of being hit, liquors, sweets, games, rewards, medals of honor, or fine dinners seemed to her things all the better for being forbidden some days. She had noticed, judging with the logic of a cunning little animal, that everything that was very good was accompanied by a feeling of doing evil. Real pleasure was only to be found in concealing one's enjoyment. Eaten on the sly, angelica was better than Sunday angelica, taken in front of society with the restrained gesture of a sensible lady. When their maid's cat stole meat at the service, it was sometimes the meat that he had already been offered and had not even wanted. Laure Lordès knew how to keep her mouth shut, refuse a second plate of cream, and, at the service, bend over the plate, stick out her tongue, and *lap it up* like a cat.

3

Laure fell ill with languor around the age of ten. She hardly ate at all, seeking out impossible dishes, raw vegetables, or cakes that she craved come soup time. Her mother would not let her, as they say, dig her heels in; she did her utmost to find for her a cinchona that was not too repulsive. Her father felt her pulse with a ceremonious emotion that he did not bother to conceal, and which impressed the little girl, making her withdraw more and more into herself. Classes, catechism lessons, visits, and errands to the farm they owned near Pivasse, a hamlet close to Estérac, were eliminated; piano lessons, drawing classes, and embroidery lessons with the neighboring lingerie maker were eliminated.

Perhaps all this should have been replaced by gymnastics lessons, but in Estérac, gymnastics had such a well-established reputation for indecency that no one gave it a second thought. The house call doctor spoke of growth and nervous disorders; he ordered a ferruginous wine into which Monsieur Lordès religiously introduced one of his latest creations, so as to perfume it.

In the courtyard, where she went to play, she breathed a lukewarm, musty air, masked by the scent of the robust angelica trees. She would walk solemnly, reflecting on the sadness of being isolated, to amuse herself, she told herself that she would have dearly loved a little brother. At the study, there was a young clerk of fifteen, a lackey so sickly that he could have been mistaken for a child; but Laure would not go near him, instinctively hating cripples, for he had one mucilaginous eye and examined people with a disheartening stare. From time to time, in the large green window overlooking the courtyard, the clerk's eye would appear as a bloody stain against the glass, and Laure would shudder with a disgust she made no attempt to conceal. Besides, this clerk could only see to write, her father claimed, and he still had to rub the paper with the tip of his remarkably sharp nose. She made her way to the dark corner where the sacred plants flourished, penetrated their obscure canopy, and stretched out somnolently in the shade of these tasty branches, which impregnated her with their strong odor like the scent of the flower's secret mating ritual. What was she thinking? Nothing good. She went round and round in her life, trying to break through the confines, finding it already too narrow. So do the young beasts in the cage, twisting and turning to discover a way out of their nasty beatings. Without bitterness, she did not reproach her parents or teachers for the punishments they had given her; she could not conceive of a life free of punishment, that is, free of the desire to do wrong. Her most profound wisdom was a colossal indifference to anything that did not present her with the immediate enjoyment of gluttony or coquetry. Savage as a redskin, her various civilizations were summed up in the desire for forbidden fruit, ribbons, and, above all, glass baubles! Pearls, buttons, and sequins delighted her. She had invented a silent game of extraordinary simplicity. It consisted in peddling pendants from an old chandelier relegated to the back of the attic.

These faceted pieces of crystal, these prisms that she placed over one eye while looking at the sky, filled her with bliss. Her father had explained to her at length the curious experiments that can be produced with the aid of a prism, and the cigars lit under the magnifying glass heated by the sun, and the very precious decomposition of the solar spectrum, but the child, without batting an eyelid at Monsieur Lordès's pedantic demonstrations, answered nothing, took the dazzling shapes, then ran off to play with her glass baubles in a less learned manner. She would line up bits of cut crystal, first the smallest, then the biggest, call the wall "monsieur" or a chair "madame," and the ruthless trafficking would begin.

"If you wish, monsieur, I will sell you three diamonds for three knives. Ah . . . ! You do not want to? Well, you keep your knives, I will keep my diamonds."

She had little enthusiasm for her dolls. A being who says "mommy" and "daddy," all one's life, all around, seemed a rather unpleasant prospect for a lady. For a little girl, the simulacrum of such a being did not interest her in any way. She would arrange to have the most beautiful doll in town and put it in a dresser drawer without worrying about it. The gilded, illuminated books exasperated her and were no different from doing lines, and the supposedly instructive games sometimes lulled her gently to sleep on her father's lap. The notaire dreamed only of the precept: *to instruct by amusing*. It was his fetish, his monomania. He used everything as a springboard to launch into three or four technical phrases designed to astonish his schoolgirl; unfortunately, the schoolgirl, who was annoyed by this macabre clowning, could only see the way to *amuse herself by learning*, and she quickly gave up serious games, returning to the glass bauble. Madame Lordès shrugged her shoulders. A girl always knows enough when she can count pearls to a hundred.

One Sunday, the cook beckoned Laure from her doorway. She abandoned her bag of diamonds in the angelica and ran to the kitchen. In the half-light of the vast room, near the stove still burning like the alchemist's crucible, Laure spotted a boy of her own age holding a basket the size of a huge nest, full of birds' eggs.

"What's this?" she asked curiously.

"Ah! Mademoiselle," replied the maid, "this is your mother's remedy, a real treat I assure you. They're magpie eggs for making an omelet. In the countryside, it's said that a magpie egg omelet cures languor."

The boy had randomly collected magpie eggs, blackbird eggs, goldfinch eggs, nightingale eggs (the brown ones with red dots), and dove eggs.

Madame Lordès entered, followed by the notaire. The mother was ecstatic, and the father burst out laughing, while agreeing that women's remedies often have unexpected effects. He trampled on the idea that, since the egg contains the principle of poultry meat in its thinnest volume, the eggs of birds, such lively, agile creatures, should . . . He became confused and glared at the bewildered peasant.

The maid prepared the frying pan and melted creamy goose fat while the children cracked the eggs with their hands that were adept at handling microscopic objects. The eggs amused them with their lentil-sized yolks and whites that would not have filled a thimble. It was a real truant's picnic.

"Have breakfast, my children," said the notaire with importance, "and you, Laure, my little one, be kind and do the honors.

You must thank this boy for the trouble he has taken, and forget that he is not of your class."

He went out.

Madame Lordès discreetly let them finish their supper alone. Laure could already sense that the remedy was working. She questioned her host feverishly and showered him with spoonfuls of jam, which she put on her own bread for him to taste. They exchanged names. His name was Marcou, a diminutive of Marc. He was about to make his first communion, like she, and he knew things about the catechism that she did not. The maid patted them on the backs, repeating, "Bless my soul, a little husband and wife!" Greatly cheered by the pure wine they were allowed to pour over the omelet, they decided to play with diamonds in the courtyard.

She strut in front of the peasant, dressed in a new blouse and strong studded shoes. She led him under the angelica trees, and they sat down in the semidarkness of the green canopy, which was as fresh and fragrant as their affluent kitchen. The boy's eyes widened as he admired the gigantic foliage.

"Are those beets?" he asked.

"You are silly," Laure replied, pinching him. "They are sweet plants that one eats on New Year's Day in cans."

"Let's get out of here! My head is spinning!" he added.

"No, let us stay here and play sleepaway. Here, like this. We've stopped at an inn on the edge of a forest; thieves are looking for us to steal our diamonds . . . Hide them under your smock. We're a gentleman and a lady. What shall we call ourselves? Never mind! Never mind! We won't have names; I cannot think of any. Besides, we're scared, so we cover our faces."

She threw her apron over his head, forcing him to lie down beside her. He obligingly imitated the sound of thieves trying to demolish the inn. From afar, Monsieur and Madame Lordès, surrounded by their Sunday visitors, heard the high-pitched cries, the furious *hou! hou!* of the children, and whispered, "Eh, the kids are having a ball, aren't they! Our Laure will have an appetite tonight!"

"You who laughed at my magpie's egg omelet," added the triumphant mother.

But soon silence returned, a singularly profound silence. The angelica trees, motionless in the warmth of this spring afternoon, seemed to be accomplices in a mystery. Their appearance was so impenetrable, their leaves so enveloping and their aroma so dizzying, that one might have mistaken them for large, devious ladies spreading their petticoats over something that must not be seen . . .

Laure held the boy close to her. They looked at each other, their eyes drowned in languor, their skin moist and their lips dry. Their gullets could no longer formulate human sounds; they had the grunts of beasts that sniff each other out and recognize each other. Marcou resisted at the start of this new game; he laughed, struggled, did not dare give her his bare skin, even though it was chilly. He only gave in when she kissed him tenderly on the chest, where he had small breast spots, like she, which she proved by pulling aside her blouse. They rubbed each other, muzzle to muzzle, heart to heart, knowing they were doing wrong, the boy desperately afraid of the parents or the maid bursting in, and the girl afraid for the thrill of being afraid, to convince herself that she was doing something forbidden. They did not know the name of the game, nor why they played it. Their need to rub each other was driven like a sudden appetite for green fruit. They savored each other with inflamed teeth, scarcer saliva, in the same way as those who taste barberry for the first time. It was delicious and painful, and they immediately understood that it would never end, that they would not be able to appease this maddening hunger for tangy sensations, that they were biting into the void.

Not only was the game resumed each time the boy returned, but the pretty little Messalina-in-the-making also invited the gendarmerie captain's sons to join in—two big sneaky boys whose father would take them to the notaire's to eat angelica . . . Until the day that Marcou demonstrated these audacities that got the maid to throw him out—the clumsy one sacrificed to those better mannered, who knew better how to hide their instincts as filthy, skirt-sniffing young animals.

"Well, well! Little Marcou does not come back anymore," Madame Lordès remarked one Sunday at the dinner table.

"My word, madame," retorted the maid who was distributing the bread, "it is for the best. These peasant boys have such filthy manners!"

Laure took a piece of bread from the basket, fixed her eyes on the maid, and whispered in a soft voice, "Louise is right, *Maman*, this little boy has bad manners. He says bad words. I do not want to play with him anymore."

And the maid, magnetized by those black eyes, sparkling with liquid moistness, felt moved and did not want to explain anything to her masters, out of respect for one so affected by naivety.

He returned. One market morning, he was seen sitting on the stoop, his head bowed, all heartbroken, showing a human sadness that was painful. Laure, standing by an open window, examined him with a withering stare, pursing her lips, she would never forgive him his clumsiness. What a clumsy fool! To jeopardize the whole future of such a well-invented game! At least the gendarmerie captain's sons knew better than to take ridiculous initiatives. Marcou was devouring her with his eyes. He would have come in through the window had it not been for his terror of the notaire. His new coat puffed around him like a blue balloon, and his skinny legs, finished off with big, dusty leather shoes, gave him a most pleasing appearance. Laure burst out laughing and turned her back on him. Someone arrived to close the window, and Marcou withdrew slowly, a fold creasing the middle of his forehead. He was alone now, given over to the dreadful consolations of little men too soon awakened. While this naive heart clutched at the anguish of a first heartbreak, Laure Lordès asked for her hat, the one with the mauve satin bows, to go and pay a visit.

Little by little, along this Rue d'Estérac, a new kind of epidemic developed. Either because this part of town had an unhealthy exposure, or because, situated below the church square, there was more shade, more stench of streams, more corners of moldy walls, more indulgent carriage doors, the children of this street died one after the other, especially the little boys. Families were not immediately frightened by the disease. If the children lacked appetite and color, it was because they ate too much fruit or sugar. Mothers came to the Lordèses to beg the notaire's wife not to spoil them on Sundays.

Madame Lordès smiled aristocratically. She enjoyed her role as protector of the young ruffians. She did not mind if they experienced indigestion in her home. If Laure sowed treats on this young herd of gourmands, she was quite free, and that only proved the goodness of her heart.

"We're not rich," declared Monsieur Lordès, "but when we treat our young guests, we always have a box of angelica at their disposal. Children are children, for heaven's sake!"

And the big kitchen, on public holidays, filled up with ragamuffins. They put extensions on the table and made crêpes. From the study, the notaire supervised the courtyard games, that is to say, he talked with his friends, pointing out from time to time the "soldiers of the future" who were simulating the assault on the green plants, or the "future housewives" who were undressing his daughter's doll in a corner. Laure, always wary of females, would try to gather them around a respectable game and then ran wherever her duties as mistress of the house called her. She seemed to love noise and furious arguments, and would escalate any quarrel to escape for five minutes, followed by a favorite.

A cordial understanding reigned among those most enamored by her charms. Stripped of vanities and boastful quarrels, this miniature of humanity bore a striking resemblance to the other.

On a certain Thursday, during which Laure hid herself completely under the leaves because it was raining, the office clerk came to the angelicas; there he encountered the sons of the captain of the gendarmerie who were waiting and almost seriously ruined the recreation. The boys lost their heads, stating that Laure was there. The clerk said nothing of what he had seen: he withdrew, making no attempt to return. Laure was informed, and she shrugged her shoulders, repeating, "You are fools!" for she hardly feared that man's one eye that disgusted her so.

Now entering her eleventh year, Laure continued her classes. For her development, she was always allowed a host of fantasies, and the worst escapades were tolerated under the specious pretext that a child in training needs movement (and also so as not to disturb the maid). Sometimes she was entrusted with errands to suppliers. Sometimes she was asked to inform her mother that she had detention. During her lessons, she got news of the brothers from the sisters. She knew where Jacques played marbles and which streets Jean took to go to Sunday school. In this way, she was always late. The catechism was a wonderful meeting place. It was a success with everyone, and the boys and girls could mingle without being blamed when they gathered in the square. The maids would gossip on their own, while the older children would slip each other notes and the younger ones would elbow each other. In the catechism class, amid the jostling of empty chairs, Laure prepared her recruits, made her choice, and offered them pictures of piety from her drawing folio. Her allure was so serpentine, her gestures so supple, so enveloping, that one would have had to be a fool to resist her.

Some were sentimental, swearing "a lifelong oath of friendship." Others, jealous, cried when she was unfaithful. Depending on their temperament, she was either their darling mother or their darling wife, but she almost always spoke to the boys younger than she, dreading the already trained boys of thirteen and fourteen who stared at her with mocking or obscene grimaces. To these she commanded respect with regal attitudes, absolute indifference, and often coldly polite phrases.

One day, the son of a college professor mischievously weighed her hair, asking if it was "the tail of his papa's horse." She delivered him a formidable pair of slaps, and the sound reverberated throughout the church. The curé interrupted the lesson to chuckle deeply into his large book. Here was one who did not pull any punches! Hand games, naughty games! And he scolded the boy, the notaire's daughter not being, after all, any ordinary girl.

The white dress ceremony was a triumph for Laure Lordès. Her little men, awestruck, contemplated her all Sunday, dressed in muslin, lost in a halo of candlelight, and prettier than a saint. Snacks were served in all of the houses, and fine wine and generous liqueurs flowed for the chosen few.

These divine joys, mixed with regrets, were the cause of much emotion. Mothers dabbed at their daughters' eyes, telling them about heaven and the sacrifices they had made so that their little ones could wear costumes worthy of the solemnity. Laure, knowing that it would be particularly noteworthy, publicly asked her parents for forgiveness for all of her sins and misdeeds. Perhaps she seriously thought to rid herself of the load, which she considered heavy, seeing as she found the opportunity. Madame Lordès sobbed, murmuring, "My poor angel! Ah! Ladies, I feel nothing but contentment."

Monsieur Lordès, despite his well-known republicanism, had to leave the salon, too emotional not to burst out in front of the neighbors. He fled to the courtyard, near the angelicas, and wept like a calf. Those white muslins had turned his heart upside down: the effect of *œufs à la neige* when one has eaten too much.[1]

---

1. *Oeufs à la neige* ("snow eggs") are a dessert with egg-shaped meringues floating in vanilla custard sauce.

4

Laure, who was no longer called petite and whose skirts were lengthened, remained well-mannered for almost a year. Her mother had revealed certain things to her in suspicious language that made her tremble. She even imagined for a moment that they knew everything.

Madame Lordès kept telling her, with a look of compassion on her face, that a young lady of thirteen should not be running the streets. "There are some minor ailments that happen to you around the fifteenth spring, sometimes earlier in the region of Midi; it is appropriate to lower one's eyes in front of a young man. There is nothing more natural, for example, than playing with dolls, because you will get married and have children. But before marriage, you must be careful to avoid opportunities for coquetry, and not to jump onto a gentleman's lap to cuddle him, as you have had the deplorable habit of doing." In general, mothers, already too old to relate to their daughters in the intimacy of these solemn moments, excel at making these kinds of mixed sentiments. They say what is unnecessary when it would be better to either remain silent or to clarify things brutally. Madame Lordès did not fail to cloak her discourse, as befit the occasion; she had pitying and mocking faces, knowing looks sent to their maid with laughter underneath, and Laure, thinking only of her games, tormented herself for a long time with the idea that she had been caught behind the angelica. But how? Who had told? She made the most meticulous inquiries, even innocently questioned the clerk bent over his paper. He turned his red eye to her, and with a truly frightening expression, replied, "Well, what is it? You are bothering me!"

No, the clerk, no more than anyone else in the house, knew nothing about her morals. So what did her mother's double-entendre phrases mean? She brooded on this for nights on end, in the absolute shadows of her percale curtains. Racking her brain to guess the mystery being hidden from her, she stopped sleeping, stopped eating, and turned pale. Finally, she discovered, in the monstrous logic of a lecher, that her childish antics, which she thought were simply forbidden games, were supposed to happen between grown-ups, under the labels of "love" and "marriage."

From there, she considered that motherhood could well come out of these different exercises, and she almost fell ill, so much did her perplexity increase. What was the dangerous exercise? She spent her time poring over dictionaries, recalling details and women's conversations, questioning the maid and the seamstresses who came in during the day, creatures always ready to tell dirty stories. She was only slightly reassured by an old beggar woman who told her, half jokingly, half angrily, that children were only made when they were old enough. Children could not make children, that was obvious. Madame Lordès was astonished by her daughter's sudden change of behavior. Laure cloistered herself, wasting away, shunning opportunities for coquetry, as instructed, but for some unsuspected flirtations at home. The poor dear, thought her mother, she's being overly rational. Like all beautiful natures, she went from one extreme to the other, becoming enthusiastic about virtue; soon she would be talking to them, no doubt, about becoming a nun. How often the mother, moved, had contemplated her daughter reciting her ten rosary beads in the morning, and how often, moved by old memories of reading, the mother had attached silver-white wings to the little devotee's back, while Laure wondered, interrupting her prayer with a vague look in her eyes, "Am I, or am I not, pregnant?"

This hideous fear of motherhood, weighing down this young adolescent body, bent and broke it, and the mother, blissfully admiring this prodigy of reason embodied in a thirteen-year-old schoolgirl, repeated to the father, "Our daughter is already a portrait of me." The unfortunate thing is that thirteen-year-old girls are never a portrait of their forty-five-year-old mothers. No electric current flowed from the slenderness of Laure to the thickness of Madame Lordès. What can stale senses teach those newly aroused? And besides, considering the many stages of affectionate motherhood without bias, what lessons could one find there that would guide a fresh soul against the shame of the body . . . ? When a daughter is three months old and represents nothing more than a bundle of flesh in a state of panic, women cannot get enough of caressing this little inert object; when the daughter is twelve and actual tenderness would be a diversion for her, the mother, most of the time, weans her of caresses, first because it is not customary, and above all, because the child, already too familiar, is showing her will, and mothers no longer have such a keen interest for her. But it is not when she feels nothing that a child needs caresses and noisy tokens of affection; it's when she feels pleasure—my God, yes, the word can be used loosely—*pleasure* in being caressed that we must sacrifice ourselves to her and surround her with loving care. But mothers call this age "the ungrateful age": in the twilight that descends their children's faces and makes them wince, they haven't seen the dreadful wrinkle of unfulfilled desire fade; mothers are beasts, they take after the beast before they take after the angel, and yet their vanity shows them their portrait reduced only to the form of the angel. "So, poor little angel, you are getting ugly, you are getting willful, capricious: my kisses no longer have the same pleasure in roaming over your gangly little person; if your lips hunger for females who wish to prelude the games of love with innocent play, go to the pretty streams, in the shade of footpaths or mint, with booties or bare feet, and, seeking out angels of another sex, city ruffians or village ragamuffins, develop together either your normal appetites or your unnatural ideas! Caress! Caress! Something will always come of it, if only disbelief in the significance of virginity! We honest mothers do not need to know, since we are careful now if we were not once . . . !"

Laure, full of the troubles of a thankless age, ended up bedridden. The doctor advised the parents to get some fresh air, and Monsieur Lordès remembered, very appropriately, that their farm, near the hamlet of Pivasse, was located in excellent pasture.

The young flirt was brought to the countryside. And it was there that the girl found her first serious toy: Marcou Pauvinel, her farmer's boy, Marcou, who, thanks to her, had really become a very special kind of brute.

One morning, the teenagers met in the vegetable garden; Marcou was pulling weeds, and Laure was enjoying a slice of fresh butter.

"We're not kids anymore, eh, Marcou?" she said in a benev-olent tone, having nothing better to do in this lost land than to renew the old conversation.

He crouched on his heels, arms drooping. "No, we're not kids anymore."

They did not dare laugh at each other yet, very embarrassed. Roses were blooming all around them, so fresh that each one seemed to send out a sunbeam from its heart, and it rained pink light on the lettuce.

Laure added, "One cannot play anymore when one is our age."

She thought of the piercing cries of women during childbirth in this innocent corner of nature. In Estérac, recently, the hab-erdasheress had given birth to a child, and all of the neighbors had heard her. There was silence, and the roses seemed quieter than other flowers. Over the garden, the sky was as clear as silk.

"We sure had fun . . . !" said Marcou, looking up.

Laure felt like calling for help. Ah! It is only the first sin that counts . . . and she had committed her first sin with Marcou. It could reclaim them, that sin of rubbing up against each other . . . and he was ugly, this peasant, he was *a man*. Without him, she would ignore the shameful desires of her flesh, and the cries of childbirth would leave her cold.

"No, Marcou, it is not possible, I do not want to," she declared feverishly.

The boy had not asked for anything, but he flinched. In the darkness of his soul, he understood that she was thinking of the little angelica game. He chuckled. "What do you not want, Mademoiselle Laure?"

He was no longer the little pink "piglet" bringing magpie eggs to Estérac. Marcou's hips jutted out from under his clothes like two stakes. His red hair fell over his greenish eyes like a bramble on a precipice, and he extended bony, muddy legs that could jostle you, but when he raised his brow, his eyes lit up with lust, his blond lashes white as a sun's silver lining.

Flattered by the title "mademoiselle," Laure laughed too. "There is no need to explain, Marcou, just shut up!"

He pulled up a blade of grass, a species of wild oat, and sucked it.

"I'm not saying anything, I'm just working . . . One must work to pass the time when one is bored."

He kicked his bundle of weeds, then stretched out like a lizard on the path, blocking her way. With a slow gesture, he now amused himself by sweeping his strand of wild oats up and down Laure's legs, stopping at the knee and going down to the ankle, not uttering a word. To save herself, she would have had to climb over his sprawling body, but she did not have the courage.

"Marcou, leave me alone. I'll tell my parents." She gave him a gentle kick.

"You will not tell them, Laure," Marcou replied softly.

"I am too much of a young lady, I made my first communion."

A breeze blew in, spreading the fragrance of the garden. Laure felt her brow grow heavy. Marcou's gaze lured hers. In the pure silence of the roses, in the midst of this little Eden, she uttered this dreadful sentence as one would throw garbage onto a heap: "No, you see, Marcou, I am afraid of having a child."

"You are silly, Laure, children are not conceived through playing."

"You think so?"

"Of course. I know all of the games. If you wanted, we could love each other like mates."

And still he tickled her with his blade of wild grass.

"Yes, that is an idea, two lads who love each other as friends," murmured Laure, her eyes gleaming.

Marcou immediately turned red, then pale. He straightened up and took her by the hand.

"I have a *hiding place*," he said. "Let's go. There is no danger where I lead you . . ."

They crossed the garden, the courtyard, and Marcou said loudly as they passed the farmhouse, "Come and see our oxen, mademoiselle, they do not bite."

It was a superfluous precaution, as Mother Pauvinel, busy sorting linen for the laundry, was not worried about the young lady. In the vast ox stable, they hesitated for a moment, their palms burning as they rubbed their still undecided hands.

"It is so dark in here!" sighed Laure, thrilled.

"Like being in church. It is getting late. Shall we go up to the attic, on the hay?"

They climbed a light wooden staircase that trembled beneath them, and when they were in the dry hay, in this great ocean of dead waves, they found themselves so happy that, at the same time, they let out a little howl of joy. The dormer window in the attic formed a blue moon, streaked by the flight of swallows, and doves came to peck at the edge of this hole in the sky as if at the edge of a nest. Laure rushed headlong into the hay. Marcou joined her, lifting up armfuls of dry grass, covering her with bursts of this great bath of withered greenery, drowning with her in an abyss of intense delight that scorched their skin.

He wanted to undress her. Laure resisted, since for her, modesty consisted in clothes. Anything but that. They argued, growling like two young dogs, showing their whitened teeth across the grass, biting either hay or flesh, slapping each other soundly and kissing cheeks with grimacing muzzles. Finally, he knocked her over, deprived her of her smock and gradually stripped her naked. Laure, gripped by a superstitious terror, thought she would be punished for her nakedness. She mechanically made the sign of the cross. Through this blue hole, God was watching her, she felt it, God who sees everything, sin or good deed . . .

"Do not! Do not! I do not want to. It makes me ashamed now . . ."

The truth was, it scared her, and she cried for half the day, huddled in the hay, not daring to go back down the stairs without him! Without him, for the lover had been forced to abandon her to go and tend the oxen . . . !

5

In the glow of light through a stained glass window, the young *abbé* preached modesty, and with a slow gesture, scattering rays from the end of his muslin sleeve, he blessed them, calling them the sheep of the good shepherd. Very upright, his head pale, his eyes almond shaped, he had the silhouette, minus the dragon and the sword, of the knight of Saint-Georges seen at the far end of the nave. Laure listened to him without hearing him. She had come here, followed by her maid, because it killed time and church is the only salon you can have in a small town. She seldom went to confession, taking communion three times a year, but never missed an exercise during the Month of Mary, as she always hoped to find an "opportunity."[1] An inner fire consumed her; she feigned great cheerfulness about everything, disguising it out of habit, and despair gnawed at her; she no longer knew what to do with her skin. A woman before her time, already ready to marry, despite the apparent ingenuousness of her seventeen years, Laure no longer had the pretext of childish games to soothe her fevers; she no longer vacationed at the

---

1. For centuries, the Catholic Church has set aside the entire month of May to honor the Virgin Mary.

44

home of the Pauvinels. As her classes ended, her companions dispersed or returned to the confines of family life, she remained isolated between a father always busy with paperwork and a mother preoccupied with frivolous details. In the study, scribbling, nose glued to his work, always the same clerk, that Lucien Séchard, nicknamed "the Cyclops," a cripple, whose red eye had so revolted her at various times of her childish antics. In the street, no one passed by . . .

What Laure was looking for was a slave, a man who would love her for the allure of pleasure, who would not disrupt the course of her life as a decent girl, who would submit to her every whim, and above all, who would be as innocent in appearance as she. And, as she watched the young abbé walking away from the pulpit, *she thought this.* Behind her, her maid, a befuddled old creature, a kind of sister to the poor, was making a monotonous sound with her lips as she prayed the rosary.

Since the departure of the fat, bouncy, giggling cook Louise, a sort of odd bird was accepted into the house, and nothing cheered up the silent courtyard any longer, the dark foliage of the vineyard, the angelica against the blind walls; nothing seemed to laugh around the Lordèses, neither people, nor animals, nor plants.

Greener than ever, the windows were rarely opened, the notaire fearing the drafts because of his rheumatism; Madame Lordès, ill and quite obese, only went from her armchair to the kitchen, where the pitch-black furnace burned eternally without casting a glow.

Laure dropped her brow into her hands. Hymns were sung, and fragrant vapors wafted from the flower-decked altar on which stood, in a gaudy earthenware cachepot, an angelica given by the notaire's daughter.

No, this could not go on. The nights were too awful, and it was foolish to struggle like a virgin when she was no longer a virgin, thanks to the fatal inventions of Marcou, the lout who had made her a woman long before her time! No, she was renouncing modesty and the conventional somnolence of innocence under the white veil! Any love would be less shameful than her solitary depravities. Love was in her blood, that was for sure, and she would mutter dozens of rosaries later, when she bore resemblance to the old maid praying behind her! Why should she have to wait so long for a husband? And with husbands a plenty on the streets of Estérac! You would not believe how even-tempered these city boys were. Where had they found relief from their fevers? As children, they had pined after her braids; today, they all fled from her or greeted her from afar. So were there corners for kissing that she did not know about yet? For getting married? She was not keen on it, having guessed that marriage did not satisfy creatures of her ilk. She dreamed of another life, a convent, if you will, but one where there would be two of a different sex, perpetually tête-à-tête on velvet cushions.

She was looking for an opportunity to give herself away and had laid all her plans so as not to risk any scandal. Oh, she would know how to dictate her terms, she possessed all of the necessary knowledge, and she lacked neither wit nor beauty. Yes, this young abbé was tempting her now. The more she thought about it, the more she realized that salvation was at hand! There were rumors about him; he was thought to be in disgrace in Estérac, a very small town for him, coming as he did from a major city.

Until something better came along, he replaced the curé, who had become incompetent.

The thought of sacrilege did not faze Mademoiselle Lordès; she learned some odd things about curés, as her father did not mind speaking ill of them when the captain of the gendarmerie dined with them. "They're men like any others," said these two gentlemen as they sipped their coffee, leaving Madame Lordès, who did not like these piquant speeches, but who always ended up laughing heartily to herself . . . Men like any others, only they kept up decorum and only had fun when it was assured. Since young girls and priests were forced to feed a beast deep in their bowels: Lust, without ever admitting its ravages, could they not unite against the enemy? Put their beasts together, park them in the commune of pleasure? Laure raised her brow and examined herself, her eye sliding sideways under her eyelashes. She had been freed from her smocks and was dressing according to her tastes, in very tight clothes, molding her curves, which appeared simple and childlike at first glance. She wore a brown woolen dress with a black draping jacket, tight around the waist, a Parisian model that her mother had let her choose at La Reine Berthe, Estérac's chic store. Her heavy hair, braided into a single enormous plait, rolled back and forth across her shoulders, as if endowed with a power of its own, flapping at her sides or snagging people as it passed. Wearing an otter hat in winter, a peacock feather hat in summer, she had no other hats. It was not a question of economy: she felt that this kind of hairstyle emphasized the length of her eyes and left her face free for the day when she wanted to rub it against the face of a neighbor. On that day, would she have time to untie her braid, and where and how would they meet? Fawn-headed or bird-headed, she did not care about fashions. Her mother received a newspaper called *Le Courrier de l'Élégance*, which she never opened, eschewing the readings and engravings that make women out of wood.

A singular beauty, her face was elongated while retaining the look of a serious, remorseful child. She had a rounded nose, a little wrinkled at the tip, a nose of a panther or cat, her drooping lips chiseled on both sides into voluptuous commas; her complexion, very matte, shaded under her eyes; her eyebrows, shaped into arrowheads, pointed at the corners of her brow, were lost in the root of her hair; her eyes were endowed with extraordinary mobility, as their pupils retracted and became nothing more than a line, a thin black fissure crossing the brown eyes striated with yellow.

Laure was revived, hourly, by a series of mindless little counsels that mothers think to repeat for the honor of the body, and Laure, mad about her own body, did not bite; she loved herself too much, moreover, she was not always logical when she had to be. Ostensibly, she lived by Estérac customs. What more could one ask of her?

Quite satisfied with the result of her examination, Mademoiselle Lordès moved her prie-dieu closer to the choir balustrade. She had a privileged seat, in the highest ranks of public figures, and could hear the Latin phrases that the abbé murmured. The priest's voice was harmonious, tinged with disdain as he turned to his flock of pretty simpletons and old devotees. In this delicate springtime of the church, among the waves of incense and bundles of flowers, how many withered hearts for how many fresh daisies lit the luminous golden background of the altar? Ah! If he heard confessions of naive women who were determined to tell him everything, he too must possess terrible knowledge! He knew the secrets of the languors that take to bed on rare lazy mornings, and the irresistible desires when, in the street, one brushes against the handsome boy in the neighborhood. He knew everything and was therefore capable of anything. Laure, through the lightning-spiked wisps of smoke, gazed at the young man adorned with his crown of brown hair.

What was he thinking, he whose fiery eyes would not willingly lower? The false enthusiasm of the organ's majestic sounds excited the young girl's imagination and led her to lean over the balustrade to get a better look. Their eyes collided. It seemed to her that the priest had twitched his eyelids for a second. Laure turned to face her maid.

"Joséphine," she said, "you will have to go back alone, I want to perform my contemplations."

The maid slowly unscrewed a boxwood egg, put her rosary back in its shell, and joined the group of women leaving. The candles were extinguished, and the last devotees moved away. Laure remained at the altar, meditating. The altar boys, in turn, ran off, jostling each other to move faster. The young abbé, on the threshold of the sacristy, was removing his lace rochet, taking precautions to keep up appearances in the process. Laure was watching him.

She crossed the space separating her from him with a quick step, without making the traditional genuflection of devotees in front of the altar, and entered the sacristy.

"Monsieur l'Abbé," she said in a faint voice, "I would like to talk to you."

"I would like to take this opportunity to thank you for the beautiful plant that you donated to our Month of Mary. It looks like a palm tree, this angelica . . ."

Laure leaned against the doorframe. As she remained motionless, her face looking very pale in the dim light, the priest sensed that something was wrong. He asked, suddenly worried, "What can I do for you, mademoiselle?"

She replied, placing her hand on her chest, "It hurts!"

"You are suffering! Ah! My God!"

And he was frightened by this creature, almost a stranger, who came straight to him for help. He had already come across those begging eyes and that feline, love-tortured mouth, and he had already said to himself, as an observer of women, that this girl must be suffering physically or hiding some moral torment. She looked mysterious in her dark clothes, like a bronze urn, but so graceful and strong . . .

"Excuse me, Monsieur l'Abbé, I am afraid . . . I could not cross the church, I would fall . . . my maid has left . . . Please allow me to sit down and do not leave me, I beg you."

Stunned, the priest mechanically stepped back and closed the door, never taking his eyes off his strange visitor. In what danger was she? Or was he?

A pilot light burned in a small alabaster vase, illuminating them with a murky glow.

Laure moved toward one of the carved wooden stalls in the sacristy, then suddenly, with a faint cry, she fell backward, toppling over from her full height and risking a broken spine in the process. Her head struck the tiles and bounced; she no longer moved, lying still like a dead woman without anything being disturbed in the exquisite order reigning around her; her hair framed her head, extending her otter cap like a blanket of fur; the folds of her skirt enveloped her properly, and she took on a more ideal pallor beneath the darkness of closed lashes.

As a man who is human before he is a priest, the abbé took his part in the adventure; he slipped the bolt so as not to give rise to useless comments if anyone entered, and ran to seize a burette from the credence.

Upset, he repeated, his fingers trembling, "What a story! Goodness me! The poor child!"

He caught hold of a piece of muslin that dragged along the ground, rubbed her temples and nostrils, and tapped her palms. Laure still did not move.

"And there is no fresh air here," he added. "If she has died . . ."

Distraught, he put his ear to Laure's chest: her heart was beating very fast indeed. He hesitated for a second. No, he could not do that. Opening a bodice, even for a good reason, was too scandalous. He knew himself well, he would not touch a woman's breast without losing his sense of right and wrong, and this girl had such a strange beauty that it would be prudent not to expose himself to any more foolish temptations.

His conscience held him back, now, on the dangerous slopes; he dreaded a new storm, and, moreover, recalled the last sermons of the bishop: "Let us not give in to slander, Monsieur l'Abbé, that is all there is to it."

He sat in one of the stalls, cold sweat running down his back, staring at the unconscious woman, counting the minutes. The sacristan could come, an extreme unction could be requested . . . a marriage could be declared; the bell could also collapse from the top of the steeple, a stained glass window shatter into a thousand pieces. He expected everything, except to get out of there without scandal. And for a few seconds, he lived several lives. It concerned his position, which he had made his honor, his voluntary sacrifice. He did not want to succumb to those wretched women's bodies falling, as if raining, from the heavens, where they would probably never be welcomed. No! No! He got up to shake her, to push her out, dead or alive. And then he stopped again, thinking of that charming sister he had so desperately loved, that other woman for whom he had stripped himself of his fortune, his share of earthly happiness. Oh! The little sister, the little fool . . . cherished as in biblical times . . . Did she not have black eyelashes? His head bowed, his eyes closed, his fists clenched.

When he was called Armand de Bréville instead of Monsieur l'Abbé, he did not yet know that you can suffer from lovesickness even in fraternal affection. He knew it today, because every time he approached a woman, he remembered the dear sweetheart just by the emotion he felt . . . All of the mistakes he had made thinking of her . . . Oh! The little sister with the heavy hair braided behind her shoulder, the one who shared his games, the one who said, "I want a golden bunny!" and who, thanks to the spontaneous renunciation of her brother, had obtained a handsome husband, a man of money . . . The young priest saw again the avenues of a park, luxurious greenery, a romantic château, and two little white arms tied around his neck: "Brother, carry me!" Oh, women, women! He was not a virgin and he had not had a mistress; he had loved while ignoring love, and he suffered cruelly, with scornful lips, as is fitting for a well-born boy to suffer. As for God, that eminent figure in his world, he respected him. That is all there was to it.

Laure made a movement. The abbé awoke from his reverie.

"At last!" he exclaimed, leaning over her.

The girl opened her eyes and looked confused.

"I am embarrassing you, Monsieur l'Abbé," she said. "I will try to get up."

She straightened up, clutching her knee.

"I will explain, Monsieur l'Abbé," she continued, her voice very gentle. "It is a nervous illness that throws me to the ground without my having the time to foresee its attacks. I fall anywhere, and I am always very afraid of being left alone. My maid was far away, I could not see anyone . . ."

She breathed, circling her arms over her forehead to arrange her hat, smoothing her hair.

"You must not talk about this accident," she added, "because I am ashamed of my illness, and my parents would be upset if it were discovered . . . You, monsieur, are a confessor, it is not the same thing, a confessor is like a doctor . . ."

She is hysterical, thought the abbé, moved by these phrases uttered in a low, timid tone, mixed with a kind of childish resignation.

"Why should you be ashamed, mademoiselle? God is no doubt testing you terribly, but he has his eye on you. Our sufferings erase our sins. Saints have claimed that our physical ailments redeem us from the years of purgatory."

He spouted these somewhat empty words while examining this supple creature who rose with such chaste gestures and maintained such a dignified bearing. He was delighted to know she was out of danger, but a profane curiosity nagged at him about hysteria. He was now in the presence of the mysterious evil that had once tortured the possessed women of Loudun, an evil that produced both pain and pleasure. Ah! If he had dared, he would have questioned her. Instinctively, Laure chose the most interesting situation for a woman destined to seduce a priest; and, besides, could she not be in the specious category of feigning hysterics?

"You know, Monsieur l'Abbé," she continued, "I do not care. I do not want to get married, but my poor parents are sorry to hear that I will not find a man who wants me. Then I will have to enter a convent, perhaps . . . ! It bothers them."

She headed for the door.

"I thank you, monsieur," she said humbly, "and forgive me: I did not consider that it was improper . . ."

She fetched the key, shaking it in the lock for a moment. The abbé rushed over, very upset. "I slipped the lock," he stammered, "because I was afraid of curious onlookers."

And he stepped aside to let her pass. She took off, shuffling like a wounded bird and leaning on every chair in the church. When she reached the porch, the abbé, who was following her with his eyes, felt a chill run down his spine. She could fall victim to a second attack, break her skull, despite the thickness of her hair. It was silly, this cassock preventing him from offering his arm to sick women!

Charity must, of necessity, take on worldly trappings in certain circumstances . . . or you no longer have charity!

When the padded doors closed with a deep thud, he took a breath. His conscience took over again. After all, he had had a narrow escape. The sacristan would know nothing of this painful accident, and the altar boys, always so depraved, would not comment on it . . . Let us not give in to gossip . . . In his turn, he left the church, forgetting to bow at the altar, according to sacred custom, because he was alone.

The next day, the abbé de Bréville went to see the notaire.

He thanked Madame Lordès for the angelica and asked, in a detached tone, about Mademoiselle Laure's health. The latter came bearing cookies and liqueurs, her mouth laughing, her eyes somber with dark shadows. She spoke little, but when the priest withdrew, she accompanied him to the staircase, and, as he said his last goodbyes, she placed a finger on her smile, looking fixedly at him. He responded to this sign of intelligence with a discreet wink. No, of course, he did not want to betray her, this child so concerned with her parents' dignity, but he very much regretted this little secret between the two of them; when he confessed it, he would be embarrassed or awkward.

For her part, Laure wondered if he would ever discover her. *I hope he understands me,* she thought in exasperation. *We'd make a lovely couple! It is going to take a long time, I am afraid. So many obstacles to overcome, my God!* She had confession, chapel visits, and then . . . Where would she go from there, if he remained incorruptible? He must be aloof, she supposed, just remembering the care he had given her. If he thought she was innocent, he would guard against temptation; if he thought she was perverted, perhaps he would distance himself from her out of disdain, and Laure made her calculations while counting the stitches of a tapestry work destined for her mother's party.

A month passed for the girl, creating chimerical plans. One morning, she thought of dressing as a man and sneaking behind the Estérac parish church, where there was a terrace shaded by hazel trees. The servant of the abbé was an old Beguine woman like Joséphine, their cook; what's more, she was said to be as deaf as a post.

She abandoned this mad idea that very evening for another extravagance: she would write to him, tell him of her great passion, force him to respond by threatening him with scandalous suicide. She got up at night, started a draft of a letter, and realized that the words, on white paper, were revoltingly crude. She could not string these things together . . . either because she did not have the art of sentence structure, or because she was ashamed of undressing her soul as the Marcou peasant used to undress her body. She resolutely gave up on love letters. Reflection after reflection, she came to deplore the theatrics of the fainting spells. How could a sick woman tempt a healthy man! Ah, if they did not come to an understanding right away, the game was lost, for opportunities to meet were too few and far between. She had fits of tears deep in her pillow, fits of fury, clawing at her breasts and cursing this priest who now stretched over her life like a mortal shadow. And on Sundays, when she listened to him preach in his harmonious voice, she would start dreaming again, caressing a naked figure amid the austere folds of his priestly vestments.

On the eve of a religious ceremony, she went to find him in the sacristy to ask permission to confess in the evening after the Angelus. He greeted her timidly, replied that he was busy with a dying man, a landowner whose house was three leagues from town, and asked her to come back the next day at Low Mass. The next day, the conceited old priest, the infirm one, heard her confessions. She despaired utterly, and from then on abstained from the sacraments.

Laure, in her peignoir, holding both ends of a kerchief to her clammy throat, spoke to the clerk in a jerky tone, not even looking at him.

"You understand well, Monsieur Séchard, it is for embroidery . . . You have to write on it: *Musique,* in large round letters, with initials. I do not have a good enough hand . . . I would write it crooked." She added familiarly, "No! It is so hot! We are sure to have a thunderstorm."

To avoid seeing him from the front, she positioned herself behind the young man, who was spreading out a transparent paper in his records.

From the back, he looked almost like a man, if one did not know his red eye and sulky, crippled face. Bent over this new job, he applied himself as well as he could. The mistress wanted to make a music roll and embroider from the round; it was a good idea she had, his mistress; he would prove himself worthy of the trust placed in him! A grimace twisted his mouth. From time to time, he would suck on his penholder, all worn out by this habit, then start a letter, turning his hand in circles with the casualness of a character very adept at making frivolous loops. Laure, still planted behind him, was examining his carefully combed drab brown hair, parted by a line on the side that had certainly been drawn with a ruler and exuding an astonishing scent of jasmine. The clerk was perfuming himself. She felt like laughing, then said in a soft voice, "You are very skilled, Monsieur Lucien."

"Oh! Practice, mademoiselle," he replied, as a pink tinge crept up the flesh of his neck and onto his nape.

But, just as he was about to complete an elegant delineation, his quill spat out, flooding the paper with a series of little messes.

"What a shame!" murmured Laure.

"Bah! I will do it again," said the clerk calmly. And he put his nose to another leaf.

"How you bless me!" sighed Laure, putting her hand next to his to spread out the paper.

"I am very happy, very happy. Besides, it is going to thunder, and I have never been able to transcribe when it thunders."

"Hold on! Do you get nervous?"

"Sometimes!" retorted the young man with an air of mockery.

And his eye went up to the girl. Laure tried to bear this one-eyed gaze, shivering slightly. Full of frozen tears under its bloody patch, blurred by eyelashes growing in there like thorns bristling at a wound, that red eye looked terrible next to its forget-me-not-blue brother, ridiculous, though one knew not why. And his face around the purple blotch looked decent. A nascent mustache blurred a well-shaped lip, the teeth were healthy if the smile retained an expression of wicked sadness; the skin, of an ivory hue, must have been extraordinarily pleasant to the touch; it had the satin of those vellums he used for precious copies, all of the delicacy of a woman's skin . . . Laure smiled at him. He lowered his head, punching a hole in the transparent paper at the letter *u*.

"But, goodness," he cried, "I am full of mistakes today!"

"You want it too perfect," retorted Laure.

"No, no! It is the storm. Hold on! I think I will wreck everything."

His dip pen fell. He drew in a painful breath and wiped his forehead. The study window was open, overlooking the courtyard's well where the angelicas baked as if in a furnace. Despite the half-closed shutters, one could smell the penetrating scent of their greenery. A ray of sunlight crossed the solemn cabinets with gold, lending gravity to the dance of playful particles. Laure dropped onto one of the leather seats.

"And to think that our house is one of the coolest in the city."

She slipped off her kerchief, revealing the top of her unbuttoned peignoir, and tossed her hair from side to side.

"I think," Lucien murmured, curling his shadowy mustache in a grotesque gesture, "I think that your father will not return home without drenching his jacket."

Laure, both hands hanging, stretched out her legs and brought her pointed feet together, stretching herself out like an arrow ready to release.

"And Maman! If you saw her, Monsieur Lucien, you would feel sorry for her! A real laundress. She is smoking! She is in the kitchen roasting us a chicken. Ah! It is quite a day to turn a spit! And Joséphine nearly had to take off her petticoat..."

At the thought that Joséphine, head always covered, wanted to take something off, they burst out laughing. Laure pulled out her handkerchief to fan herself. Lucien sucked on the end of his feather with a sort of chuckle. Suddenly, the sun's rays took on a gloomy leaden shade, one of the shutters slammed furiously down on the other, and all of the cabinets shuddered.

Laure jumped up to the clerk's desk. "Are you not afraid? I thought the window would break! Then . . . you are not nervous, whatever you say . . ."

"It depends . . . I have only restless legs. Oh! It is shaping up nicely . . . We are in for a storm."

He rose to grab a third sheet of paper. For a moment, they stood face-to-face in semidarkness. All one could see of the young clerk was the shape of a lovely boy, dressed in a cheap but fashionable suit, the shape of a nineteen-year-old man, a little thin, yet very virile looking.

Mademoiselle Lordès gritted her teeth under the sinister gaze she sensed without daring to look. "You are lucky, Monsieur Lucien. I am trembling. Here . . ."

She held out her hands. He hesitated, the time of a flash, then, fallen back into full shadow, more sure of his means of action, the young man seized the hands offered to him and drew the girl against his panting chest.

"Why are you trembling? Maybe it is I whom you are afraid of . . ." His voice trailed off in sorrow. He had just laughed; he was going to cry.

Laure was overwhelmed by his voice. "My poor Monsieur Lucien!" she sighed.

"Oh! Do not deny it," he continued. "It is only natural, I am not handsome, and you, you are such a pretty girl . . ."

"Lucien, you are wrong, I am not afraid of you . . . Like this, in the dark, you do not look too bad, I assure you."

She had turned away a little, leaning against him, pressing against him with her whole body. She hardly knew what she was doing, caressing herself on him, simply like a cat who has found a corner of furniture that pleases it and rubs its muzzle on it, convinced that the piece of furniture will not complain about the game. Given the opportunity, she was not averse to coquetry in front of a mannequin of a man. Suddenly, the clerk leaned over, wrapped his feverish arms around her and folded her in a kiss.

She straightened up angrily. "You disgust me! What's the matter with you? I am not your prey, Monsieur Lucien Séchard . . . !"

He grabbed her wrists and said in a hissing tone, "Oh! I know you . . . come now, I know everything you are, Mademoiselle Laure!"

"You know me, do you?" she roared, turning around with fire in her cheeks.

"Treacherous, eh? Here you are, angrier than when I kissed you. Ah! You miserable little fool . . . you little wench, you little fool," he chanted, placing his finger on Laure's mouth three times to prevent her from protesting. "Yes, I know everything . . . everything . . . I have only got one eye, but I can see clearly . . . You have driven me mad, what a pity! You have lost my respect . . . Ah! If you were not beautiful . . . I would take my revenge! Say again that I disgust you . . ."

"You know everything," she stammered, "and the proof . . . ?"

"Proof?" he retorted, sneering. "Listen to me without looking at the door . . . I have got you dead to rights . . . Proof . . . ? You little fool! Yesterday you went to the vicarage terrace . . . Instead of going to buy wool from the haberdasher; you blew a kiss, just like that, with your fingers, to Abbé Bréville, who was reading his breviary under the hazel trees . . . You are in love with a priest. If that is not shameful . . . And that priest has not only noticed you in return. You were once in love with the peasant Marcou, the one who carried peaches and grapes in the vacation season . . . You were not more than ten years old, and you let him kiss you. I saw it, there, under the angelica trees . . . Oh! I could have killed you . . . ! It hurts to look when you cannot play the same game . . . Why did you come here . . . to annoy me? *You are no prey for me* . . . Such a good story . . . I am just a dog who is bothering you, you would like to have me chased away . . . I would be replaced by a handsome clerk, curly-haired, muscular, a clerk from Paris . . . but no, they cost money, clerks from Paris, and your father is too stingy; he will keep me because he pays me less than another, you hear! And I will stay here, for my bread! I do not care what I earn . . ."

And he added, seized by a painful longing that suffocated him, "I do not care, because I have always loved you, I have always wanted you, me, the horror of a boy whose face disgusts you . . ."

Laure, at once furious and charmed, began to cry. "Oh! Be quiet . . . ! I had no idea. Your eye looks so odd. It is like you are sulking at everyone . . . You spied on me, that is nice! First of all, you are wrong. You saw nothing . . . You could have told, you beast!"

"Indeed, I should have denounced you to your father. But then I would no longer have enjoyed the show . . . Sometimes this one, sometimes that one, and you would give them cakes on top of that . . . It drove me mad. Are you crying? Often I cried entire nights, biting my pillow."

"Lucien, we'll be friends from now on; please forgive me," she murmured affectionately, wrapping her arms around his shoulders. "It is true that I am in love . . . and I do not really know who I am in love with, I have sensitive flesh, my skin flushes immediately . . . Is it my fault! I do not understand a thing. You will not betray me, will you, Lucien, my dear little Lucien? But . . . how can I explain to you, I cannot look at you."

Lucien Séchard buried his face in her loose hair. Lightning followed lightning, glinting between the shutters like the reflections of sharp blades.

"My God!" he sobbed.

"Take comfort," she continued, seeing herself as mistress of the battlefield, "you are a man. Some things are impossible in the end!"

He shuddered to the depths of his tormented being. "You said 'impossible'! Come now! I want, you want! What is impossible now?"

"No! No! I am telling you the truth, Lucien! See reason!"

There was silence and he knelt down, making himself a blindfold from the fabric of his cloak.

"Even if I stay like this, always, at your feet, imploring you?"

"You are an idiot."

"Even if I only kiss you at night!"

"Ah! In my room, so my mother can catch us."

"Even if I wear a mask."

She giggled. "You really do have ideas, Lucien . . ."

He raised his brow. He leaped, seizing a penknife from the bureau. "I do not care that you are beautiful for the others," he cried, beside himself, "because I am too ugly for you. I will blind you!"

Laure, terrified, rushed to the door. He ran after her, seized her hair, and pulled it brutally.

She stammered, "Tonight, tonight, in front of the living room window. Oh! My eyes, my eyes . . . Do not gouge my eyes out, darling . . ."

And, freed, for he had thrown away the penknife, she ran off down the corridor, reattaching her kerchief.

Lucien Séchard staggered back to his office. He slumped in his chair; a stream of tears flowing from his blue eye, and the other, red as an ember, burned in the most atrocious manner. He mopped his face with his handkerchief, irritating the wound without paying any attention, happy to dig into it more, to aggravate it until he could rip it out once and for all.

In the courtyard, large drops of water fell and splashed onto the angelica, tears of the storm after tears of love; everything sobbed, everything collapsed around him, and he had foreseen that it would end like this! His head was too hot. No, he would not go to the rendezvous. What's the use, my God! Promises cost little when one is a pretty girl capable of leading the life that Laure was leading. She had come to see that he had poison in his veins, and now she was laughing at him.

He lay across the table, fists clenched. In love with the curé d'Estérac! What a curse! This dance had been going on for a year. She gazed up at the sky, while he, below, kissed the hem of her dress, begging for a caress. The world was too unfair. She, who feared scandal, was talking to a cassock and risking compromising herself, in the middle of town, in front of the terrace of a vicarage! If things continued like this, she would be standing naked in the middle of church on the day of the sermon . . .

Lucien, still hiccupping, gathered his papers, sorted the next day's work, and finished his transcription. From time to time, he recalled their scene and wondered how he could have said all of those things to her. They had leaped from his lips without his even realizing that they had escaped. Someone else had spoken for him. What a story, my God! And never again would he find this opportunity . . .

Five o'clock struck on the old black marble clock, where Justice weighed a sword on its bronze scales. It thundered terribly outside. The clerk closed the window and opened the door, for he was suffocating. Monsieur Lordès returned: a cabriolet brought him back soaked, and he heard the cries of commiseration from Madame Lordès as she rushed to her husband to sponge him dry—and prevent him from dirtying the staircase.

From the salon, Laure said very loudly, "Papa, one would not throw a dog in the street in this weather. You should invite Monsieur Séchard to dinner."

The parents burst out laughing. The notaire, once dry, went upstairs, and, discarding his briefcase full of paperwork, made the invitation. "Say, my boy, would you like a bite to eat, in the kitchen, without fuss? You cannot go out in this downpour . . ."

The clerk then realized that he was the dog, and, holding back his last tears, refused.

For weeks, Lucien Séchard devised the most complicated schemes to mitigate the effect of his eye. He asked his mother, a widow of strict morals, if English taffeta would cost much.

The latter, who could not even see her son's wound as he had been one-eyed since the age of three, laughed in his face and called him a great ass, adding fiercely, "You are not going to flirt with girls with what you earn for us, are you?"

He went to a chemist's and bought some of the pink fabric in secret. In his room, he shut himself away as if to commit suicide; he cut out circles of different sizes and pasted them onto himself in succession; but either they were too small, and a purple halo encircled the pink taffeta, or they were too big and covered the cheek. Then, the eyelashes, those thorns that protruded from the wound, growing crooked, gnawed at his flesh, festering to the point of bleeding when he was overexcited, the slightest irritation affecting his diseased eye (and one would have thought that all of the misfortunes that befell him had to pass through this gaping hole!), the eyelashes prevented the pink circle from fitting properly over the eye socket. He had to renounce English taffeta. He tried emollient lotions, hoping that the inflammation would subside. Not all punctured eyes, after all, had the appearance of blazing embers! The lotions brought on a yellow malady, a sort of pus that ran for two days, threatening to spread to the healthy eye, and earning him exclamations of disgust. His mother counseled him to stop leaning over her glass when he offered her wine, and Monsieur Lordès entrusted him with his records in a *particular* way.

He tried no more remedies, limiting himself to calculating the effects on his face. He leaned to one side, lowered his brow, scratched his hair to get a chance to put his hand in front of his wound. This eventually complicated his life to such an extent that he neglected his work. Always hoping that he would meet Laure at the right moment, he would perpetually scratch his hair or his eyebrow, striking his temple in a gesture of deep reflection. When he crossed the corridor from the street and went up to the study, he could meet the girl, and he prepared a series of movements rehearsed the day before in front of a mirror. First, he knotted his tie, curled his mustache, and tossed back his hair. At the desk, he rested his elbow on the paper, leaned his head on his hand, pulled out his handkerchief, and then shook it at eye level.

One day, the notaire said to him, impatient, "Sacrebleu, you are giving me vertigo, Séchard, with your fidgeting."

"Excuse me, monsieur," murmured the young man, "I have a headache."

"I imagine so, you are putting eau de cologne on your handkerchief. It stinks!"

These observations subdued him. With Laure nowhere to be seen, he fell into a dreary despair and thought for a moment of writing to her. The prudence of a man raised amid compromising paperwork held him back. If he wrote, he could not send his letter through the post; besides, where could he deposit a love letter, since he never went anywhere but the study? When one of the living room windows was open, if you stepped over the balustrade from the street, you would have reached the piano, and only Mademoiselle Lordès played that instrument; but good Joséphine wiped the keyboard every morning, and she would inevitably discover the letter. Should he wait for a new opportunity? Laure had asked her father for her embroidery pattern back; Lucien knew, now, that she would never return . . .

She continued her chase of the curé, redoubling her devotion, going to church every Sunday around dusk, when the priest was isolated, far from his altar boys and old habitués of the confessional. Ah! It was a devotion well understood, that of Mademoiselle Lordès! The former curé was dying, he was not confessing young girls still, and with the new one having completely replaced him, he would have to take her under his tutelage, receive her confidences; and she hunted him down with the patience of a wild beast who knows that sooner or later she will lay her claw on her poor, trembling victim!

Lucien Séchard, with his single eye, could see the ups and downs of the struggle through the walls. He knew the toilette for the rendezvous, the parasol for the walk under the terrace of hazel trees, her graceful negligence of morning masses, the bouquet that was placed on her bodice on the day of a possible confession; and he guessed, from the girl's mad aspect, the disappointments, the rebuffs, the fits of nerves at night, also the solitary abandonments, all of the exhausting caresses that he shared at a distance, calling out for her very low...

At home, the parents did not suspect a thing. Madame Lordès fattened up, Monsieur Lordès ran around the countryside for contracts and returned with rheumatism. Joséphine peeled vegetables in the middle of the courtyard, in fine weather, in front of her stove, and in the rain, and sometimes this servant took up her rosary and mumbled a dozen prayers while peppering a stew.

One morning, Laure opened the salon as the young man passed by and stopped on the threshold, desiring to utter a word. They were face-to-face with one another. Lucien immediately made a mad gesture, tossing his hair back with a quick turn of his hand, and the young girl, hesitating, reminded herself that he wanted to hide himself from her. She closed the door. Lucien faltered up the study stairs. He was in despair, for she had had the expression that one always has when looking at a toad. Lucien wept, his brow buried in his stamped papers. That evening, at four o'clock, the notaire went out and left him to scribble alone. The clerk remained sad, and yet he sensed something coming: behind the walls of the study, behind all of the dusty paperwork, a gaze was blazing. Laure was watching him, as was her habit, alas, from watching the priest... She was gradually turning away from the latter to examine the former who loved her, who would not run away from her warm velvet eyes and who would hold out his arms to her...

Slowly, the office door opened, just as the salon door had opened in the morning; an electric shiver shook the young man, and he saw her standing there, her finger on her lips. He did not stir, did not disturb his elbow or his hand, masking his eye with his moist handkerchief.

"Do you have a headache, Monsieur Lucien?" Laure asked, her voice soft.

He replied dully, "I always have a headache!"

Laure glanced briskly up the stairs, then closed the door; but this time, she was locking herself in. "Monsieur and Madame Lordès have gone out," she said in a deeper voice, imitating Joséphine when she dismissed an unwelcome visitor.

The clerk almost jumped. "And the maid, where is she?"

"She is in church for a small dozen rosary prayers, Monsieur Séchard."

Laure was now close to him, brushing against him with her hip. He got up abruptly, pushed the bolt, and pulled down the shutters, while Laure sat in her father's armchair.

"So we're going to have another storm, Monsieur Lucien?" she said, smoothing out the folds of her dress. You remember the last one, eh? How it thundered! This is October, so it is not so hot, is it?"

She laughed a strange laugh, half mirth, half sob. Lucien grabbed her by the waist, knelt before her and laid his aching head on her lap. The unfortunate boy was suffocating. "Are you here to talk to me about the rain and the sun?"

Laure slid down the backrest, falling from the top of the green leather like a drop of water sliding down a broad leaf. In an instant, she fell into the young man's arms. Lucien, dazzled, no longer dared.

"Come on, you great beast, you can see that I am closing my eyes . . . !"

7

Mademoiselle Lordès stood by the gilded choir screen. She was the last to arrive, and she had come to make critiques. No! She did not like this Month of Mary. It lacked greenery, shadow, and mystery. Too many artificial flowers and not enough ornamental plants. All those paper lilies made the altar look like a fashion boutique, but she would not be adding an offering. Since the old curé d'Estérac had died, she had deserted the church and was not interested in pleasing this indifferent young priest, so lacking in zeal for his flock. Around her, devotees, laden with multicolored gifts, scurried like ants. Laure hardly knew why she had come. She had gone in thinking that this man, Armand de Bréville, was lucky to be hiding under a cassock, because without that black shirt, she would find a way to get at him, to take revenge for his disdain. Her eyes glinted in the direction of the sacristy, where she saw the abbé chatting with a lady. In this way, the abbé was joking, even laughing, occupied by a person of the female sex.

He, usually so haughty, so calm, walking shrouded in a nimbus that prevented him from seeing, was laughing! Anger invaded Laure's brain, anger made up of ancient desire and recent jealousy. Joséphine, the Lordès's maid, had pretended, while directing signs of intelligence to madame regarding mademoiselle, that this young priest was emancipating himself; he visited the less respectable parishioners, wandered the countryside, gathered ragged women in his home to distribute bread, and had even gone so far as to use church funds to pay for a young mother's trip to the town center of the arrondissement. His conduct was that of an exasperated man. His ambition dashed, appointed to a modest parish where he could not make the worldly connections necessary for advancement, this little priest would end up in a bad way . . . And many other things transpired that one did not dare to say in the presence of a young girl.

Laure scoffed at the gossip, but for her part, she reproached him for a host of truly deliberate and hurtful insults. He had not come to their house on New Year's Day, had not noticed her absence from the holy table and confessional, and finally it was he, the coward, who had precipitated her into the miserable state in which she was languishing, he who had thrown her into the arms of the monster Lucien Séchard, the Cyclops. Without the unrequited passion that the fool had for this man of the cloth, she would not have fallen, she, a beautiful creature, on a crippled man . . . !

Laure trembled with rage. Her heart, still closed in the midst of the blossoming of her flesh, could scarcely distinguish pleasure from love; besides, what she loved above all was certain pleasure, and today she was quite sure that the pleasures of the Cyclops disgusted her, whereas the priest, so beautiful, whose eyes cast such extraordinary glimmers, represented to her a perpetual promise of bliss. He still dominated her life; she thought of him in the hours of humiliation, and when she seemed sweeter to the unworthy lover, it was because she was dreaming of him.

Laure leaned on the choir balustrade. Now they were taking down the statue of St. George to substitute it with that of the Virgin, and this delicate operation was not without amusing moments. The young sinner took sacrilegious pleasure in seeing all of these people becoming agitated before God as if before *someone else*. The women, gradually returning to their chatty habits, exchanged their impressions as if in a common washroom.

Voices rose, they fought over brooms, towels, sponges, and feather dusters. The more serious shook out the carpets and altar cloths, and removed the cobwebs; the more experienced contented themselves by arranging the painted paper bouquets and organizing the candles' girandoles. The sacristan, an old dried-up man with the pointed face of a weasel, went from right to left, giving advice, raving and taking off his Greek cap, sometimes in front of the altar, sometimes in front of a notable lady. When the Saint George statue was brought down, he mopped his brow, saying in a penetrating voice, "That's not made of bloody feathers!"

There was a slight laugh.

Monsieur l'Abbé approached, he came and stood close to Laure, and, not suspecting that she was staying to spy on him to try to make him ridiculous in his flock of devotees, he exclaimed briskly, "But that is not it at all, the Virgin Mary looks like she is stepping out of a sack. She needs to be raised."

Laure added in a very stiff accent, "From a ragpicker's sack, you are right, Monsieur l'Abbé."

He turned around and was dismayed by her ardent gaze. "So here is one more good worker," he murmured, lowering his eyes and striving to smile. "And it is good of you, mademoiselle, to come and help us, you have been so scarce of late . . ."

With a feverish gesture, Laure pushed back her heavy hair, which was still whipping around her sides like the tail of a wild beast. "Monsieur l'Abbé," she said coldly, "you have no shortage of devoted hearts around you."

"Yes," he replied, his tone cheerful but his face pale, "I have only praise for the eagerness of my dear parishioners, they spoil me . . . Yet there are some who forget me, who forget God . . ." he added in feigned unction.

"It is undoubtedly your fault, Monsieur l'Abbé," Laure retorted, her glittering pupils piercing his eyelids.

He straightened his head, looked at her in horror for a moment, then had the terrible urge to launch himself at her, to chase her away, to crush her. Laure guessed his confusion and leaned forward. "I am going to right my wrongs, Monsieur l'Abbé," she said with sudden gentleness. "I want to confess, and as there is only one priest left in Estérac, naturally I have come to fetch you."

He was so shaky that he had to lean against the railing. No one was listening to them; the routine of cleaning the altar continued in familiar conversation, exchanging news from outside and events in the kitchen.

The abbé faltered under the imperious gaze of the young girl, still standing there, awaiting his decision. "I hope it is God who brings you back here, mademoiselle," he replied, running his hand over his already damp forehead. "I will be with you in an hour."

Laure bowed and went to the side of the confessional, leafing through her prayer book with an air of detachment from the things of this world.

The devotees completed their work as best they could. They piled pot upon pot, paper roses upon silver lilies, and here and there they hung silk banners that made the dazzling display resemble the storefront of one of those fairground merchants where the flag gives one the right to choose the biggest porcelain. The Virgin emerged from the pile of roses like an upstanding woman, embarrassed to be selling such merchandise. The sacristan put Saint George near an obscure piece of furniture in the sacristy, the ladies meditated for a minute, resting from their exertions, and then withdrew, whispering a few pious invocations. The church fell back into gloomy silence. All that could be heard through the open doorway was the slow, nasal wail of a poor man kneeling with his begging bowl in his hand, pleading with guttural inflections.

The abbé de Bréville entered the confessional, where Laure was waiting. As soon as he drew back the wicket, she said, raising her pretty profile to him, "I frighten you, Monsieur l'Abbé!"

He murmured contentedly, "Say the *confiteor*, my child."

"So you despise me?"

"I beg you, my child, to begin with the confiteor. We are in the court of penitence."

Laure said the prayer with clenched teeth and burning lips. She had definitely taken her revenge, and since this indomitable young man had not wanted to see her, he was going to hear her . . . Confession allowed for anything.

"My father," she began with mocking humility, "I am going to scandalize you, because I am already a great sinner. I am still only twenty, but I have committed many faults, and I do not have much hope of divine mercy: Father, I have a lover . . ."

The abbé de Bréville shuddered violently and stammered, "We are the ones who can hear everything, and God teaches us to forgive everything . . ."

Ah! She had a lover! He clung to the hard wooden stall, digging his nails into the jambs. Lord, how suffocating it was in that coffin, and how dark it was around him! "Courage, my child," he said.

"Yes, my father, I am guilty of having given myself to someone without love, for the sole satisfaction of my senses. I will never love the man who possesses me, and yet I can no longer rid myself of the bonds of my sin. Do you know our clerk, he who is nicknamed the Cyclops, Lucien Séchard?

"Father, have you ever come across dead dogs on your way, along a path, in the fields? I saw one, when I was a little girl, near a farm where I used to spend my vacations, and this dead dog had puffy eyes, full of earth, covered with swarming insects, bits of dry grass . . . Well, my father, the look of my lover is that way, I swear, he has the eye of a dead dog!"

She paused to smile, and the priest saw her teeth glinting through the wire mesh like a knife. "Yes, Father, I accuse myself of being the mistress of this one-eyed man, I who only love beautiful things and who was made for a handsome boy. At night, I wake up thinking that the red eye might burst in the darkness and scatter like fireworks, flooding me with sprays of sparks or droplets of blood! I think of it when I eat, I think of it when I drink, and I cannot chew my bread and I cannot swallow my wine; I think of it when I look at myself in the mirror; I think of it when I look into the pond . . . The eye of my one-eyed lover follows me everywhere; it stains the sky and then it is as big as the sun; it is, in the evening, the moon rising behind a cloud; it runs through the meadows when I walk, it is on all of the flowers; it is on all of the dresses I wear. Father, never was the torment of the damned more appalling. To escape it, you would open hell to me and I would throw myself in, quite happy, thanking you, and that, my father, is the love that I enjoy! I must, don't you think, be insatiable for touch, be repelled by nothing, to be satisfied with this lover . . . Oh! I do not reproach him for his ugliness! He loves me tenderly and does all that he can to conceal his shame, but I think that I would see him, such as he is, even if he were to bury himself a hundred feet underground . . ."

"My God! My God!" uttered the confessor, dropping his forehead into his hands. "And why do you not break this degrading attachment, my daughter? If this boy has seduced you in spite of yourself, he has committed a crime, and it would be your parents' duty to expel him from their home without his being able to claim or avenge himself. Would you not like to marry this clerk? So . . . he is threatening you? Are you afraid of scandal? Tell me, my child, do you want to break it off . . . or are you afraid . . . ?"

"You do not understand, my father! On the contrary, I am his mistress out of goodwill. I gave myself to him because I did not feel strong enough to resist him . . . I even went looking for him one day when he was not thinking about me and did not hope to find me . . ."

"You must leave him . . . leave him . . ." repeated the priest feverishly. "Laure, my child, confess everything to your mother, and with her, I will take it upon myself to expel this monster from the country! You are young, sensitive, a little mad, you will recover from your errors and repent. Yes, I understand well, I understand too well . . . Under the empire of the senses, what are we not capable of . . . My child, you must break this odious chain . . . You must . . ."

Laure nodded softly; the braid of her hair slipped from her shoulders over the confessional grating, and the confessor felt its scent envelop him like the fur of a great beast settling upon him.

"I do not want to break it off, my father," she continued. "No, I cannot ... I do not love him, and I do love him; it often seems as if I hate him, for he drowns me alive in a frightening purgatory. He is my punishment as well as my pleasure ... but ..." And here she sighed. "He protects me from a more serious danger. I am grateful to him."

"Danger?" murmured the trembling priest.

"Yes, my father; it was for love of another that I gave myself up to Lucien Séchard, I thought it better to damn myself alone than to damn the other with me ..."

"Be quiet, my child!" stammered the abbé, making an angry gesture.

She resumed, humbly submissive. "And then, my father, he is so good, this boy, so passionate, so delicate ... At night, when I cannot see him anymore and I come to forget him, I think of the other man, the one whom I love so much ...!"

"Laure, silence ...! I forbid you to speak of these things ... here, in front of me ...!" cried the priest, beside himself, and forgetting that the beggar chanting at the entrance porch could have keen ears.

Laure straightened up. Her nostrils flared and she gave a cynical look. She had touched her adversary to the heart.

"Why should I remain silent, Monsieur l'Abbé?" she replied, neglecting to call him "my father" as long as he called her "Laure." "I accuse you by accusing myself, and that is justice! Did you come to console me, to chase away this wretch when it was not yet too late? Did you pity my tears when I cried at night, because a curé does not marry, and that one is not allowed to find him handsome, to say so to his face . . . You are afraid of scandal! Do not worry, my precautions are well taken. I have changed my room, and I am sleeping on the first floor instead of the second floor of our house, where my parents sleep. What is more, Lucien Séchard is so hideous that no one, I assure you, will dare gossip about him . . . or me! You do not like scandal! My lover is very discreet. He is neither a married man nor a priest. Everything is going as well as can be expected . . ."

"But, wretched girl, have you forgotten that the work of the flesh was instituted by God for the reproduction of the species, and not for the sole purpose of pleasure . . . ? One day, you will wake up . . . pregnant?"

"Oh!" Laure retorted quietly. "He knows secrets!"

"Lord! Have mercy on her . . . ! Have mercy on me . . . !" moaned the unfortunate man. "I will not be able to absolve her . . ."

And with a brutal movement, Armand de Bréville pushed open the stall, no longer wanting to look at the beast of lust that happily waved its black, perfumed tail behind its round shoulders.

"I do not give a damn about your absolution," said Laure to herself, shuffling out of the church. Hearing no more movement from that dark box, that large coffin standing upright against the walls, she got up and headed for the porch. There, she gave the pauper two pennies for his blessings and walked home lightly, her conscience cleared of sin.

In the evening, however, a strange sadness took hold of the young girl; she had been avenged, but that would not get her far: Lucien Séchard was guarding her, spying on her, tyrannizing her perpetually with the fear of her shame being revealed; he threatened to kill her if she drove him away. He had sensed it, this priest, that she was looking for victims, for she was a victim herself and could hardly boast of her triumph: it would do her no good. No, she did not love Armand any more than she loved Lucien; she ran around to triumph over men, driven by an irresistible force; a blossoming monstrance of flesh, she carried love inside of her like a God and remained unmoved under its rays.

She still missed one thing: the joys of the heart . . . Did she have a heart? Very vaguely, as one suffers from a microscopic thorn embedded in the tip of one's finger, she believed in the presence of this object when she pressed on it to count her palpitations, and she felt an anxiety not to love more, always desiring another sensation, a more acute pleasure. A rage came over her at the thought that this priest was decent, and she admired him a little, not, this time, for his soft, almond-shaped eyes, but for the sort of toy that he let her break, for his heart, so mysterious, a closed vessel from which she had finally released the overflow of passion. She did not sleep. The next morning, she got up very early, put on her penitent's dress, wrapped her hat in a lace veil, and resolutely went back to church. She followed the Low Mass with edifying attention. What was he going to do, bruised from the day before, when he saw his torturer again? When Mass was over, Laure began counting her rosary beads. Would she again use the confessional as her battleground?

She was approaching the altar, watching for the abbé to take off his surplice, when he sent the sacristan to her. "Monsieur le Curé is waiting for you," said the man in greeting. And nonchalantly, he added, "Mademoiselle will have her work cut out for her."

Laure, stunned, watched him walk away. What work was he talking about? She crossed the large carpet adorning the altar steps and remained undecided before the sacristy door. She shuddered with a truly new emotion: on the threshold of paradise, she could not have been more confused. Behind the cascading artificial flowers that represented the Virgin's altar and her own existence, she was about to reap the sincere flower of love, the flower forbidden above all to nonbelievers. Their exquisite pleasure, rubbed with incense, would truly give them a foretaste of heaven; they had waited a long time to exchange the divine kiss of the chosen ones, one wallowing in the mire, the other isolated in prayer, but they were going to be united in church, having envied, from afar, the chaste brides dragging their immaculate dresses over the paving stones strewn with boughs, and the serious husbands, so proud of their charge of such feminine souls. Laure knocked gently on the door.

"Come in," replied Armand de Bréville.

She tiptoed into the room, as if into a sickroom, and was immediately seized by the scent of roses. Amid the transparent muslin, white rose branches spread out to form a cross, which the young abbé was consolidating with reeds. The ogival window of the sacristy opened onto a vista of graceful hills still in the blanket of morning vapors, and a curtain of poplars bordering a road wrapped the awakening town in a soft veil that tempered the vulgar details. Standing out from the light background of the ogive, the priest, slender, elegant, and supple, appeared darker, more severe in his melancholy, and his passionate, dark-rimmed eyes were wet, like roses, with a colder dew.

He indicated a carved stepladder, a former monk's chair, to the young girl, and said, striving to smile, "Would you like to help me today? I know you hate artificial flowers. Last night, I picked all of the roses in my garden because I could not sleep, and I am starting a job that frightens me . . . It is to weave a very fragile cross, mademoiselle . . . the cross of human vanities, a cross of flowery brambles. It was missing from my altar, and I count on you to provide it . . ."

Laure stared at him, astonished. He would be choosing a charming pretext if he wished to succumb in a bed of perfume, but why this icy aspect?

"At your service, Monsieur l'Abbé," she murmured, removing her veil and tossing back her hair. "Shall I close the door?"

"Yes; we will be alone, I am afraid; all of the confessions came yesterday, and I have got no baptism this morning, no catechism . . . I have nothing left to do . . . but prepare this cross. Here are some scissors."

He passed her the scissors as she bent over the table, brushing his hands against hers. Armand de Bréville slumped into the purple velvet armchair where the bishop sat on religious solemnities. His back was to the window: his eyes, having wept all of his tears, could no longer bear the light outside. He remained there, resigned, bent under a degrading weariness, chatting like a man of the world and no longer concerned with his dignity as a priest. Except for one thing he did not want to do, he no longer resisted, he confessed his love, he confessed his cowardice, reserving himself to draw new rigor from the very shame of his confession. She would not rape him; that was all that he had sworn, in short, *not to let himself be raped*, and his Jesuitisms of conscience assured him of peace now. He had foreseen that she would come, she had come; he would receive her and feel no more fear than when breathing in the intoxication of roses.

Laure arranged the arms of the cross and covered them with flowers, then slipped a few fallen petals into her bodice.

"We need to talk, Laure," stammered the young curé in a slow voice. "You have confessed . . . brutally, and you still find me upset by your stories . . . little-girl stories that I should not take seriously. Only I, your confidant and sole protector, since your parents do not know what I know, want to save you, if possible. You are only twenty, Laure, and the holy books say that you are at the age of generous impulses. I will not talk to you about the love of God, nor of our sacraments. Let us abandon sacred things so as not to soil them through contact with evil passions; we will have recourse to them later, when we are less distraught." He paused, putting to his brow the freshness of a leaf that he was mechanically tearing. "I say *we*, because there are two guilty parties here . . . I may even be more guilty than you." He lowered his tone. "Yes, my poor child, I feel for a woman, whose name I do not have to mention in front of you, what you feel for Lucien Séchard. This woman, like the clerk of your father, has a hideous wound, she is tainted with the fatal sign of lust; but, if I am forbidden to love her, I am not forbidden to try to pull her out of the mud . . ."

Laure knelt at the young man's feet, presenting him with a clump of roses. "You are very hard on your child, my dear father!" she said.

Armand smiled a bitter smile, letting his hands fall away. "Yes, my child . . . or better still, *my sister*!"

There was silence. Laure buried her face, pale with lust, in the long, frail hands of the priest; she cradled her head in his lap. "Oh, how I love you!" she breathed in a savage accent.

"Laure, my beloved sister," continued the abbé, closing his eyes, "I can see only one way to protect you from your senses. You must get married. I am not mad . . . no . . . no . . . I calculated, last night, all of our chances of salvation, and I think that I have found the right one. You cannot marry your lover; your parents, yourself, would not want you to; and the scandal would be inordinate. You will have to marry someone else, and I will look into it. I know a very estimable young man, a future notaire who would buy the practice of your father. Answer me frankly, Laure, would you accept a husband whom I would propose to you . . . ?"

Laure looked up. "I will accept death from you; but, in the meantime, what is my reward?"

"You will obey me!" he said in a distressed tone.

"And this husband, we will reveal my stories of . . . girlhood to him?"

"He will never know, you will break up with Lucien Séchard, you will send him to me if he threatens you with a row, and eventually you will come to love your fiancé."

Laure exclaimed, revolted, "And if I refuse . . . ?"

"Then, I will ask my bishop for a change of parish, it is that simple."

"You will always despise me . . . am I not pretty enough for you, brother?"

The abbé bent to her offered lips. "I suffer martyrdom without complaint, demon; I have already committed the sin of intent, and I do not want to fall prey to you. My dear sister, get up!"

"Let us go anywhere, my beloved brother, to the depths of a convent, we will love each other . . . and do penance afterward . . . Speak . . . ! I accept responsibility for your sin! I want . . ."

"My sister! My sister!"

He repeated the word painfully, gazing at her with an intoxication that paralyzed him, and she threw herself into his arms, little suspecting that at that supreme moment, even more depraved than she—fervent of body, he—fervent of soul, dreamed of incest.

They remained entwined for a second; Laure melted completely onto his mouth, like a crushing fruit. With the scent of roses in her hair and on her fingertips, she surrounded him with an extraordinary vertigo, pushing him toward an abyss that he imagined to be cool and dark, like the luxurious foliage of a great park. Sandy paths of gold spiraled before him; bare arms, a forest of bare arms, knotted around his neck; he was caressed by a floating braid of black hair that took on the dimensions of a fiery smoke, and he could no longer escape, for a mutinous child's voice cried out to him, "Carry me, my brother, carry me, carry me!"

Laure saw him faint, she felt pity for this proud, passionate man, exhausted by fasting and struggles.

"Forgive me . . . I am a cruel woman," she stammered, rising to her knees as he fell back, half-unconscious, onto the armchair. "Oh! I have hurt you."

"No, dear little sister, you were right, on the contrary, to say that . . . You have broken the spell, the demon has fled! So be it . . . I will carry you . . . all the way to heaven."

Laure clasped her hands together. "I will obey you, do not cry anymore!"

"You swear it to me, my sister?"

"I will swear it . . . on one condition," and she kissed the tip of the priest's scarf, "that your wisdom will do you no more harm in the eyes of God than my folly, Monsieur l'Abbé!"

They smiled at each other, and, revived, the young man rose, moved toward the threshold of the sacristy, and said, "When I have the strength to take up my cross again, I will be back. Finish your work, my dear sister! Flowers fade fast . . ."

8

The two betrothed gazed out over the landscape, not daring to share their thoughts. After this grand ceremonial dinner, they had been left alone on the terrace, and the moon was rising, drowning them in a soft melancholy that prevented them from finding the appropriate, or simply banal, phrases. Henri Alban was looking for something graceful, in harmony with the beautiful evening, while caressing his cigar case, which, out of politeness, he could not open. Laure, fidgeting, her eyes moist, waited for a loving exclamation that never came.

At their feet, the town of Estérac slept in a mist studded here and there with the small golden dots of lamps, and seemed like a lake with dark eddies reflecting stars.

When the moon emerged, not very round, with a slightly reddish light, the look of a sad eye on the brow of this spring sky, still full of brooding clouds, Laure twitched involuntarily; she moved closer to him and began to tremble in earnest.

Was it the freshness rising from the garden, or the strange gaze of that moon whose pallor was mixed with blood, that made her tremble? Was it because she felt too happy and her joy suddenly made her anxious?

She could not say.

Henri examined her furtively. He was discovering a kind of beauty he did not like. This profile of a woman, with a short nose, a chin pierced by a wide, line-breaking cleft, a narrow temple, long eyes, so long that they had the appearance of a tent between whose silky edges a wild cat might peer, both surprised and disturbed him. It baffled all of his prejudices about the eternal feminine, his notions of an orderly, methodical young man. He would have preferred a less well-built woman, with less developed hips and a more regular figure, more *like the others*. The hair, for example, made him proud, and he said to himself, *It is not the mouse tail of our poor Parisian women, who have only just enough to accompany their hats*. Despite this essential quality, he pointed out the faults with the meticulous care of a reluctant fiancé.

She was original, easy to clean up, and promising enough for good motherhood, but she cared little for her toilette, wore old, clinging fashions that were no longer worn, which made one appear naked amid a hundred women dressed in complicated draperies. Finally, she smelled of lavender, like pure linen, she was serious, calm, like an ignorant woman who knew only one thing: that she had time, her whole life to learn; and she smiled a constrained smile, like a child who is about to leave her family.

The prospect of their honeymoon in Paris, this return to the luxury of honest pleasures—theaters, expensive restaurants, car rides through illuminated streets—charmed him for a second. He already enjoyed his amazement and delight of a young provincial let loose in toyland. Certainly, it would be a memorable date, she would remember it for a long time, she would make discreet allusions to it, on winter evenings, when they would hear the breeze blowing and would huddle together, she preparing a layette, he reading his newspaper . . .

If the business of the practice prospered, they would go back to Paris, treating themselves to a few excursions and trips to the seaside. My God, in the meantime, he was going to settle down in a pleasant way. Not a great fortune and with unique in-laws: Madame Lordès always said *passed away* instead of *died* and soaked her bread in gravy; Monsieur Lordès joked like a collection of poems distributed at the fair; but the girl would quickly be trained to nicer habits, she did not have their vulgar language since she was perpetually silent, a proof of taste, and if she liked her home, her children, he would not ask her to do impossible things. Oh! That sweet little home that he had been dreaming of! A well-kept English cart, yet not pretentious, harnessed to an amiable broodmare not difficult to manage, able to bear the brake on the downhill slopes and to take the sugar from the hand of her master, without ever needing the whip!

Brought up by a cranky aunt, a maniacal spinster, and his father, a sorrowful widower, Henri Alban wanted to found a real family, as depicted in the works of Charles Dickens, his favorite author. Armand de Bréville, for his part, vouched for the future, and Henri, no more devout than he needed to be, for he did not go to religious services, thanked his friend the priest from the bottom of his heart. Only they, in their black petticoats, could discover the pearl in the oyster!

Still, he would have liked to smoke. The cigar prohibition spoiled his engagement party.

Laure murmured in a low, troubled voice, clipped with hesitation, "The moon scares me. See, monsieur, how red it is?"

Henri leaned over the terrace, propped on his elbows, and smiled. "I am not looking at it, mademoiselle, I am looking at you..."

He felt it was absurd, this introduction to the conversation, but in provincial circles . . .

"She is red, red," repeated Laure, who was turning pale, moving closer to him.

Henri took her wrist, very slowly, not wanting to startle her, and added, "We are going to be very happy, are we not, my dear little fiancée?"

Laure gave him her hand and, without realizing it, one by one, her fingers entwining with those of the young man, joined their palms.

During this display of trust, Henri remembered that the last mistress whom he had had, the only one perhaps whom he loved more than a beautiful object of art, used to press his fingers in this way in their hours of intimacy, and he laughed outright. "Are you nervous, Mademoiselle Laure?"

"I do not know, Monsieur Henri."

"Because you are afraid of the moon!"

"Close to you, I am no longer afraid of anything," she repeated.

Henri brought the hand of the girl to his lips and kissed it lightly. Laure almost fainted. This was the confession, the definitive confession, and she could already see herself in his arms, nestling on his chest.

Her head bent, begging for the young man's shoulder, she wanted to cry out to him, "You are handsome, I adore you, come away to the grass over there! I will prove to you that I am beautiful, and it will be worth a church wedding where I know a priest who will curse us instead of blessing us, a jealous monster who, standing, under the porch, will have the right to spit on my white dress . . . !"

The fiancé murmured, "When we are married, we are going to buy a victoria ... I think that we will be able to do that with a bit of savings, and we will go to the city on holidays."

Laure said dully, "I do not care about carriages, Monsieur Henri, I am not ambitious." She tried to be absolutely plain and to disguise her indignation from him.

He was amused by her ingenuity. "It is not for ambition that one has a victoria, dear girl, it is for the convenience of dealing with clients. A notaire cannot travel on foot, I assure you."

"Ah ... ! You think!" Tears welled up at the edge of the girl's eyelids. What was he talking about?

"Do you like fashion?"

"I only have one dress, and it is always new," answered Laure. And her haughty pout added, *This dress is my skin, you do not seem to be in a hurry to see it, eh?*

Then she reasoned with herself. She wanted to run when he walked, did not even dare venture into the mysterious land of engagement. She had to come back to reality, reserve herself more, not throw her freshly blossomed heart at him as she had formerly thrown herself. Late-night modesty invaded her and paralyzed her limbs. Sorry now that she did not find herself more naive, more desirable, she would have gladly fallen to her knees to beg his forgiveness; but it was too late now, she had only to let herself be married. What she had accepted the day before as a safeguard and a rehabilitation, she accepted today as a definitive expiation; she would bear the full weight of past faults, remorse, and his wrath *if he realized it*. If he did not (a twenty-six-year-old man never has much experience), she would give herself so well, love him so much, absorb herself so much in him that she could still become an honest woman.

This love had taken hold of her suddenly, at the very hour she had seen him enter their home, there, behind the haze, in that corner of darkness where the greenhouse lay, in that grave where she had been born. Suddenly, it had seemed to her that she saw an extraordinary man.

And he showed her nothing more attractive than anyone else. He was blond, a slightly dull ash-blond, with regular features, a white complexion and a sober mustache; his mouth puckered at both ends in a disgruntled crease that gave him a look of disdainful mockery, but he was charming when he smiled. Laure loved him above all because she instinctively sensed his absolute contrast and dreamed of conquest. She would be the master, he the pupil. Turning her husband into a lover would bring her the most exquisite human bliss.

Then she stopped reasoning, and after a few weeks of ordinary courtship, in which the stuffy white camellia replaced burning declarations, she loved him madly, in a whirlwind of contradictory desires. Sometimes she wanted to confess her past to him, sometimes she forgot she was not a virgin, feeling the candor of a little girl frightened by a monsieur. And then she would have superb bursts, brief immolations where she would trample his heart under her feet, vowing to enter religion and pray for him. She ended up imagining a God through man, and was shedding her former wickedness. She wept whole nights in front of his photograph—which she did not put under her pillow for fear of marring it. She softened over useless things, in which her passion was mirrored for lack of a better and more ardent mirror: the death of an insect she had just crushed, the end of a flower fading at the bottom of a vase; and tears welled up in her eyes as she gazed at the stars, as numerous as the agonies of guilty hearts.

She loved! She loved! She possessed all of the satanic desires and all of the purities of angels . . .

How could she offer him her poor, withered self?

Would she play a comedy all the more provocative because she knew the spice of all of the refusal techniques, or would she tell him the truth, the better to surrender herself, the better to annihilate herself in the brutal caress of the furious male, who would kill her by forgiving her.

She thought without cessation about that sinister wedding night! And around her, she activated a flame that would perhaps devour her that night.

As for Lucien Séchard, she could not even remember his entitlements . . . Since he had not asserted them straight away, he must have been planning some ridiculous scene, and she took care to destroy its effect on the evening of the solemn day . . . No, Lucien would not dare. Besides, he had no proof.

Every time she passed the study, the clerk rushed in, shutting the door so as not to expose himself to any more encounters. She had broken it off for good. Another week and Lucien Séchard would be gone, she would be free . . .

Once, Henri Alban had said to her, speaking of the one-eyed man, "The poor boy, one would think he had fallen into gooseberry jelly!"

And with good grace, she had laughed, laughed out loud.

However, Laure was worried about Henri's coldness. She was troubled by it while acquainting herself with this overly respectful style of love. The priest, choosing a quiet man of tranquil senses out of the secret jealousy of a lover deprived of carnal pleasures, had no idea that he was providing the passionate young woman with an excitement more terrible for her than the impetuous caresses of a boor. Laure drew her main cerebral joys from this respect for her future husband. It was a double attraction for her to feel the slightest touch on her fingers and to know, at the same time, that everything was desired, that she would have to give up everything . . . She simpered, granting her hand, and offered her body in that small, open hand. What young girls do not usually know, she knew, and she completed sentences, she finished gestures, she knew the meaning of all of the signs. Torturing herself to fathom the mind of this cold man, she invented questions even more ingenuous than usual. She found equivocal situations to try to make him lose his restraint and judged him on a word, on a smile, already molding him in her image, endowing him with a hypocrisy equal to her own. The madness of the senses had matured her for more delicate follies, the pleasures of the imagination replacing brutal results. The monstrance had at last melted into its own radiance, the divinity was incarnate in her, and she no longer held out the host to the lips of the faithful without having tasted it herself. Her violent desire for sacrilege, when she lusted after the curé d'Estérac, was transformed into a legitimate fervor, and the priest had merely prepared her nerves, her blood, and her flesh to receive an aphrodisiac from which she would inevitably make poison. The unfulfilled dream was to inflame the chaste husband at her touch, to dictate terms, and it was not exactly good motherhood that was promised by her hips swaying under the taut skirt, her breasts pointing straight at the men.

The moon covered them with its sad eye, and the two betrothed chatted quietly on the terrace. Laure, suffering martyrdom as he recoiled from her approach, laughed the foolish laugh of a virtuous young girl. Henri spoke of the miseries of Parisian existence for boys who do not feel at home, of the hermetically sealed stoves in which asphyxiation simmers, of those stoves with their appearances of top hats, and he praised the Christmas logs piling up in the big provincial fireplaces; he told of the delights of beef stew when one came out of restaurants where one paid a lot to eat so little ... Then he talked about their contract, realizing that she was interested in the serious side of the marital question.

This contract was a masterpiece in which everything would be foreseen by their parents; he added, index finger raised, "Even our death!"

"How," she murmured with an irony the depth of which he did not suspect, "must we die?"

"There is no telling what might happen, my dear," he replied, overcome by a touching emotion. "If one of us were to die, *I would be* naturally very unhappy, but the best interests of our children would come first ..."

This sentence, full of naive selfishness, was spoken in a very soft voice. He was not aware that he was saying anything dreadful, and Laure, by chance, was reminded of the torture that she had inflicted one particular night on Lucien, the miserable lover forced to conceal his suffering.

She endured the sentence by way of expiation, and thought this: without remorse, life would be unbearable, the stupid things that we have done are the only justifications for these inconsistencies!

And, very humbly, showing herself to be even more sincere, she said this, "Of course I can die, we are all mortal!"

It occurred to him that decidedly she was talking like a fool.

Madame Lordès snapped them out of their sentimental chatter. "Please go home, my children! Some peasants could spy on you, it is not proper," she shouted.

They returned, hand in hand, swinging their arms in imitation of rebellious schoolchildren. And they hitched up the cabriolet they had borrowed from the mayor of Estérac.

The Lordès family, their daughter between them, set off from La Bourdaisière, the fiancé's estate, waving handkerchiefs in the moonlight, Laure murmuring inwardly, *He does not love me yet! What I consider respect is only indifference. He is marrying our practice!*

And, straightening suddenly and menacingly, she turned to face the house, which stood out white against the dark sky. *You will love me, Henri, I want you to! I will make you love me, otherwise I will turn into the worst animal you have ever seen, me, whom you already take for a beast.*

A week after the engagement dinner, on a Thursday, the Albans in turn descended the hillside of La Bourdaisière to visit the Lordès family.

At the house of the notaire, they cooked earnestly; it was appropriate to drink plenty of aperitifs, and the liqueurs, all from the very back of the cupboard, soon formed a rainbow on the table of the solemn salon where the succulent plant, with its glassy hair, exuded the chill of a drowned woman. As Henri's aunt entered, she felt cold and kept her shawl on with a bad-tempered air; the father Alban, to escape this assortment of sugar, and the *angeline*, and the last peach maraschino containing, by its creator's own admission, a soupçon of prussic acid, fled to the gendarmerie to see some horses. Henri, out of politeness, accepted a few various poisons. Laure, her eyes downcast, was busy grouping the bottles and occasionally passing a plate filled with dry cakes powdered with aniseed and ginger.

The plate of cakes exhausted, Laure was asked to play *her* Métra waltz.

She obeyed, her eyelids still half-closed, as if continuing a sleep she dared not shake. Henri turned the pages for her, her father beat time, his aunt nodded her head in approval with several discreet exclamations, and her mother cried out to her at the critical moment, "You know, your arpeggio, do not miss it, eh!"

But she hardly woke up, only becoming aware of their presence when the notaire said, in a voice that seemed to vibrate under a bell, "Now, Monsieur Henri, we will leave the ladies to it, and I will take you to the practice, my clerk awaits you. The poor Cyclops, it is his day for receiving guests too . . ."

And the two men went out.

The day before, Monsieur Lordès had settled his account with him once and for all. They had exchanged the usual banal words. "Oh! I have never had anything but praise for you, Séchard, put 'er there, my boy."

"Monsieur, I thank you for all of your kindnesses. I am sure that I will not find a better boss, either in the capital or in the arrondissement."

"What can one do, Séchard? Destiny ordains that we part."

"A cruel destiny, Monsieur Lordès."

"Yes! Yes . . . ! Ten years of loyal service . . . If I did not marry off my daughter, Séchard, you would never leave me."

"Ultimately, one cannot do what one wants in life!"

"Here, Séchard, let us embrace . . ."

And the boss had hugged Lucien, avoiding, as he had explained to his wife that evening, touching his face to that one eye that distilled red tears.

He had been invited to dinner for the second and last time, but he had excused himself, feeling that his place was taken at the kitchen table, despite their sympathy.

"You will eat with us!" said the notaire in a show of generosity.

Sit next to Laure, next to the fiancée? No, he could not, and the clerk shrugged: he refused again.

Henri Alban, entering the study, found it very calm; the *amateur* clerk and the low-paid clerk held out their hands, brushed their fingertips against each other and immediately began examining the different arrangements of the green cardboard boxes. They knew each other from afar; Henri felt pity, Lucien respect. The notaire, seeing the two of them heartily engrossed in paperwork, slipped away to join the blasted horse-racer at the gendarmerie to lecture him. The study door closed.

"To the left . . ." murmured Lucien Séchard, "all business concerning the city, and to the right, all business concerning the countryside. There, on that glass cabinet, you will find the stamp, the bottles of ink, a supply of blotting paper . . . Office supplies are almost nonexistent here . . . You would think there would not be much work to do . . ."

"I know, very few clients and bad clients," said Henri, frowning disdainfully. "Papa Lordès neglects his practice for the liquor merchant's craft, and he has his routines . . ."

He finished his sentence with an impatient gesture and lit a cigar. He retained a bitter taste of the green liquor that irritated him.

Lucien replied, "Oh, he is a good man . . . a blind one."

Henri almost burst out laughing. This one-eyed man calling another blind seemed very funny to him.

"You are joking, Monsieur Séchard."

Lucien raised his blue eye and his red eye; he said with a strange grin, "I am sure of it, monsieur."

The examination of the musty files, cardboard boxes, blandsmelling drawers, and copper-bound books lasted a while, then Lucien Séchard consulted his watch.

"I still have a few minutes," he said, "because I do not get out of here until five o'clock and I am paid for today until the evening. Oh! The boss will get his money's worth, I promise . . . I will wait for the time, as always . . ."

Henri, comfortably seated in the armchair of Monsieur Lordès, nodded his head in approval of this scruple. His cigar was excellent, and he did not mind joining the ladies at the piano. They would talk business for a while until the time came for this honest fellow to make his proper exit.

"So, monsieur, I have just time to instruct you in *the rest*," continued Lucien, sitting down in front of the young man and inclining his face to his chest, as was his custom whenever he found himself in front of someone.

"The rest?" Henri repeated mechanically, crossing his leg.

What did that emphasized word mean? Did their practice have dark secrets? Was he going to tell him the story of a fantastic will, give him charitable advice about some dangerous mania of the boss? My God, this clerk was disturbingly precise.

"I am listening, my friend," added Henri, analyzing the one-eyed man's pitiful expression and becoming increasingly convinced that *the thing* resembled gooseberry jelly.

There was a silence. Lucien was biting his lips, already calculating the scope of his revelations and not hurrying himself. Henri was smoking, very anxious, not knowing why.

"Monsieur Alban," continued Séchard, clipping his syllables with pauses, "you may become the clerk of my boss, but you will not become his son-in-law. I would like to explain these things to you without making too many speeches. I do not want to stay in this house unnecessarily, as my minutes are limited, so I will confine myself to what interests you specifically: Mademoiselle Lordès, your fiancée, has a lover."

Henri stumbled back in his armchair, dropped his cigar, and, pale-faced, exclaimed, "Monsieur, you are a wretch!"

"Indeed, I am a wretch," sighed Lucien, gasping. "I am poor, I am ugly, I am a coward, and yet I must declare the truth, for it is written that he who knows of a legitimate impediment to marriage must reveal it on pain of mortal sin. Your banns have been published, the white dress has been sewn, how can you break it off without a scene? I pity you sincerely, you did not hurt me . . ." Lucien stopped to take a breath. "No, you did not hurt me. The time has come, and an hour that has been paid for, monsieur, the time has come to tell you: your fiancée has a lover, the worst kind of lover, a wretch, very poor, very ugly, very cowardly . . ." He stopped again, choking, hands trembling. "I tell you, she has a very unworthy lover, monsieur."

Henri Alban stood up abruptly. The red eye glinting in front of him no longer made him smile. Either this boy was distraught with grief at his departure, or he was taking revenge for terrible reasons that needed to be cleared up immediately.

"You are lying!" Henri stammered, picking up his cigar to contain himself.

"So," murmured Lucien, without moving from his seat, "you do not care for her much . . . Why do you not grab me by the throat? Eh! I deserve to be strangled, monsieur! Oh! You do not care for her much; I would not have responded, I would have struck. This lover, monsieur, it is I, I, Lucien Séchard, the Cyclops . . . Listen well, it is I, and I want to die."

Henri sat back, his face flustered, no longer daring to stare. He tried to mock the boy, who was begging for a good blow to the head. "It just keeps getting better! And do you have any proof of this, Monsieur Séchard?"

"I have no proof, but ask Laure and you will see!"

"You are a despicable fool, my poor Séchard, you are sick!"

"No, monsieur, I am a despicable fool who is doing just fine. I took your fiancée because she offered herself to me, here, on this very chair you have just sat down in. She is a girl, I swear to you, a horrible girl, and so charming! I cannot marry her, but no one in my lifetime will. I have suffered too much. I am taking my revenge because she took my heart out of my chest . . ."

In a muffled tone, he stammered another unintelligible sentence, breathing heavily, fighting back a rising sob, then he arranged some papers in a box, checked the time on his watch, and headed for the door, putting on his low-visored cap. Henri let him, painfully frightened, thinking only of the possibility of raving madness.

"Monsieur, I will warn you of my departure," said Lucien, taking his hat off. "I am leaving half an hour too early because I still have a duty to perform. For the scandal to be complete, I must kill myself. There is a well behind the church, I am going to throw myself into it, I will poison the water with my corpse, they will pull me out, and the whole town will know that I killed myself leaving this practice. Can you imagine the speculation and gossip? No, I have no proof, but love is proven by death, monsieur. I bid you farewell."

He put his cap back on, opened the door, and left.

Henri, his eyes fixed on him, stared in dismay. Either this wretch was telling the truth or he was putting on a remarkable act. Unless madness, a very strange kind of madness, had given him a sudden passion for his fiancée.

When Lucien was on the stairs, he said again, raising his voice, "Do not forget, monsieur, to question Mademoiselle Lordès. The most clever women betray themselves; she will betray herself one day, quite naturally."

He descended the steps and disappeared around the bend in the railing.

Henri remained in a stupor for a moment. If it had not been for his desire to cry, the clerk would have appeared to be reading him a copy of a notarial deed. But for a second, he had revealed an emotion so deep, so distressing even for the listener, that the young man could not deny that this grotesque man had an extraordinary gift for sensitivity.

As soon as Henri heard the heavy front door fall, the methodical, correct Henri leaped up and tumbled into the living room. He was suffocating, he wanted to reassure himself immediately, find Laure, ask her for explanations . . . and above all find out why no one had ever told him about this cripple's nervous breakdowns, because he was mad . . . mad . . . Then they would fetch the sufferer from the well.

The old ladies, the aunt and Madame Lordès, were in the kitchen, absorbed in household chatter. Laure remained in front of her piano, hands clasped in the middle of the keyboard, no longer playing, as if petrified, trying to catch either the last vibration of a note or the sound of the footsteps of a man as he fled along the street.

Had she heard him leave?

Henri hesitated.

Was this girl to become the victim of an odious revenge of a dismissed servant? Would he sully her mind by asking her about such things?

This *charming* girl, as the monster put it, and yet *horrible*! How well she maintained the attitude of a child trying to decipher a complicated piece of music, with her large floating braid, her half-closed eyelids, and her mouth clenched against her fine teeth, which could be seen glistening through the crimson! What terms would he, the fiancé, use with the chaste young girl?

And only that day, thinking of that one-eyed man's dreadful wound, did he realize that she had beautiful eyes, the likes of which he would never meet again . . .

"Mademoiselle," he stammered, coming closer, "I want to talk to you . . . right now, oh! Right now . . ."

With a swift movement, she swiveled on her stool, her hands still clasped on her knees, her eyelids still lowered, her little feet stretched, pointing, and her vague smile.

"My God," he exclaimed, finding only this cry, "Lucien Séchard is going to kill himself . . ."

"You think so, monsieur?" Laure replied curtly.

Suffocated, Henri added, losing his head, "Because he was . . . your . . . Do you understand, Laure . . ."

She stood up, all white. "Ah! He told you . . ." And she inclined her bust, staggering, ready to slip into his arms, murmuring, "So much the better, I prefer it, I will be your mistress instead of your wife, that is all . . . Let him die!"

But she fell full-length onto the carpet, the young man having jumped back.

9

In the crowd around the well, the curé d'Estérac stood motionless, beneath the silver cross carried by an altar boy. His lips seemed to be chanting, and in reality, they were quivering in disgust without saying a single prayer. Agonized by the creaking of the rusty chain on the pulley, he would occasionally put his index finger in his ear, in a mechanical gesture that was not very religious.

It was raining.

The fig tree shading the well was glistening with oil-like water. The backs of the two men, in shirtsleeves, who turned the crank, were sweating. The women who had come to watch, hair uncovered, exchanged appropriate expressions of sorrow, and the well-dressed gentlemen, hatless, hunched their shoulders.

There were about fifty of them in this small, angular square, bordered by a wall with honeysuckle sticking out of it, and darkened by the thickness of the fig tree and the height of the church. They were just behind the sacristy. A stained glass window towered over the people, showing them its crown of radiant thorns in the red flames of a sacred heart of Jesus.

This well, very ancient, was adorned with carved, grimacing figures with snub noses, polished to a shine by rough-hewn workers on a day of jubilation. A wrought-iron frame soared over the gaping hole, parting like two black lace curtains and falling in fanciful, torn curls.

Foreigners had once picked half of these iron flowers while visiting the beauties of the little town, and a local collector wrote to the mayor every year asking for the rest.

These archaeological matters were whispered among the local notables, some stamping their feet in the mud in annoyance, others nudging each other, repeating indignantly, "Let us see it! Let us see it! Be quiet! This is about a dead man, not about selling scrap metal! Gentlemen, please behave! The curé is not happy."

The rumors about the well died down, while the concert of women, moaning over the dead man, continued above. "What a misfortune! His mother is going to find him rotten! Oh, poor thing!"

"We used to fetch our water from there! An infection, my dear . . . !"

"You could no longer bend over without giving up your soul . . . !"

"Oh! It is a story that would make me leave this street . . . !"

"I knew him well, I said hello to him often . . . !"

". . . Me, I cook my vegetables in river water . . . !"

The curé, still shivering, made a gesture of violence.

The women near him fell silent, but farther on, Joséphine, the Lordès's stubborn old cook, continued to grind out her words, scattering them like raindrops. She told them her tenth version, the best one, because the drama ended up being stripped of personal reflections, so tired was she of repeating it.

"Madame and I were in the corridor. The aunt of Monsieur Henri was walking ahead of us, saying, 'I like to dine late.' Madame replied, 'The rest of us have an early dinner . . .' And all of a sudden, Monsieur Henri came out of the living room, his arms raised . . . Here, like this!" And the old lady raised her skinny arms, waving them. "He was as white as the surplice of Monsieur le Curé. He shouted, 'Aunt, let us get out of here! I want to get out of here now!'"

Joséphine planted herself, one fist on her hip, ready to collect a standing ovation the moment the curé made another angry gesture.

A neighbor resumed, her tone lowered, "Oh! It is proper! She went with all of the little boys in the neighborhood when she was at school . . . One-eyed or lame, all became her godsend, and if it had not been for my great derelict of a son, who told me about it this morning, I would never have suspected it."

"Such a sweet girl . . ." added another, "always taking her communion and never leaving her mother's skirts."

"And to think that poor Madame Séchard is in the church waiting . . . eh? Did we look hard enough for that body that has been stinking up the place for a month?" murmured a crying man. "If the Alban family knew, they should have told us . . . !"

A woman, holding a child in a diaper, wiped her eyes, stammering, "Maybe it is just a cat or a dog! Still, he should have thought of his mother; he is going to cost her plenty . . ."

The pulley creaked more and more, and the men sweat under their shirts which stuck to their skins. The curé paled as the ferocious denouement drew nearer, and he, too, thought of a woman waiting, huddled in his church, not daring to show herself in the full glare of the scandal. At last, the head of a man emerged, that of the courageous well-digger who had been taken down, straddling a plank, sneezing foul-smelling water and spewing putrefaction from every inch of his clothes.

"He is there!" he shouted in a voice that seemed to rise mournfully from the bowels of the earth. The man shook himself, throwing appalling odors at the attendants rushing toward the edge; he added fiercely, "Respect, you people! Do I smell like roses, you pigs?"

And as he was beside himself with rage at what he had glimpsed in the darkness of this hole, he forgot the presence of the curé, swearing all of the names of God that he possessed. Armand de Bréville stepped forward, summarily blessing the well. Then, turning, he muttered through gritted teeth, "Let us say a prayer, my friends, for the deceased whom, alone, our Lord Jesus Christ has the right to condemn. *De profundis . . .*"

The women knelt with a feverish intensity, the men uncovered themselves, some pouting. The sewage worker, sheepish, his hair bristling along his temples, kept his profane position, straddling his plank, but his fingers wandered in numerous signs of the cross, and all could hear the monotonous sound of water rushing into the well through his trouser legs, falling in huge tears on Lucien Séchard's rotting flesh. Now it was a matter for the gendarmerie, the mayor, the justice of the peace. The altar boy, happily carrying his staff, made his way to the left; the priest followed, bowing his brow. When he entered the porch, he gestured anxiously, holding the child by the arm.

"What is that?" asked the latter, his curiosity getting the better of him.

"Hang the cross, the same as always, under the keystone! Come, give me that and go!"

The boy ran off, delighted to find himself free, and Armand closed the quilted door with a sigh of relief.

Madame Séchard, seated at the altar, moaned, her face buried in her mourning shawl; she prayed aloud, reciting the litanies of the Virgin, displaying her pain openly without thinking too much about the fact that no one was left in the church. She was a tall, bony woman, with a mean look and a yellow face with prominent cheekbones. The curé touched her shoulder.

"Courage," he stammered, his eyes fixed elsewhere, "courage, poor woman, and let us pray together for the despairing . . ."

"He was in the well! He was in the well!" roared the mother, whose grief suddenly increased by the depth of the abyss into which heartbreak had plunged the suicide victim. "As I said, we should have looked there right away. Ah! The poor dear child . . . ! The murderers . . . ! They killed my son . . . ! And I will kill them too . . . Yes, all of them! Father, mother, daughter . . . Oh! Wench! Wench, I will kill you . . . !"

The nimbus of the saints quivered, the wings of the angels vibrated, and the statue of the Virgin, amid a halo of stars, took on a sullen, more resigned aspect.

"Courage," breathed the priest, clamping his hand on that shoulder as hard as a wooden limb. "We must pray, madame."

"No, I have had enough," screamed Madame Séchard, seized by a blind rage. "I have had enough! I want to see him again . . . Do not torment me, Monsieur le Curé; he is my son, and what is more," she finished her sentence in an explosion of sobs, "and what is more, I want him back dressed, I do not want anything taken from him; if he killed himself with money on him, I want to find it, that money . . . to sue them, do you hear me! Yes, I will take them to court, that is my idea . . . Leave me in peace!"

She dashed madly forward, brandishing a brown cotton umbrella, and was soon out of the church, pounding the ramparts like a drunken woman. Outside, the clamor grew louder as her high-pitched voice repeated, "The wench! The wench! I will kill her!"

Upright on the threshold of the sacristy, the "wench" stood there, very pale, the tail of her hair pulled back in a collar around her neck, ready to strangle herself so as not to fall alive into this mud mixed with human decomposition. Laure was dressed in a singular costume; she wore a draped skirt too long for her, a sort of bodice of an Amazon buttoned with tiny buttons, and her hat veiled with a marvelous embroidery on white tulle. Armand de Bréville pointed to a confessional. She crossed the choir, entered the part reserved for the confessor, and locked herself in. The curé stood by the narrow grate, hidden by a red drapery.

"They found him," he said laconically.

"I know," replied Laure in a calm accent. "I followed the operation from the back of our prie-dieu in the sacristy. I could see very well . . ."

Sweat bathed the brow of Armand. He sponged himself feverishly with the edge of his surplice. "Do you have everything you need for the journey?"

"Of course, I cut and sewed all night, used two cassocks and all of the trimmings of an altar cloth for my hat. I was very worried about the hairstyle, but I am fine with it, thank you."

"Laure! Laure! Quiet yourself!" grumbled the priest, exasperated by her indifference and cynicism.

"I am safe," replied Laure. "They can scream for all I care. And you, are you afraid of complications?"

"I am going mad . . ."

"Too bad! If you do not keep your calm, you will hand me over to all of those brutes. My parents will come after me, naturally. They drove me away, but they regret it, and they will search for me endlessly. I do not want to go back to them . . . Ah! That would be too clumsy of me! If they think that I am dead too, then all is well! No, I am going. Once I am in Paris, at his place, no one will have the right to take me back, because I have been of age for three weeks . . ."

"What if Henri Alban were to drive you away too?"

"He would never dare!"

"Laure, Laure, you damn me, we damn each other! It will be known that I protected the escape of the guilty child! I am helping you to disgrace yourself even more, and it is a hideous role you are making me play . . . Laure, I implore you, go home to your parents, I will take care of reconciling them with you . . . Later, when all is forgotten, you will—"

She interrupted him with a light laugh. "I do not forget, I still have the claws of my mother branded on my chest! You are ridiculous, my dear curé, with your eternal remorse. You have not sinned, you are not my lover, I do not think! Indeed, what you are doing is Christian charity, nothing more!"

At that moment, the funeral procession was passing in front of the porch, the corpse was being led to the town hall, and they could hear the distressed wails of a company of women and the raging complaints of Madame Séchard, who was being prevented from rolling onto the stretcher where a monstrous body lay under a sheet. A clamor of she-wolves rose, engulfing the sonorous vessel of the nave, echoes sowing syllables among the shadows. The refugee distinctly perceived a name, that of her parents, who were publicly scourged by a whole series of insults.

"You see, Monsieur le Curé," she sneered disdainfully, "I have to leave and never come back. These people are brutes!"

And Armand de Bréville, with the danger receding, went to the altar to prostrate himself, imploring divine mercy since he could no longer hope for human mercy.

The Lordès family, indeed, had driven their daughter away. The scandal had hit them like a thunderbolt, and they had not had time to think.

One evening, the half-mad father and the mother, almost rendered senseless, both pushed her into the gutter of the street and shouted at her, "Get out of here, prostitute, get out of here, our house is an honest house."

The haberdasher across the street, cooling off on her doorstep, and the notaire's neighbors, all being aware of the sensational story of the beautiful girl who had given herself up to a one-eyed man, had seen her tumbling down the stoop scantily clad in a percale underskirt and camisole, and all closed their doors by general consensus. And that bundle of white rags, looking like a snowflake whirled by the wind, had fled, without a word, without a cry for help, they did not know which direction! And yet, Laure fled, battered and bruised. The father had seized a cane after the horrible scene, and the mother had torn her up with her own fingernails. They no longer remembered the beautiful, proud angelic girl so long-awaited, so well cultivated! This was no longer *the little girl*, no longer Laure, no longer Mademoiselle Lordès! This was a bitch that the dogs would come and sniff out under their roof, a prostitute whose vices suddenly burst forth like an internecine fire . . . Perhaps they should have remembered their ardors of yesteryear to create her, before destroying her, their ardors to make her pretty and seductive, to run through her veins a rich blood fortified with spices from all corners of the world, aphrodisiacs produced from all of the hot countries where love is seasoned with red peppers; but they were old: extinguished ardors are hardly forgiving; when it comes to legitimate opinions, indulgence does not count. Above all, they blamed her (the drop of bitterness that made the cup overflow) for the solemn departure of their maid, Joséphine, who had flung her apron at them in the middle of the salon ...

Then Mademoiselle Lordès, finding the church at the end of a mad run like a beast stalked by a pack, threw herself into it, head down, imitating Lucien Séchard's furious fall into the abyss. Fortunately, the church remained empty at that hour of the evening, containing only its young curé, constantly in prayer since the scandal grew around his parish. Laure showed him her bruised arms, her throat covered in scratches, by the light of a candle.

"Protect me," she cried, "if you do not want me to kill *myself* also!"

And he had installed her behind the good Lord, in the sacristy, locking her up in the confessionals when he feared either her imprudence or visits from the sacristan, arranging bunks for her with priestly vestments, altar cloths, surplices, and mounds of lace, ransacking the Lord's treasures with the conscience of fulfilling a pious duty, tearing the embroidered silk scarves offered to him on religious feasts to provide her with a belt and put her in a more decent state, bandaging her little wounds with the large tulles with which the Virgin was veiled, the holy batistes that covered the ciborium.

At night, she slept in an ancient chest where sacred vessels were kept; the church safe, to which he alone had the key, was as wide as a bedroom, as deep as the den of a wild beast. Through the velvet blackness of its obscurity, golds and gems gleamed, and she had quickly arranged a sort of marvelous bed with a pile of crimson cushions *à crépines*, fleur-de-lis carpets used on procession days, brightly colored stoles with reverse sides of white moiré, of yellow salina. Two banners, that of Jesus and that of Mary, formed her curtains; her neck rested against the Easter chasuble, and she buried her elbow in the sequined silk that was stretched over the monstrance during the ceremonies of Perpetual Adoration.

Sometimes, bored by her imprisonment and inability to see, she would grope open jewel cases and play, dipping her feverish fingers into the precious stones. Here and there, a lightning bolt would flash under the slender beam of a slit in the sideboard, and she would turn ciboria, patens, and drinking vessels over and over, without qualms, out of a naive desire to touch glass trinkets, a childish glory of being the mistress of forbidden objects, and she alone knowing that these objects were no more alive than others, that they bore no witness to their character as blessed, reborn vases, never to be treated familiarly.

At night, she would get up, get out of her silky bed and wander the sacristy under the stars. If the priest had not taken the precaution of locking her in, she would have climbed up onto the altar to put her ear to the lock of the formidable, tiny door of the Lord God.

Ah! He was a convenient neighbor, that one! No noise, no light. He was always asleep! The first night, she had thought that she should be afraid, but the second night she had laughed, a silent laugh, contemplating, in the moonlight, an empty monstrance that shone less brightly when looked at closely . . . She was much quieter in the sanctuary of her judge than in her maiden bed. Surrounded by the discreet scent of incense, she rested like the true idol restored to its primitive place, her knee on the heart of the priest and her thumb on the throat of Christ.

It was simple and natural. A well-deserved stopover between the life of lies that she had led at home and the life of free passions that she led there. She was the animal king, the cursed and petted beast, the beast that lodges where it can and makes a cozy nest out of the ugliest mess. It was enthroned above prayers, for it was innocently fierce—like God. Besides, if God was not happy about the rivalry, he could speak . . . And she questioned the mysterious silence of the church, which answered nothing.

During those eight days, a deadly length for the priest, her jailer, she had dreamed of her conquest, Henri Alban! She knew his address in Paris, and she would go and find him, saying simply, "Here I am," laying down her coat. First, she wanted to heal her wounds, to erase her mother's scratches. As for suicide, she stopped thinking about it, not admitting to herself that to stop loving is sometimes to commit murder. She ate what Armand brought her secretly, fruit, bread, pâté, cakes, and drank from the cruets of the Mass. Then she would stretch her limbs, yawning, leafing through Latin books as a distraction, to see the colored pictures, and finally, smiling mischievously, with a shifty eye, looking right and left, she would go into a dark corner, slip behind a mortuary drapery, spangled with white tears in exclamation marks, and use an ancient Roman stoup as a chamber pot. This was done gracefully, with the hypocritical air of a pretty, lustrous beast, loitering for . . . the pleasure of loitering. She tended to her person as usual, drew water from the baptistery, washed her hands and face, and performed her ablutions with the same peace of mind as if she had stopped under a tree! The unfortunate priest tortured himself to make her comfortable, and no longer dared to enter when she, already combed, was waiting for him at around five in the morning, as one waits for the manservant who is to bring you chocolate.

"Laure, did you pray?"

"No, brother, I am hungry! What news?"

"Here are some strawberries, pie, and a chicken wing. Oh, my poor child, I could not sleep last night; I thought that there was a fire and we had to sound the alarm. Come, do not stay there. My sacristan or the altar boys would just have to go ahead with Mass . . . No, the news is not good. They are looking for Lucien and they forget to look for you, my poor friend!"

She laughed and joked with him about his night terrors, but no longer tried to tempt him, as she wanted another man and thought he was a fool not to *take advantage of her.*

One night, Laure stood at her window, that is, at the stained glass window of the sacristy, an antique stained glass window stamped with a flamboyant crown of thorns. The square behind the church was still deserted, and the well under the tall fig tree seemed to be sleeping the bad sleep of a monster that crawls deep into the earth, letting passersby see only its gaping maw. It was warm and mild, and the heady aroma of honeysuckle wafted around the girl . . . Suddenly, as if the wind, in order to allow this atrocity, had suddenly leaped from north to south, the honeysuckle aroma took flight, and from the well exhaled an appalling breeze, a rotten breath that landed wetly on her cheek. She threw herself back, hands clasped.

"Is it possible?" she exclaimed.

Seriously alarmed this time, she scrambled to the bottom of her stepladder, teeth chattering, fists in her nostrils so as not to smell the stench of death. In the clouds, a reddish moon stared down at her, and she murmured, hiding her face, shaken, "The sky is one-eyed!"

Two days before the discovery of the corpse, she asked the abbé for thread, needles, and scissors. She prepared her traveling costume, and it was agreed that she would cut it from cassocks. She had the coquetry to embellish it with a brand-new black silk scarf, and her hat, a toque held by the cap of a barrette, was a miracle of patience; she wrapped it in a white tulle veil, gloved in purple gloves, and stood in the middle of a showcase displaying the Holy Gospels, and found herself charming. However, she no longer opened the cross window where the heart of Jesus shone, adorned with his crown of thorns, and she burned incense as soon as the priest had cowardly offered her some.

He could not expect an easy voyage. To reach the midnight train at the main station, they were forbidden to take the main road, and they could not leave the church before eleven o'clock in the evening. This meant an unpleasant journey, in the middle of the harvest, with the risk of running into either peasants collecting the harvest or gleaners. The priest dressed like a workman: gray blouse and cotton pants, then put a straw hat on his head. But Laure would not part with her white lace veil, which drew the attention of people, and the curé had to bow because he was now secretly worried that she was indulging in the profane game of the existence of a sinner in a church.

As they crossed the square, walking with wobbly legs, they met a drunkard. He examined them and said, "They are lovebirds, what!" and he grunted obscenely.

They both nearly fainted and set off at random down the first of the alleys. They imagined that houses, lampposts, and hydrants were chasing them. The priest, disoriented without his robe, took little steps, got confused, could not find his way, turned, came back, could not read the names of the roads on the posts. In the open country, they began to gallop. Laure had pulled up her skirt of sheets, too heavy, it beating her calves, and she was discussing setting it down to move faster . . .

They rode along the main road, reassured for a moment, met a farmer driving oxen, and had a panic that rolled them into a millstone. They lay flat on their stomachs, their eyes dilated, their chests gasping.

Laure grabbed Armand's hand and put it on her breast. "I think I am going to suffocate!"

"No, no, it is the air, the fresh air. You understand, you have been locked up for eight days without air . . . My God, how your heart beats!"

They were on familiar terms, suddenly really brother and sister in the face of danger, no longer thinking of the dignity of the priesthood.

"Where is the money?" asked the young man.

"Oh! Do not worry, I have got it right here under my scarf . . ."

"It is just that, if you lost it, I would not be able to get any more at the spa . . . it would be a lost opportunity . . ."

They got up, the oxen were far away. After an hour, they saw the station and the red lanterns. Laure stiffened, turning around on the path.

"Let us see, here . . . what is wrong?"

"Oh! Nothing! Nothing! It is that red eye. Here, carry me, I cannot walk anymore. My legs are so limp . . ."

And the curé carried her for some hundred meters, murmuring, "How heavy a woman is!"

Arriving at a level crossing, the young man stopped.

"Laure, we must part here, you poor little thing! Say goodbye!"

He let her slide gently, holding her arms with a convulsive movement.

"You see," he said, trembling with another emotion now that they were saved, "I carried you, as you once asked me to! Alas, in hell . . . I, who wanted you respected and happy, obeyed you, you who obey the devil."

"Yes, you were good, my brother," replied Laure, "I will remember!"

"Will you write to me, sister, and always give me your address?"

"Yes, I promise," she asserted, her eyes fixed on the station.

She wrapped her arms around his shoulders, which he himself pulled up, distraught, and they kissed on the mouth. It now seemed to the young priest that he was a man like all men, without his black robe, stripped at last of the holy and funereal livery. Could he not also abandon his miserable existence, flee with her, save himself from the public curse, taste happiness? Oh! How weary he was of the road traveled and the despair of his love!

Laure exclaimed, "I hear a bell. Say, do not make me miss the train!"

To miss the train! Ah! Yes, that would mean risking not being able to join him, the fiancé chosen by his solicitude as a good devoted brother . . . him . . . Henri Alban!

He recoiled jealously, and Laure's arms untied. "I wish God would punish me alone, my sister," he stammered. And he found, despite his upset, a confessor's phrase: "Go in peace, my child . . . !"

From the road, he saw the train that was taking her away; and when this train had disappeared in the hollow of a valley, an immense pain tore through Armand's brain: he began to laugh . . .

The next day, Laure was in Paris, on Rue Racine, in a student hotel, striding purposefully up the stairs to Monsieur Henri's room. "The tall blond fellow, is he not, mademoiselle?"

She entered. He was smoking, standing against a chair, and he grabbed the chair, brandishing it at her in an almost instinctive gesture. "You . . ."

"Yes, my parents chased me away to be your mistress."

"Are you pregnant?" he mocked, glaring at her.

She smiled quietly, put down her veil, toque, and gloves, then sat down on the floor beside the chair, not rebelling. "I have a bit of money left," she said in a firm voice, "and I will rent a room in this hotel. Every morning, I will be your servant, and every evening . . . I will wait for you. I do not need you to hide me. I could have lived somewhere else . . . but I love you. If I do not have you, I will fall ill!"

And he did not dare throw her out, because she was uncoiling her hair.

When he was convinced that she was not pregnant, Henri rented a modest apartment on the sixth floor of the Rue de Seine. Perhaps content, deep down, to possess a love nest of his own, he consented to let himself be loved . . .

Like an honest boy who does not want to betray the hideaway of a woman, nor inform her parents of her new vicissitudes, he feigned heartache, postponed his plans as a future provincial notaire and returned to a Parisian practice. He would occupy himself with another marriage when *the latter* had decamped with the large sum of money that would surely be offered by one of his close friends. For the sake of human respect, he kept his room on Rue Racine. Their home, a former studio of a photographer, became a sort of glass cage where he would hear the rare bird sing, the bird from exotic lands whose ardent song he did not understand . . . And Laure remained faithful to him, believing herself happy for a whole year, until that night of nervous derangement when, on a crystal roof, she saw cats dancing in the moonlight . . . !

10

On all fours, the young woman gazed at him, truly moved by pure emotion, almost rapt in the ecstasies of motherhood. Isolated from all that could give her ways to react, to "see reason," according to the bourgeois expression of Henri Alban, she had come to love this frail animal with the love of a female for her young, and she spent long hours crouched on cushions, posed like a beast herself, her hands splayed, her fingers spread, her hair always beating her shoulders like a panther's tail.

With her mind constantly occupied with the minutiae of a challenging rearing, in the month that she had owned this cat, she had experienced all of the joys and pangs of primipara. She had found him in the street, near the mouth of a gutter, clinging to the sidewalk, and as she caught sight of this silky, needle-spiked ball of fur, her heart had suddenly opened up to an immense tenderness for a tiny infancy. The newborn did not want to die! He clung on, using whatever gymnastics he had learned in the womb of his feline mother, and mewed in a relatively formidable voice, the voice of a cursed creature accusing society, blaspheming before the final kick. Laure had taken him in, tucked him into her bodice, and defied public opinion.

And she had saved him all the same. More tormented than a recent mother stricken with fever, more patient than a nurse, for a month she had arisen at night to make him drink, to offer him a sponge to suck on; she had kept him warm in the tepid cradle of her arms, not stirring for fear of waking him, wiping his little droppings with meticulous care and not complaining when the hairy marmot forgot himself in bed. She had bought a night-light lamp equipped with a container for *tisanes*, on which her milk was kept at the desired temperature, and she would be terrified when a hail of mewls rose from the cotton-lined basket: the young woman would rush over, imagining he was cold or asking for his bottle. Henri would get angry and call her mad, scandalized by this other kind of sensual exaggeration.

"It is absurd," he repeated, "absurd! When you do not have a good enough reason for your insomnia, you invent one! Do not sleep any more if it amuses you, but at least do not keep me awake!"

He thought that her passion for a beast made her more contemptible, moreover, he calculated that the self-imposed seclusion for the sake of her childish toy made her more than ever a harem woman, the cloistered lover shunning the crowds, the places of worldly pleasure, where wanton creatures like she were supposed to gather.

He could not understand the peculiar character of this madwoman. She thought herself faithful, this overexcited woman, and at the same time attached herself to the only man who did not care about satisfying all of the fancies of her senses! Would she, now, take him for a cat, sharpening his nails and appetites in that electric fur coat? *No such luck*, decidedly! If she continued to shut herself off between her love for him and her exaltation for an animal, he would never find the opportunity, surreptitiously sought, to break away.

On this day of summer, Laure remained at home, gazing at her cat far from the noise, in a half-darkness conducive to daydreaming, having drawn the blinds on the windows, worrying little about the escape of the young man, who had left in the morning without telling her which way he was going. He refused to take her with him, so she stayed there, perched in the house like an abandoned female dropped in the gutter after a night of wicked caresses.

Of course, she was expecting the icy companion of her life to return, she knew that habit would bring him back to her, but she was suffering cruelly from these successive abandonments, and, her heart increasingly swollen by an outburst of abnormal tenderness, now she felt the need to indulge in the games of an affectionate little girl who consoles herself with a doll.

Very simple, she could have become a divine lover if someone had loved her, for she was, in short, much less of a woman, that is, less perverse than any other. But she would have had to be cajoled, guarded, enveloped in voluptuous attentions, and unfortunately her heart fell on that murderer of love who is called an "orderly man."

Yet this heroic, guilty woman had decided not to betray her lover, despite the coldness he showed her. No, she revolted at the idea of deceiving him! She would resist temptation with all her might, and if the demon screamed in anger deep inside her, roared in her unfulfilled depths, she would bestow all of those tender caresses on the microscopic infant, the child of her mind. And she would courageously begin that heartbreaking struggle of love that exalts itself against love that mocks. He would not give a damn about her, but he would not find the opportunity to leave her; she had become even more submissive, snuggling in the shadows, giving him permission to lock her in her cage, and she would create a childish affection, a ridiculous motherhood rather than drain the overflow of her kisses elsewhere . . .

Half bristles, half fine needles, the fur ball rolled with the comical allure of an infant risking its first steps. The kitten stood up, pricked up his ears, rounded his back, carried his tail high, ruffled like a tuft of feathers; and his pink mouth, like a sneezing insect, spat furious curses.

A little Egyptian god newly reinstalled on his throne by the morbid enthusiasm of a sad woman, he was aware of his worth, trying his hand at mischief, clawing into the unctuous flesh of her arms, or watching her out of the corner of his eye.

He was, in fact, a fine breed, not too bastardized by cross-breeding with stupid, narrow-minded angoras who have the softness of lazy kings, a sort of angry Jumièges fit for the per-petual convent.[1] This one was more directly descended from the mighty wildcat, the brother of the tiger, the wildcat that pounces on the back of a gazelle or a doe and carves his own meal from the panting meat of his mount as it gallops along. He had a broad, slightly square head, the skull of a young thinker, straight, thin ears, concealed under floppy tufts, imitating faun-like horns, and, when he folded them back, they adorned him with a baby's bonnet. His fur was russet, almost yellow under the neck, almost brown on the back, and he was ringed with cir-cles of black velvet. The paintbrush of the geniuses of Memphis, contemporaries no doubt of his first incarnation as an idol, had drawn, from his eyes to his ears, a series of hieroglyphic lines signifying sometimes anger when they crinkled, sometimes

---

1. Robert of Jumièges (died circa 1055) was the first Norman archbishop of Canterbury, deposed and exiled from his archbishopric in 1052.

gentleness when they opened into a wheel whose hub became topaz, emerald, or sapphire. The mustache bloomed white, with black peduncles—a conqueror's mustache. Still downy with the hair of early youth, one guessed it would soon darken, have less white legs, brown nails, red nose and lips, and perhaps a spotted muzzle like that of a leopard. In any case, he would be a terrible beast, a superb cat who deserved the nickname of "Lion" that Laure bestowed upon him . . . And, while waiting for more glorious epochs, he would make little leaps, playing with a paper butterfly that the young woman, still on all fours in front of him, would wave in the breeze of a fan. She never tired of following him, alternating butterflies with cake crumbs and drops of milk; and when he grew tired, she would put him to sleep on his cushion, on her dress, no longer moving, listening to the faint sound of the purr that he was learning to make; then, sliding her cheek against the carpet, lying down in a dead posture, she would spy on his awakening, ready to start the games all over again.

The apartment that she occupied was wonderfully laid out to serve as a nest for two libertine creatures, lazy like this woman and this cat. The former studio of a photographer was draped on all sides with *crêpe de Chine* blinds, a pale shade, the color of a silkworm's cocoon, neither very yellow nor very white, turning to mother-of-pearl tones in places too faded, with a seductive swan-wing sheen. To save money, Henri, the reasonable man, had furnished the apartment in furniture bought at Drouot Hall, his job as the clerk of a notaire providing him, incidentally, with excellent surprises at judicial sales, but he had not chosen anything for himself.[2] A young man, forward-thinking, he liked

---

2. Drouot is a Parisian auction hall opened in 1852, and still in operation today.

new, solid things and ordinary colors renowned for their good tinge.

Laure preferred the softness of touch to the brilliance of hues, never inquiring about fashion, and she had a caprice for those ivory silks that were similar to the shimmering specks one finds on moss in the woods. A spring and a ribbon were used to raise all of the blinds with a single gesture. The glass cage glowed with light. One would find oneself suspended in open sky, flooded with sunshine on sunny days, as if through a lake on rainy days, with no neighbors, no intruders, overlooking the dreary houses of the street and the smoky distances of the city, suddenly transported to a secluded corner of nature.

A plain wool carpet covered the floor. To the right, behind curtains of the same fabric as the blinds, lay a bed upholstered in old gold satin, covered by a cloth of real otter and pillows of white satin stamped with an unknown diadem. To the left, a leaning mirror reflected the bed, and at either end of the room the two sumptuous layers, the real and the fictitious, provoked you softly, with an air of silent resignation. All along the studio, various cushions were scattered, some piled up to the height of a seat, others scattered at random according to the cat's games.

Laure had finally realized her dream of a cloister paved only with velvet cushions, she had erected her own temple, she had her own altar . . . minus the devotee of her beauty, because, alas, the man who presided there did not care for this brunette's spectacle, which he called very banally "the yellow room." There were no knickknacks, statuettes, tableware, or pianos around the yellow room, as Laure was not interested in fanciness or art. When she wished to take in an interesting sight, she drew her blinds and gazed up at the sky. Sometimes, tilting back her head, she would look up at the ceiling, remembering her curiosity of yesteryear for strange glass trinkets, their ceiling iridescent with opaline glimmers like a phosphorescent crystal. The vestibule of the studio, a sort of small salon, was reserved for Henri, and the young man had arranged it as a smoking room. At home, the prospective notaire read, reflecting on the future, and worked on legal questions to rest from his most recent cerebral convulsions. In this cozy retreat lay a recently made Louis XIII carpet, on the mantelpiece stood a standard lamp bearing with, in addition to its moderating nozzle, a sight-preserving shade, a chronometer, a thermometer, and a cigar cutter—an exquisite invention for men of order. Henri's customary armchair, a medal-winning American seat, rocked him for hours on end, and he was quick to point out that this system facilitated the digestion of love.

Henri, of the current era, seriously repudiated only portable stoves, because they kill . . . and on this subject he would detail anecdotes gleaned from scientific journals, followed by tales of restaurants where one is always robbed to be fed so poorly! In impatient hours, he also thundered against the control-room matches. But he appreciated with all his soul the rubber coats, the long ulsters with triple collars . . . And, leaving his mistress at home because during the summer there was risk of meeting acquaintances from the provinces, he would go rummage around the boulevards, studying the shop fronts of fashionable tailors, happy to note the greatness of the French nation in its chic imitation of English products. Oh! The strange lovebirds, these two lovers separated by a wall, walking hand in hand over an abyss! Laure arrived from who-knows-what forest, steeped in the fragrance of magical greenery, and he descended from a hydrotherapy establishment where young men who are no longer mad are showered and pumiced to remove all of their male roughness! The young woman was happy with a simple caress given without a thought. The young man consulted his watch before making his way from the Rue Racine to the Rue de Seine, and considered if, really, it was necessary to love that evening . . . ! Incidentally quite polite with his mistress, he had a second key for decorum, never inserting it in the lock before ringing discreetly, and always expecting to find a *rastacouère* behind the yellow curtains. He was astonished by this long passivity of a wild beast that suffers and does not retaliate. He could only reproach her for her excessive tenderness, her distraught fits, and then he remained cold, his heart closed by the petty theories of Monsieur Tidy. He had loved this girl to make her his wife, not to make her a coquette. He had dreamed up such a charming mediocrity of love, at the time of his desires as a fiancé, such a sweet life as a family man, that today he should not spread himself into sensual prodigalities under the specious pretext that she was metamorphosing into a prodigal girl! There are some things a well-bred fellow fears, and he would not be so ridiculous as to refuse the graces of a body that cost next to nothing to maintain, but he would only give away as much of his own body as hygiene demanded!

Disgusted with her before he had exhausted the treasures of her person, he slept, next to her graces, the calm sleep of a husband who, by some extraordinary turn of events, has just disrespected his young companion . . . And, always with a distressing politeness, he pointed out to her that he was leaving her the best place, therefore entering the estimable category of distinguished lovers, proper lovers.

"One day, my pretty, you could get into a relationship! That is the day that you will regret me!" he would tell her with a skeptical smile.

Laure, watching for the little cat to wake up, remembered these phrases:

"My darling, you can fool me: I will not hold it against you, it is universal law."

"But, my poor friend, do you think we will always live together?"

"Love is just a word . . . and later, when I am married . . ."

"I will bring up my children in fear of an evil lust like gluttony, because sensual taste leads to sexual sensuality."

"My dear friend, rest assured, a fellow of my caliber does not leave a woman without thinking about her future; he leaves her a thousand-dollar banknote, or else he tries to 'set her up' with someone decent."

This was his sentimental and philosophical language, a language that she listened to with her eyes closed, like a creature subjected to humiliation, accepting everything rather than seeing through it, and clinging to him like the dog who knows that her master wants to lose her at every corner.

Oh! She could see it, the thick wall built between them. She had sworn to melt it under her fierce kisses, she wrapped her arms around him believing that she was squeezing the man but only holding gracefully carved stones—stones, it is true, with very rounded angles, hurting her just enough not to damage her heart too much, but stones nonetheless . . . !

Dusk was falling. Still the little cat nestled on her skirt, purring like a bee with imprisoned, fluttering wings. A silence of abandonment surrounded this monotonous noise, barely perceptible even to the ears of Laure, the mother of the little slumberer. She felt alone, outside all of society, placed above merry girls, below respectable women, in a kind of domestic dependence, and yet free to go anywhere to find herself a new cage.

What did she have in common with any sentient being? Love! But, her love, they did not share it! It seemed of inferior quality, lacking who knew what human dignity! And Laure, saddened by an initial thought whose meanders ended far away in the vague shadows of this twilight, told herself that she was undoubtedly not a woman like the others; she discovered a special brute nature, the entrails of a beast corresponding to the delicious instincts of the little cat, for cats are, it is said, simply rogue spirits who prowl around, clad in fur, striving to reclaim their former female bodies.

Seven o'clock struck. Laure got up and wiped her eyes.

"Since he did not send me a telegram," she murmured, "it's because he will be back! He cannot forget me that easily. I will prepare a surprise for him, and we will have dinner here."

With a quick movement, she threw back the thick braid of her hair, and, changing her mind, persuading herself that he would return at once, organized their place settings on a light pedestal table. She had two Japanese plates, an old Rouen dish, Venetian glasses, and a Russian tablecloth; she placed a crystal vase full of flowers in the middle of the table, put two piles of cushions together, and lit the lamp, so happy now to think that she was doing housework like his real wife. Then she ran to put on a hat and tie a scarf over her white muslin peignoir. She took her pussycat, slipped it into an elegant basket designed to hold the delicacies that she would buy from time to time for her private little meals, and hurried down the six flights of stairs with a light foot, her head full of extraordinary impatience. She chose a chicken at the roaster's while the cat, stroking his whiskers, peered over the edge of the basket, looking very serious, his pupils gleaming. She had a ham cut open at the butcher's and upset three boxes of grapes and a basket of peaches at the fruit shop.

People smiled at her as they stroked the funny little beast that accompanied her, and said, "Here is a very happy child . . . !" as if they were certain that all of the young lady's provisions were for the animal's gluttony.

She went back upstairs, her heart pounding, thinking she would find him there, but he was not back yet. She uncorked a bottle and plunged it into a cool bucket of water, laid her chicken on the platter of old Rouen, arranged her fruit on the Japanese plates, and stepped back to better enjoy the effect.

The pussycat, enthusiastic, leaped along her dress, following her from the studio to the salon and from the salon to the doorstep. He was confident, waiting for no one, sure that he would eat everything.

"Half past seven," murmured Laure in sudden despair. "He is not coming back, and he is not sending me a telegram."

She sat down opposite the chicken; the cat climbed up, his already strong claws clinging to the folds of her peignoir, pawing at it, eager to taste the enormous golden fowl that he, so tiny, did not dread. Laure, to calm him down, poured some milk into a saucer: he refused to drink, wanting a piece of meat, and she had to, despite her frustration, offer him a scrap; he advanced his claw with a growl, his fine whiskers bristling, victorious at last as he had, for the first time, sunk his tiny fangs into flesh.

"Now you will not want any more brioche or breadcrumbs," sighed Laure desolately, in the tone of a mother who sees herself dominated by the spoiled child—little rascal!

The cat rolled around in her breasts, looking tender, stroking her for more, and she gave him more, gradually stripping the pretty golden fowl of its crisp skin.

"It will not be as presentable, that is all," she said to herself, carving and trimming with the tip of her knife, while Lion, sitting on a napkin, not much higher than the Venetian glass, waited for the prey, licking his lips. She ate too, tantalized by the smell of chicken. After a minute, they each pulled the thigh to one side and detached it without a fork.

"Mon Dieu," exclaimed Laure, "if Henri saw us, he would laugh at us . . ." She added, her brow darkened, "Eight o'clock! No, he will not return . . . and he will not even have warned me!"

She had barely finished her sentence when there was a discreet knock on the door, as the young man was wont to do. She dashed forward, her cat on her shoulders, delighted, almost trembling with joy. She had been right to hope, and it would be an exquisite dinner for the three of them, the "child" climbing alternately on the laps of the two lovers. She forgot her sad musings of the day, her abandonment at the bottom of her crystal cage of yellow silk; she even forgot her quasi-philosophical reflections about women who are intermediaries between the feline species and the human species . . .

She turned the key, murmuring, "Is that you? Hurry up! You are stupid to knock . . ."

She stood in awe as the concierge handed her a letter edged in black.

"Are you sure it is for us?" she stammered, turning over the letter, no longer daring to look at the band's inscription.

"Well," replied the concierge, looking grumpy, "would I have gone to the trouble of climbing six flights of stairs to find the wrong tenant . . . ? You can read, in all probability!"

Laure closed the door and came to sit down again before the table laden with their opéra-comique dinner. She considered the letter, bewildered, and pushed back the cat playing in her hair . . .

"Yes, it is for me, certainly for me," she repeated to herself, "and it is in the handwriting of the curé d'Estérac!"

She broke the strip, opened the letter, and read the sentence printed in bold type, blacker than the rest: "Madame Marie-Antoinette-Caroline Lordès."

Her mother was dead, and Armand de Bréville, remembering her address, which she had given him as soon as she had settled in the Rue de Seine, laconically sent her this cruel announcement . . . She awaited the lover, and death came, the ironic death, with its procession of dark memories, all of the grudges, all of the curses . . .

The young woman threw the funereal paper opposite her, on Henri's napkin, her dry eyes taking on a fierce expression. "I have been alone since birth," she said coldly, "and I feel that I will be alone for the rest of my life. What is the use of mourning my mother! I was not of her stock, seeing as she never knew me! Besides, who is going to mourn me—me, the monster?"

She might have sobbed on Henri's chest, moved by the outpouring of an unexpected return; but now, certain that her lover would not be coming home that evening, she resolutely cut into the chicken, taking wicked pleasure in plunging her knife into the flesh, chewing with the sound of fangs like a wild beast preoccupied with the sole satisfaction of its appetites.

11

"But, my dear, you are in mourning, and I really do not know why I am staying here."

The young man rocked back and forth on the American armchair in the center of the studio, smoking a cigar and looking serious. Laure, seated on the floor in a posture of humble adoration, watched him, stroking the little cat with her distracted hands. She was wearing a crimson cashmere peignoir, as blinding as a torrent of blood.

"Oh, my dear Henri," she murmured with a smile, "girls who behave badly do not mourn their parents, and I assure you I do not feel any sadness."

"I am sorry for you, my dear friend, it is shameful . . . a total absence of heart. I noticed it a long time ago."

"Yes, I do have a heart," sighed the young woman softly, "but it is naked; the other hearts are better dressed, it makes a difference . . . by far . . ."

"Come now," Henri exclaimed impatiently, "there are women who have remorse for lack of dignity."

"Look, Henri, my mother drove me out of our house, she did not consider me her daughter anymore . . . However, to please

131

you, I am willing to wear mourning clothes, but I do not own a piece of black cloth, and I do not like to ask you for money…"

"Are you blaming me for letting you run out of dresses?" said the young man dryly, shaking ashes onto a cushion.

"No, I do not need anything…on the contrary, I thank you."

Henri absorbed himself in thought for a moment, and then, with hard features and fixed eyes, he said, "I am not a prince. Mourning like this is done inwardly, and you admit you do not care…So why should I meddle in the affairs of your family!"

Nodding his head, Henri took a few more puffs.

"An odd curé, all the same," he added, "this curé d'Estérac! I thought that he was more responsible. He tries to marry off suspicious girls and sends them news from their homeland… When he was very young, he had a terrible imagination…Oh! Imagination!" And Henri made a mocking gesture.

"He has been good to me," murmured Laure.

"Well, I think it's necessary to go and have a look around," declared the young man, who had not lost sight of his idea.

Laure stood up and briskly pushed the cat away. "Are you going to leave me again?"

"Do not get carried away, my dear child, I am simply going to show myself for a month or two at La Bourdaisière, wander the streets of Estérac, and do a bit of hunting as well, for my father will be surprised at my long absence. It has been nearly eighteen months since I have been back in the fold…My renowned grief must have subsided." He began to laugh. "You do not expect me to mourn a fiancée like Mademoiselle Lordès all of my life, you who do not mourn your own mother!"

Laure sat on the lap of her lover, her face flustered. "I've dreaded the vacation season, and you found an excuse…Just think how lonely I am…Henri…"

"But, my darling, you can come and go, go out, and even receive guests—honest guests, of course. Is it reasonable to cloister yourself like this? I do not think I am making a jealous scene! In the early days of our affair, I showed you all of the places where a woman can spend pleasant evenings.

"I never refused to take you there; in time, you would have made friends and formed relationships. You preferred to wall yourself up, and today you are left with no one but your cat to confide in!

"I, on the other hand, have duties that I cannot neglect. I do not walk all over my kin as you do . . . Are you still afraid of marriage? No, I will warn you, Laure. I swear I will always be decent to you. I like you, I will not leave you in the lurch; yet . . . after all I have done for you . . ."

She closed his mouth with a kiss.

"Be quiet," she stammered, "you are going to prove me right. Yes, you are very kind, very gentle, I do not blame you for anything. I understand, I am a burden for you . . . Oh, such a burden . . . I weigh on your existence as I do on your knees right now . . . and you would like to run away. To you, I am the evil spirit whom you thought was an angel . . . but you must not leave me . . ." She wrapped her arms around the young man's neck. "With you I am almost a woman, without you, I will be a machine that lives no more. Ah! If I knew how to earn money, I would pay you back for all that you have spent on me. You see, at night, when I wake up and you are not there, I seem to find myself in a big wood where I had once come as a little girl, and I hear wolves howling, it is dark, it is winter, I am hungry . . . I am shaking, and my head cannot turn toward the sky. I encounter flowers and I can no longer explain to myself what a flower is, I encounter money and I can no longer explain to myself what a gold coin shining on the moss is . . . and if I met my mother, I feel as though I would eat her . . . Ah! I would rather not sleep than dream that dream. I have tried to read the books that you read—they make me yawn right away, the newspapers—I do not care what is going on outside! I only want one thing, always the same: to touch you to be sure that you are there . . .”

“A little dose of hysteria!” murmured the young man, both flattered and annoyed by this sudden burst of tenderness.

“Hysteria,” repeated Laure. “That is the fashionable illness that you told me about, but I do not feel ill, my poor Henri, and perhaps it is the men of this age, men like you, who are ill! Do you not think that once upon a time . . . Oh, centuries ago, a community did nothing but love each other on a carpet of green grass with a great deal of sunshine all around—”

“Probably in the days when notaire clerks were one-eyed!” interjected Henri, making up his mind to be cruel.

Laure continued, looking lost, her red lips a little pale. “At the bottom of it all, it is love that consoles! Without you, I would weep for *maman*. And when love is gone, that is to say the bond that ties me to you rather than to another, there is still love, that is to say the passion that drives beasts to mate with each other . . . Go, it is useless to live honestly. You will get married and miss me . . . and while you are missing me, I will live like a beast, without remembering God. I forbid you to leave . . . you are my husband . . . !”

She pressed herself against him, snuggling into his arms and paralyzing him. He finally let go of his cigar, laughing good naturedly. “You have morals!”

“No, I have no morals, I try to remain faithful, and yet I am sure I could love you while deceiving you . . . .”

“Impossible . . .”

"Yes, to deceive a man is often to show him deference, Henri. I love you to the point of not reproaching you for your coldness...."

"If I were cold..." interrupted the young man, still laughing.

"And I am afraid of cheating on you when you are away..."

"So I have been warned... Thank you!"

Laure straightened, sweeping aside her hair that was coming undone. "Once my heart withdraws from you, I will not be able to see clearly and I will go back to the great forest of my dreams... Henri, I imagine that this dream existence is like the lives of animals. You do not think anymore, and things happen to you quite naturally, without causing you the slightest astonishment. Animals are always in the midst of the night, bumping into things that they cannot see. But also, what tranquility for them, who have no need to mourn their mothers, no need to mourn their mistakes, and who do not care about the time of the clock or people's opinions! To prowl at night in pursuit of a caress, to drink, eat, and sleep during the day... No, I do not feel like mourning, I feel like wearing a wolf's pelt..."

Henri sighed with relief upon seeing her rise. She stood before him for a moment, her eyes half-closed, as if looking through a window.

"You can go if you like," she said painfully, "I have done my best to be a wife..."

He snapped his fingers with a kind of nervous anger. "My little one, patience has its limits; I repeat that I will not leave you without giving you some guarantees or protections. You are a wild child, very difficult to tame, but I am a gallant man, I will look after your future... In the meantime, I am going hunting at La Bourdaisière. Instead of being a clerk in a law firm, where I am the fifth wheel on the carriage, I would prefer to be my own master . . . I have done enough training, both in sentimental education and as a legal expert . . . I would like to found something other than amorous theories . . . Ordinarily, lovers do not discuss their plans with their good friends; you were my fiancée . . . even if I hid my ideas from you, you could always guess them, could you not? Calm down! Besides, no matter how you care not for social decorum, I tell you I do not like sleeping with the daughter of a woman who died last week . . ."

Laure had opened her eyes. She bent down, because the little cat was asking for its food. "Love is as constant as hunger . . ." she said, speaking to herself. "Come on, Mimi, it will just be the two of us!"

She ran to the cupboard where she kept her favorite's sweets, and pretended to look for a cup of milk that she could no longer find. Tears may have fallen into the milk, but Henri did not notice, and Lion drank them all greedily, reveling in their bitterness.

This flight was, moreover, merely a test; he wanted to force her to spend a month alone with her wild cat ways and thought that at this rate she would throw herself at the first perverted fellow she encountered on the boulevard. Laure was going to end her days as a common whore, for she knew neither how to be chic nor how to be honest, and despite her beauty, which he readily appreciated, in his weaker moments following fine dinners, he told himself that she would make a pitiful courtesan, spending too much on physical indulgences and not knowing how to provoke financial expenditures. No organization, no method; an exhausting ardor, and such forgetfulness of manners!

He lit a cigar.

"You will write to me by general post, my sweet. Try not to ruin anything at home, it is bad enough that that damn priest knows your address. In the provinces, an old scandal is quickly rejuvenated, and the funeral of your mother must have renewed stories..."

"I will not write to you!"

"Why? I would have liked to read your letters, it would have amused me..."

"Paper in place of your skin or mine, what is the point!"

"Laure, you are sulking."

She smiled.

Laure, submissive as a placid servant, packed his trunk, pulled the shirts from the wardrobes, and folded the clothes, restitching a button, checking the freshness of the ties, polishing the vermeil utensils of the toiletry kit, and adding, with discreet care, mints in a small corner of the bag.

"You would have taken care of your husband," said Henri, stroking her hair.

"I was born to be your wife!" she replied sadly.

"You are exaggerating a little, my poor sweet."

"If only you'd forgiven me, but honest people are more stupid than animals."

He gazed at her, searching for the meaning of her words, and decided to laugh. "You are priceless," he declared.

And, piece by piece, Laure's heart was torn apart by the polite banality of his month-long departure, which would be, even if he came back to her more loving, the last farewell...

In order to throw their bitch into the water, some well-born individuals insist that she be afflicted with mange; Laure, being a well-behaved animal, would find a way to catch mange.

Henri thought, *When one does not care about death in this way, one is quite capable of criticizing one's lover. I will have to be careful to make a definitive break. I should have prevented this liaison from turning sticky.*

Laure waited for the supreme caresses of farewell, her eyes glittering as she gazed at the silhouette of a man who was about to disappear from her life, and perhaps from her heart. For her, nothing existed but the present. What did she care about the promises of the future, the happiness of the past? As long as she could brush against him with her fingertips, she felt that a sincere love would elevate her above women of the wrong sort; tomorrow, she would fall more deeply into the forgetfulness of herself and of him, into the oblivion of everything that once gave nobility to her passions ever since she had loved. She accompanied him home, carrying his travel bag.

The Rue Racine room was plain and furnished simply, like the room of a student. Already their love no longer had free rein, and they found themselves at home as strangers. Laure sat down on the small iron bed and pulled back the long braid of her hair. Henri, who, extraordinarily, did not smoke, sat opposite her on a chair, the same one that he had brandished in anger at the beautiful girl who had come to offer herself to him on the day of her arrival.

"I do hope," murmured the young man, taking hold of Laure's hands and patting them, "that you will not be sad . . . A month passes quickly, my dear."

"I will not be sad," she replied bleakly.

"Let us see, are our little accounts in order? I will leave you one hundred francs. Will you have enough while you wait for me?"

"More than enough, I hardly ever go out or visit the stores. Apart from getting Lion's milk . . ." And the girl smiled.

"Yes, I know, I know, you are a model economist. Did I give you the second key?"

He searched all of his pockets.

"Here, take it, I trust you, and sometimes one needs the second key . . . when one loses the first."

"You are giving me back my freedom?" she asked, putting on a carefree face.

"First of all, silly little girl, you have always had it . . . The rent is in your name, you are at home up there, and I have nothing to do with the changes it will please you to make. I am not leaving you today; in a year, I can give up Parisian life and . . ."

"In short," interrupted Laure, her voice suddenly broken, "you are beginning to test me . . .."

"Certainly, my dear, I treat you very gently . . ." replied the young man, kissing her hands.

Laure inclined her head, willing to acknowledge him and . . . not reproach him for his gentleness.

"I am going to gauge local opinion," he continued in a more lighthearted tone. "Your father must feel very isolated after the death of his wife . . . In an indirect way, I could advise him to sell his business, to go live elsewhere, and elsewhere, time healing the deepest of wounds, you could join him . . . It would be in your interest, my dear, because you are still his heiress despite the scandals and your bad behavior. Later, you would find yourself a husband, a simple man who would love you . . ."

Henri Alban paused to stroke Laure's chin, not remembering that for a moment he had embodied that "simple man."

"You are a madwoman," he added, his voice very affectionate, "and yet you have a charming character, it seems to me you are destined for the good life of a mother . . . Oh! Little children! That is what would train you, tame you, put a good head on your shoulders . . . I envision you with six children and a pretty cottage in the middle of the woods. You would have cats, dogs, chickens, cows . . . You would get up at dawn, so you would sleep at night and not have bad dreams . . ."

"Indeed," said Laure, crossing her arms as if to lock her heart and defend it forever against the virtuous attempts of honest people.

"Come on, darling, I am right, I am talking to you like a true friend. Youth does not last . . . And you, the daughter of a notaire, should not find yourself on the sidewalk one morning . . ."

He got up, took a few turns around the room, put the candle behind the bed curtains so that no one would glimpse the shadow puppets with which they, he and she, would *probably* adorn the window panes; then, checking his watch on the way, he returned to sit next to her.

"Will you answer me, you little grumbler?"

He slipped his hand into her bodice, carefully pulling out the two dazzling breasts of this brunette who, despite her bad behavior, was the most beautiful instrument of pleasure one could desire, especially on the eve of a long fast.

Laure, arms down, passive, smiled; only her smile looked a little like the fixed grin of a tigress, with a vague notion of biting.

"Please, my dear Henri, do not worry about my father. It would upset me . . . Let us leave my future alone . . . You are too good."

"As you wish," replied the gracefully inclined young man, "but I am trying to prove to you that I am totally devoted to you, that I love you at last!"

"Then," declared the young woman through clenched teeth, "you had better not say anything."

This time, she cut him off with an accent so short that he looked up in fright.

"Do you still prefer action?" he breathed, trying to put his arms around her. Laure shrank back, pulling up her blouse, looking haughty.

"And the shadow of my mother?" she sneered.

"Little grumbler . . . !" He knelt down, holding his cuffs, his eyes full of a languor that was not at all feigned. "We are going our separate ways . . . That is not nice . . . !"

"Why do we part?"

"Because I cannot abandon my family completely for my mistress. Come, Laure, is it impossible to reason with you?"

"I do not know how to reason, Henri, I give myself or I refuse myself . . ."

"And, at this hour, you refuse!"

"Yes!"

Henri, too gallant a man to engage in a vulgar struggle, straightened up, ran his feverish fingers through his hair, and opened the window. For a minute, the noise of the street shook the room, distracting them; Laure arranged her toilette, and Henri whistled.

"I will order the car," he said, risking a glance at his mistress.

"It is eleven o'clock, my friend, and you have just time to go."

The boy brought down the suitcase, and the young woman folded the overcoat and blanket, taking care not to forget a black satin cap that the traveler wore to sleep.

Henri felt slightly irritated; he could not explain the caprice of this girl, so starved for love ordinarily, who would have happily drained him to the bone the night before, and who tonight, under the specious pretext that he was being more affectionate, more charitable, was letting him go hungry, his nerves irritated, in deplorable conditions for traveling . . . They made their way to the Orleans station without exchanging a word . . . Laure, stretching out with her eyelids closed, neither moved nor cried. Henri smoked.

Bah! It is a tactic! She is hoping that I will be back within a month, he mused. *She is getting herself all worked up, the lout.*

"Do you want the car to take you home?" he asked with his usual politeness, when they reached the station.

"No, I will walk home, it will do me good."

He had a vision of suicide, remembering the one-eyed clerk plunging to the bottom of the well.

"Eh," he growled, grabbing her shoulder with a brutal movement. "Do not be silly, some responsibilities are unpleasant, you know!"

"I will not cheat on you!" replied Laure, ashamed of what she was thinking. "Are you afraid that I will cheat on you, Henri?"

The young man burst out laughing. "I am not worried about that, my little pussycat. You are too stubborn . . . Come on, I have been reassured; let us kiss and say goodbye as good friends . . ."

"What responsibilities were you talking about?" she murmured, appalled by his composure.

"Ideas . . . Ideas à la Lucien Séchard, *parbleu!*"

"What! You imagined that I had a wish to kill myself, and . . . you were leaving all the same . . . ?"

In the night, away from the lanterns of the carriage, he did not see the flood of tears escaping from her eyes; his retort was full of impatience, for he now feared that he would miss the train. "Laure, you are of a prickly sort: you will never make your fortune like that . . ."

Settled on the bench of the smoking compartment, as the train rattled along, he finished his sentence with this mental reflection prompted by a regret in his senses: *And it is a shame . . . Such a pretty girl . . .*

Laure fled, the tail of her hair hitting her rump, her nails digging into her chest. He was gone, and when he would return, she would be the prostitute instead of the lover, the wife of his heart! He would never love her, never ever . . . unless his kind of wretched love was the kind of love of honest men . . . and she had no right to demand greater affection from this race cursed by her own, the race of wild beasts.

He was the orderly boy, the estimable gentleman, the moderate man, and he came from a modern family who launched them into society in batches to try to counteract either the neurotics or the brutes. Ah! This man knew nothing of the impulses of the senses or the follies of the imagination! Equipped with a special meter calculating the pulsations of love, he had a reserved heart, a cold brain, and worked like an honorable mechanic! With the correct and seductive appearance of a puppet that one would not have wanted to be grotesque, he was the masterpiece of his fin de siècle! An original invention, a hothouse plant from which all of its poisonous principles had finally been extracted! He lacked the prejudices of the province, but retained its exquisite religiosities, such as: respect for the shadow of his mother, belief in a superior will that governs us, probity in dealings with money, and politeness toward women. He would be a notaire. An apotheosis of the Frenchified American genre, he would be the type applying for the knighthood of *well-being*, comfort, and, above all, education. One could not help admiring his science; to remain null, self-effacing, though always so distinguished . . . ! He was happily mediocre! He slept at night, dreamed only after eating hare, and never thought that a woman needed any other distraction than distraction . . . ! He was proud of Monsieur Carnot's Paris, proud of France, which reason and a fine social equilibrium honestly mummified.[1] He studied the manifesta-

---

1. Marie François Sadi Carnot (1837–1894) was the President of France from 1887 to 1894.

tions of electricity, no longer even suspecting that thunder had not been created exclusively to facilitate communications with the Potin grocery store . . .[2] He would marry because romantic relationships are not very safe despite numerous pharmaceutical discoveries, and he would have children modeled after him, other samples of the irreproachable modern bourgeois factory: molds from other molds, loaded in the belly with the same meter that regulates both the needs of the stomach and those of love . . . ! No, these men do not have the gift of loving, even like animals do; they are, in the scale of beings, below animals, between the mineral diamond and the mineral oyster shell!

And good Providence, which we call "chance" when it is wrong and we do not want to disrespect it, had brought together the woman of primitive times with the man of civilized times, of rubberized, electrified, scraped, polished, and mechanized times. Laure had loved Henri after scorning the brutes, her equals, or the fools, her slaves. Over there, in the land of the sun, the peasant Marcou was dying of a "languorous illness" that the Pauvinels, his sturdy parents, believed was a spell cast over their son, such a solid thirty-year-old! Lucien Séchard had killed himself, the poor one-eyed man; Armand de Bréville, almost demented, had terrible hallucinations while saying Mass, calling Laure's name instead of Jesus Christ's . . . And later, at the tamer's hour of triumph, when the dreamed-of man, the existing man, finally approached the young woman to take decisive possession of her, she would not recognize him, her unnecessarily ignited heart would no longer flame, and he would no doubt be reduced to the instinctive mating of beasts . . . they

------

2. Jean-Louis-Félix Potin (1820–1871) was an entrepreneur who founded and built a chain of successful grocery stores through the second half of the nineteenth century.

who should have regenerated the species, been like the Adam and Eve of a new love . . . !

Laure ran through the Parisian night, bumping into gas nozzles and tangling her braid on the shoulders of passersby.

On the Boulevard Saint-Germain, a man accosted her. "By God, it's all yours, baby . . ."

Laure cried out in rage, "No, it's his, his, and he does not want it anymore, he is gone . . . !"

Very serious, believing that he was dealing with a drunk woman, the man, a reveler, respectfully stepped aside. "What an idiot!" he exclaimed.

And, dizzy, Laure replied, "Come, follow me, I will give it to you . . . !"

Thirty days passed slowly. Laure, prostrate, only bothered to feed her cat and herself. The two of them took their meals lying down on the carpet, facing each other, waiting for hours for the concierge to bring them either milk or sweets, and falling back into their somnolence as soon as she turned on her heels. If it was too bright, Laure would lower the blinds, and they would rest there as if wrapped in cotton wool; if it was dark, she would pull aside the silky drapes and look up at the moon. The clock had stopped. Too bad! What was the point of counting the present moment? She no longer received the newspaper, she never leafed through a book, she never hummed. Time passed through this ignorance of human life and the noise of society, like water through a sieve. Strangely enough, Laure had no awareness of being bored. She did not even lead the existence of an animal, she lived the life of a plant, she vegetated, her brain suddenly shrunk by the crushing of her love, and the force of the blow robbed her of thought: she no longer dreamed, no longer desired, wrapped herself in her own arms, sleeping all afternoon, waking at dusk; then, uncoiling her limbs and hair, she sought air, opened the windows with a mechanical movement, then washed herself because the pores of her skin were often terribly thirsty.

Lion, at least, would play, mew, clown around in the cords of the awnings, and upset the cushions in pursuit of a piece of paper. But Laure tired of all of the games, seeming to regret all of the useless gestures, and stared into the void without trying to see. The misfortune, so little appreciable, of a separation of a month, made her a widow . . . Because a month, for those who count only the present moment, is eternity. She transformed herself, forgetting even the root cause of her torpor. During certain bouts of insomnia, she had dreaded this new state on par with death. Other young women have social obligations, a household, children, friends, dressmakers; she possessed only her love. When Henri left her, he left her alone with her singular primitive instincts, her instincts drawing her down like roots, twisting around her skull like branches with poisonous blossoms, and when she breathed in her sad isolation, far from her love that was her only company, she ended up slowly poisoning herself. She became intoxicated, astonished by the scent of her own flesh, confused by the unhealthy vapors of her rank. Remaining with herself was to fight her most appalling enemy. And yet she knew she was the absolute mistress of her actions; no one tempted or provoked her. As a child, Laure had already been afraid of solitude, her bad adviser; she had had attacks of nerves over an extinguished candle in the evening, over a room too large to sleep in, over a dark courtyard, on the way down to the cellar, across the deserted countryside, and still she could not explain whether these attacks had been an excess of pleasure or an excess of fear; she feared to be alone as one fears to do wrong, and shivers of joy shook her when she thought that, again, once she became a woman, she would still have these dangerous fears. Such creatures, always ready for a fall and influenced by the shadow of sadness, are examples of the sensitive family, but of the carnivorous kind, those who, yawning from the flower or leaf, gobble up insects as they pass. Lacking the means of locomotion, they suffocate the fly as soon as they have hold of it, or else dry up from having nothing left to suffocate in their corner of tenebrous nature.

Laure, the savage, did not want to go out anymore; she was afraid of grabbing yet another man's attention in passing on the street, she no longer wanted to get dressed because the mirrors reflected her in passing in her room, and she no longer dared move for fear of feeling beautiful.

On the thirtieth day of this voluntary imprisonment, Laure uttered the name of Henri aloud without flinching. As one sweeps away a troublesome twig, she tossed the name absentmindedly into the abyss of her childhood memories. Henri was now as old as all of the Lilliputian lovers to whom she had once offered herself under the monstrous angelicas of her paternal home . . . However, since this caprice had seized her heart instead of stirring her senses, she retained a pain from it instead of only a fleeting emotional disturbance. Yes, she would deceive him as she had deceived those poor youths, only she would be the one to suffer, that is all, and she would only tell him so when she was forced to . . . The honesty of her love was but a deception toward one who was indifferent; she would be less honest from now on, and, who knows? Henri might love her more if he returned!

That evening, she played with Lion for a long time, finding new happiness in stroking him, looking into those pretty apertures of light and giving him lessons in craftiness like a female. The little cat, always rubbing against her obliging humanity, took on the appearance of a child, becoming human, while the young woman, more bestial in rubbing against this fur of an animal, became feline, feeling the need to scratch, to howl her sorrows in a mewing of passion and anguish. Tired, Lion fell asleep and, once she had calmed down about the baby, the mother climbed, like a real cat, the ladder that led to the roof, to the great night full of stars. Laure, for this escapade, had brushed her hair, put on a red satin peignoir, and slipped on velvet slippers, but she was well aware that the roof would provide her with no other lovers than prowling tomcats. On the frosted crystal, she stretched out, satisfied, her eye on the lookout, her body quivering, vaguely happy with the promise of pleasure she sensed in the breeze. A slightly wild moon seemed to be chased by the autumn wind, and the round dry leaf, the golden-yellow dead leaf, swirled beneath russet clouds in the company of stars twinkling like white immortals. It was no longer spring, with its tears of sap and its finery of a young bride, its enormous moon, delicious to the eye like honey, but in this troubled atmosphere, vain desires whetted faster, beaten to a pulp, and the fleeing glow of the star seemed to shout, "Hurry up, I know it is going to be cold." Plumes of smoke twisted around the chimneys, covering the brightness of Paris with a veil and haloing the tops of buildings in a nimbus of mist, where red spires shone. Here and there, beneath swathes of funereal shadow, the infernal braziers of the great boulevards opened up, the silver jets of electric globes filtered through, and the forest of tin chimneys, those black trees of an eternal winter, gleamed, at times, with a vivid reflection when the moon perched, as it passed, on their tops. Laure straightened up, toured her domain, inclined, and did not feel dizzy. The idea occurred to her to climb over the little balustrade to visit the neighboring roofs. On the side of the

Rue de Seine, a yawning precipice grew wider: she moved away from the edge of the gutters, and crawled along the courtyard side where she could see attic windows.

"I can break my head," she said to herself. "Henri is not waiting for me anymore!"

And, muttering this bitter sentence, she tore her peignoir on the roofing hooks that she met along the way.

Only one attic was lit up, with a pink spot of a small, dying lamp behind a curtain. Laure was bitterly curious to know what was in the attic: whether a chambermaid undressing or a store boy shining his shoes, she would amuse herself by spying on them behind this luminous lattice, and like the shadow fairy, she would cackle at just the right moment to give them horrible scares.

She had to cross a perilous spot, the top of an inner courtyard made of iron mesh so thin that, as she climbed, she felt like a colossal spider in the middle of its web, then she reached the attic and huddled behind the glass. Eleven o'clock struck on a distant clock; the chiming, scattering in the wind, overwhelmed her and almost prevented her from raising her head.

Ah! That melancholy voice of bronze crying over her, crying over Paris, the accursed city of all shame, of all criminal passions . . . ! But Laure did not know the voice of God, and it was not a message from Henri that the bell was addressing to her; curiosity got the better of her, and she looked into the attic.

In front of a table, a workman in shirtsleeves was polishing microscopic, sparkling objects—earrings, bun pins, cufflinks— which he took out of a box and put back into another with a gesture that was always the same, so nonchalant that one could well have sworn he was asleep while working. The room was humble, furnished with a brown-covered hospital bed, a straw chair, and a few kitchen utensils, including a black-bottomed frying pan with an ugly, thick ink stain on the wall. The workman, coincidentally, interrupted his work to replace some kerosene in his lamp, and came out in full view.

Laure saw a young boy of about seventeen, skinny, with a hollowed-out chest, protruding Adam's apple, arms detached from his shoulders like those of young miscreants, capable of anything, who go with swinging hands along the sidewalks picking up cigarette butts, a type of trickster or procurer, and also a sort of good-natured devil when he bent over, with renewed vigor, the fine Parisian trinkets he was polishing. Laure smiled behind the glass, wondering if the jewelry was artificial. The wind redoubled, whipping her cheeks with her hair, and she found it hard to stand upright on the sloping roof. To her left, she could see the streetlamps as big as blazing matches, and she felt herself being sucked into that inner courtyard, so close to her, this courtyard veiled in its spider's web, black as the opening of an oven; only, the lure of the glass trinkets held her back, she looked again ...

The workman resumed his task. He dipped a rag in a bucket, looked for pliers, dismantled a stone, smoothed the metal on a powder or adjusted the jewel between the notches of a vice, and rubbed firmly. From time to time, he yawned, furiously irritated, it seemed, by a haunting idea. Finally, he pushed back the table, turned and raised his arms to open his window. The young woman crouched down, startled, fearing that he had heard something; but the boy, no doubt asleep on his feet, did not suspect a thing. He returned to his table, muttering unintelligible words. Laure ventured out again and took one last look, attracted above all by the sparkling jewels that this poor boy was carelessly handling, and she would have gladly asked permission to play with them. How happy he was, the boy, to play with this fortune!

She watched with all her gleaming eyes, keenly interested. Her wandering around the rooftops gave her back an hour of her early childhood, one of the purest hours, spent playing with stoppers of decanters, prisms in which her naive heart imagined that she could see a reflection of paradise. In those days, she would have given anything to become the little wife of a jeweler, even in counterfeits! The marvelous clarity of the fragments of the sky, the naivety of her girlish beliefs, how quickly all that had tarnished, my God! Could one not ever exist quietly without the fevers of the senses that creep into all games, even the most innocent ones . . . ?

Clinging to the windowsill, holding on with her ten fingernails and supported on the two cleft ends of her slippers, she was almost resolved to shout to him, "Do you want to share?" while she remained open-mouthed, eyes fixed. The young boy, abandoning his work for the third time, had fallen backward, seized by a sudden ecstasy. Laure felt a pain and then let out a sobbing laugh, like the wailing of the breeze, like the crying of the bell, for *this was the misfortune of all life*, among the poor, among the rich, in the abyss, or near the sky. This was the evil of the flesh . . . ! Scared to death, the young worker leaped up, shouting, swearing, drunk with joy and spite, unable to explain what was happening, but ready to believe anything possible. He had dreamed of a pretty whore who had beckoned to him, and the woman, giggling, hair flowing, arms bare, he had to have her. Where did she come from? The clouds? She laughed! It was because she wanted to . . .

He jostled his table, the jewels scattered to the four corners of the attic, and he stepped over the window in a tiger-cat leap, but Laure was already fleeing, darting over the iron netting stretched over the inner courtyard, across the roofs, clinging to chimney after chimney; she fled, light, airy, just like a "true vision." On the ceiling of the studio, she disappeared down a trapdoor, engulfing herself in a trick of enchantment, this evil fairy, this capricious fallen angel wearing a dress of fire and followed by the dark satanic train of infernal hair. The boy, sweat at his temples, shaking with nervous shivers, arms open, stopped against the balustrade of the workshop's small roof. No one! Had he been dreaming, or was it simply a thief attracted by the glitter of his jewels? No, a thief is not so beautiful, so quick to laugh at funny things . . . And, distraught, the boy went home, threw himself on his bed, weeping with rage.

A house-distance away, another joyful creature was also weeping, lying on her bed, bruising her chest as she called for a lover who would no longer return in a month!

The next morning, Laure awoke with a heavy head; it was late, very late, as the sun flooded her bed with burning rays. A good day was in store for her, for she had slept, oh! Slept like the dead! She dressed carefully, looking calm, with a wicked grin on her lips. A silly adventure, that of last night: she would find something better. What she wanted was love, not an hour's madness; she wanted to be loved at all costs, guessing that the only true aphrodisiac of love . . . is love! Henri did not love her, and he would never satisfy her; she no longer counted on him, ending up despising him. She thought that since she was "giving" instead of "selling," she had the right to choose. The young man whom she had met the night Henri left would not come back because she had seemed mad, but she would accept that.

"Here, Lion," she exclaimed, untangling her hair to comb it, "we are both beasts, and honesty does not exist!"

She tried to mock him; however, there, from her other side, a part of her recanted, made her suffer again when she thought that he would have the right to say to her, "Your only merit, my dear, was fidelity!"

And because he had the right accent to say so, a very soft accent of a man of superior education, joking coldly. Laure spun around in her nest of yellow silk, he had given her all of these things, and all of these things would serve her trade as a girl . . . One night, a man would pay her on this bed already paid for by another . . .

"First of all, me," she murmured fiercely, "no one would dare buy me; I think I would kill anyone who dared offer me money . . ." And she added, giggling, "As if pleasure could be paid for . . . I will always give it for nothing to anyone who wants it."

She fed the cat and, restless, waited for the moment to go out. She would take a car, go anywhere, and try not to come back, so as to distract herself away from this hot greenhouse where her languor increased. Around three o'clock, the doorbell rang. Laure flinched, distraught. She thought that the boy from the attic had probably discovered her retreat and was about to pounce on her, to rape her: she found him in the depths of her conscience, obscene, as agile as a monkey, he would envelop her and she would not resist, she would not know how to resist him. It would be her most ridiculous fall. Worried, she crossed her peignoir over her throat, tied her ribbons, tied back her hair, put on a stern face: she could not open the door, but an irresistible force was pushing her toward it, because behind it a man was waiting for her! She opened the door.

13

Henri Alban, standing on the threshold, in the same place where she had smiled at him, stepping aside to let her pass, a stranger begging for love, was smiling, contemplating her, looking a little vexed to be back so soon.

"You see, my dear child, that I am a man of my word!"

And he entered, taking her wrists to kiss her, as the "other" had kissed her a month ago.

"I am not disturbing you, am I? Is there not someone hiding under the bed?" he added mockingly.

Laure remained motionless, very pale, but smiling too, her face calm. This was to be expected, and although she had something dead in her heart, this unexpected return pleased her. Like a flower that is fresher after a storm, she seemed more reserved, more modest. The madness she had committed—running across the rooftops in the open air at night—had left her with a graceful melancholy that made her more supple and illuminated her with an inner light. She received her lover-husband like a pretty petite bourgeoise whose short widowhood had been filled by the healthy occupations of the domestic household.

Her home was in order; she had, to rest from all of her emotions, tidied up, cleaned, put green plants in planters and shook out the hangings, blown away the atoms of love, the dust of guilty memories. Henri took stock of the living room at a glance. He sniffed the atmosphere; it did not smell of cigars, and his American armchair had remained in its favorite spot. Lion, gravely seated on the desk, looked at him amid his books and papers with the air of an honest cat who knows nothing. Henri, having given no notice by letter or telegram, dropped in on her like an uninvited guest, and found, oddly enough, that he was not in her way.

She replied serenely, "So, you were hoping to find someone here?"

"Why, finders keepers, losers weepers, as the saying goes!"

Incidentally, he returned home, very happy to find this wanton girl after a month's abstinence; and, his blood whipped by the midday meal, high on spices of all kinds, he certainly would not refuse resuming communal life. He carefully placed his suitcase on a chair—because of his aunt's jam jars—and went into the yellow room. The bed was neatly made, the sheets without a suspicious crease, the blanket without a crumple; the mirror reflected the sky, opposite the wide-open window, and everything smelled of sunshine, shimmering with golden glints like a crystal soaked in light. He sat down on the cushions, drew her in front of him, made her turn around for him.

Laure, for her part, examined him, wondering if he was really Henri, the one she called her "fiancé." She saw him worse, changed, because she was changed, she no longer loved him in the same way and resented the fact that she had deceived him. He was too blond now, his eyes too gray, like earthenware eyes, and that disdainful smile, which she used to admire because it made her feel sorry, intimidated her, made her want to laugh in his face. However, she felt happy to see him there, confident in her; his kisses moved her like the caresses of a poor young man who arouses pity.

"You went," she says, "to get ready for another wedding. Tell me, then, about my replacement."

"Teasing us already?"

"Do you not deserve it?"

"Oh, if you think I believe in your oaths of fidelity, my little pussycat! All I would have to do is feel up the concierge . . ."

Laure was shocked by his language, which she found very vulgar, the language of a man who pays to be well served, and it was without enthusiasm that she let him crease her peignoir.

In the evening, they dined out, drank fine wines, quarreled over dessert, had hurtful words, called each other fools, then went to bed early with fevers: Henri, immediately soothed, fell asleep around midnight, and Laure, as was her custom (returning herself), kept watch, brow raised in the direction of the roofs, listening to the nervous mewing of the tomcats.

The next day, Henri went to his study, his attaché case under his arm, humming like a jovial boy who has played an excellent game of cards. He had achieved peace. The little cat had calmed down completely, his nails no longer protruding from under the velvet. No scenes of exaggerated tenderness, no sharp reproaches, and no dramatic despair. She was as loyal as a rock, yes, but she would be pushed gently by the babbling brook. She was ripe for a fall, and he would have the glory of breaking it off first, which a well-styled man never fails to do when he can or is given the time. There, his father was looking after his future in between bird dog hunts. He had been presented with a boarder woman who was not lacking in curves. The daughter of a gendarmerie captain. An exquisite eighteen-year-old, a little simple, a little awkward, yet already full of flavor, a blonde whose lips were as moist as a dew-painted bunch of cherries. Eighty thousand francs dowry, an honorable family and brothers whom one could smoke with. It was said that this young person was simpleminded, that she had spent her early childhood in a kind of cerebral sleep equivalent to idiocy; but she was charming, and Henri did not care much for women who could not sleep on cue. At least he would be her educator and answer for her eternal ignorance. All he had to do was steer a straight course between the pitfalls of vitriol and the storms of tears. He would enjoy his mistress wisely until the following spring, spend a pleasant winter, and bury his life as a bachelor just a month before the new engagement.

At the office, where the clerk, being among the more amateur, only came in when it pleased him, he distributed cordial handshakes, told of his hunts, and laughed a lot. He had the face of a gentleman henceforth mature and triumphant. Methodical people experience sudden bursts of satisfaction in the presence of a banal denouement well-executed at the theater, and they would gladly congratulate the head stagehand for having made it possible, through his combination of tricks, to say "yes" at the psychological moment. Laure no longer oppressed him, and he felt her lessen her hold on his chest; she would gradually disengage herself from him, forget her trivial need to love man for man in the presence of his chaste skepticism, and, who knows, end up loving him for money, as was appropriate in their equivocal situation. One thing astonished him, for instance, and that was her bizarre clairvoyance about the future that he had in store for her. What spirit had told her about his marriage, and why was she now reading his thoughts in his eyes?

One morning, he said to her, suddenly striking his forehead, "By the way, the curé d'Estérac has left. They put him in a little village in Combes, near La Bourdaisière, you know! He did not have his head on his shoulders anymore, and they put him there as if in penance."

"Ah!" replied Laure, who was combing her long hair indifferently. "You paid a visit to your old schoolmate . . . Did you talk about me together?"

"Not on your life! I never set foot in his house! I hate fools!"

"It is terrible, indeed," murmured the young woman. "No respect . . . !"

And Henri approved with a serious gesture.

Autumn passed in a gentle manner, the two lovers agreed not to argue; stormy questions were avoided, and they saw each other only at mealtimes or at the hours of love.

If I went away, it would be more dignified! she thought.

But a sort of mysterious superstition still attached her to Henri. She had sincerely loved only that man, and if she were to leave before her appointed time, she might regret this semblance of love that was dying between them and was preserving a perfume of permissible tenderness, like an old bunch of roses still preserves a badly bloomed bud wanting to bloom all the same, despite the rottenness of its stem.

In winter, they received a few friends from the office and served intimate teas. Henri, wishing to bring the wolf into the fold, forced the young woman to be "kind" to these gentlemen clerks, sons of families from the same ilk as himself. Three of them came in turn, all three impeccably dressed characters. One of them, Julien Landry, a sanguine, bulldog-faced man, was immediately enamored by Laure's miraculous hair and took extraordinary care to display "feelings in keeping with his fortune." In front of these men, she remained mute, keeping quiet and showing no preference. Julien Landry was to her in the "dark" what Henri Alban was to her in the "light": a lovable nullity, an estimable boy capable of anything, including raping the mistress of one of his best friends, and she instinctively hated him, waiting for his first folly so that she could have him thrown out.

"Do you find them amusing?" she said with a significant pout.

Henri replied, "They are excellent comrades. They will never make you feel inferior, I promise."

"But they are stupid!"

"Because they talk in front of you about things that are beyond your reach. My dear, you are becoming difficult for a woman who only talks to her cat!"

"Monsieur Landry was touching my hair all evening!"

"Oh! A joke without any malice. In any case, I never hear him risk a frivolous remark."

"Henri, I would rather stay in my room!"

"That would be ridiculous. People would think that I was getting jealous."

She would serve the tea, cut the brioche, and put the liqueurs on a tray, then withdraw to a corner of the living room by the fireplace, her cat nestled in her lap, never loosening her lips. They would play dominoes and piquet, winking at her and saying, "You have lost, my dear Henri . . . When you are so happy in love!" "If mademoiselle wanted to hold my hand, I only wish to lose!" And the evening went on, interminably, amid the wild exclamations of the men, forcing their character to try to turn her head. Henri would sometimes discuss bills, and the conversation would degenerate into an argument with Julien Landry, an intransigent man. The latter would bang his fist on the pedestal table, making the flasks and cups jump and waking the cat, which would direct its phosphorescent pupils in the opposite direction.

Then the young woman would calmly drop a sentence: "Be careful, monsieur, you will scare Lion."

Landry would be silent for a moment, rolling his big eyes, proud of having frightened the animal, and would come to his senses with a mocking laugh. "Oh, pussycats, mademoiselle, I know all about them, and if you would like to entrust me with yours…"

One evening, the clerk arrived earlier than usual, unaccompanied by Henri. Laure was reluctant to receive him, but out of submission to her lover, she let him in, despite her concerns. The young lout sat on the end of a chair, far more embarrassed than Laure.

"It is cold," he declared, "is it not, mademoiselle?"

"Warm yourself up, monsieur! And Henri?"

"Monsieur Alban stayed at the boss's house this evening on a business matter; we both had dinner, and he sent me over, just to put you at ease."

Laure said nothing. It was obvious that her lover did not spare her much thought, and she was surprised not to suffer more from his contempt. She arranged the dominoes table, prepared the water for tea in the kettle, and then went to the yellow room, where she was treating Lion, who was indisposed.

"It is really very chic here!" murmured the clerk, standing on the threshold and contemplating the silk blinds and the old gold bed. He took a step forward. "So, your poor pussycat, whom you love so much, is ill?"

"I think he has got a cold."

"Let us have a look. You know, I have studied animals."

He looked serious; Laure, preoccupied with the cat, had no idea that anything else could be taken care of for a quarter of an hour. She leaned into the quilt where the animal slept and woke him up to offer him some sweet milk.

"Goodness! He has a great face! He is a tiger! How old is he? You should neuter him, he is sick because you stop him from roaming, eh?"

"I do not want him touched, monsieur! He will never be tormented by anyone."

"Yes, compassion is very nice, but he will soil everything, and if he does not roam, he will become epileptic."

Because he spoke decently, Laure let him approach the bed and showed him Lion luxuriating at the bottom of the yellow satin.

"He is nearly a year old," she said, caressing her son who was growling at the stranger; "but I think he is past the age of a growth disorder, is he not, monsieur?"

"One year is the age of reason! Let us see! Show me his tongue! When the tongue is white, it is a bad sign . . . Oh, the dirty beast, he bit me!"

The cat fled under the bed, while Laure, annoyed that this fool had disturbed him needlessly, cried out, "What a misfortune! He will be cold. You do not know how to tame animals at all, monsieur."

"Bah! You think . . ."

And, pouncing on her greedily, he intended to kiss her neck, for in the time they had been studying the physiognomy of the cat, the clerk had been contemplating the hair of the young woman with feverish admiration. Laure struggled furiously, calling out Henri's name.

"Henri?" said the young man, chuckling. "He is far away! Are you really that faithful, my pretty savage?"

No, she was not faithful; but she loathed this boy, charged with a clean demise, a suitable breakup, who would not cause a scandal outside of the office of the notaire, she had a repugnance for honest people today, preferring any boor, any fool, to those well-behaved, half-wise characters whom one used to call well-behaved men. These reasonable ones, they were more coarse than the brutes from the country in their amorous outpourings . . . They possessed neither the naivety of simple peasants, nor the ardor of enthusiasts who dare not or dare too much, they were hygienically unhealthy, spending no more on gracious words than on gracious deeds. Now, she hated them!

"Let me go, or I will strangle you!" roared the young woman, wrapping her five sharp fingers around his throat.

"Boy, you are mean!" said Julien Landry, loosening his grip. "And you are making a lot of noise for a little kiss."

With a stiff posture, like a man who has just been offended, he went and sat down in the living room by the fire, warmed his legs for composure, and looked at his thumb, where the cat had embedded its tooth.

What strange animals! he thought.

Laure sat opposite him, her eyes fixed on a Japanese screen.

"Do you love your Henri that much?" murmured the clerk, who felt it was his duty to snigger a little.

"I am not accountable to you for my love affairs, monsieur. Is he the one who asks you to kiss me when he is . . . late?"

"Oh, no! That is to say . . . Eh! Eh . . . !" He became mired in a thick, oily laugh.

Laure made a gesture of disgust as she added mentally, *They support each other, gentlemen of the clergy. It was a fixed scene between them.*

She was not wrong. Henri returned home with a slight cough. The evening was painful. Julien Landry dropped dominoes under the table, pinching Laure's ankles as he picked them up. He put on an air of victory, no doubt wishing to give the impression that he was winning, but the ironic smile of the young woman explained everything. Henri guessed that she had just spurned the advances of the brute. As the clerk left, he accompanied him to the landing under the pretext of lighting his way, and in reality, he scolded him. Laure could only catch this exclamation: "*Maladroit!*"

"Why did you call him clumsy?" she asked, painfully moved.

"He nearly snuffed out my candle by relighting his cigar."

"Ah! Did you not think he looked funny tonight?"

"I found him as usual," Henri replied, maintaining a sullen demeanor, and suddenly lay down, back turned.

At midnight, Laure got up and, with no concern for the cold, stretched out, unable to sleep, on the cushions beside the fireplace where a log was burning. Her gaze hypnotized by the dying embers, following the sparks that flew silently in the vague blackness of the hearth, she wept. What could she complain about? Was she not more guilty than he? She had cheated on him in his absence and had the baseness not to tell him! All relations had to stop, the last chains had to be broken, but their poor love would end badly and cowardly! Besides, with the next renewal would come the follies of her senses, and she would deceive him again. Lion, gliding toward his mistress, sniffed her, purring.

"You are always there when I cry," she murmured, annoyed. "What are you doing spying on me like that?"

The animal stood up, placed its two paws on her shoulders and very gently licked her cheeks, drinking away her tears.

Then she felt one of those profound astonishments that soothe the most violent pain, because they upset the established order of nature. As a mother can be happy to see her child's intelligence blossom, she was delighted, felt privileged among women, consoled herself from all of her sadness with an explosion of passion for the humble, and thanked the cat for having "spoken" to her.

14

As early as April, with the first warm nights, Laure resumed her wanderings over the roofs; she took advantage of Henri's virtuous sleep to rise with the moon and went running in what she called her garden. A strange garden, planted with sheet-metal pipes, blossoming with weathervanes, a frightening solitude where a raging breeze blew, a desert of stone whose wild grasses were represented by the bristling of scrap metal and the roughness of roof tiles, a formidable land of which she became the queen at the hour of the feline cavalcade.

"You will fall into the street and cause our concierges to gossip," grumbled Henri, having caught her at the crack of dawn returning from her cat ritual.

"Do not upset yourself, my dear friend, one does not meet anyone there, and you cannot accuse me of making rendezvous there," she replied, smiling a strange smile.

Lion proudly escorted her, played hide-and-seek behind the chimneys, frolicked on the slides of glass roofs and followed his pussycats, who sometimes led him far away. Then the young woman would lie flat on her back, yawning with nervous anxiety. She took a veritable bath in the white moonbeams, tossing and turning in the stellar coolness as if in a wave where strands of pearls might have languidly unfurled. She gazed at the dark city from the top of her fragile terrace, with the disdain some small children have for objects too big for them to hold with both hands.

After all, seen from the stars, Paris was a dark, closed box. Smoke twisting and curling around it was enough to plunge it into nothingness. If it burned intermittently, it was like a bronze cassolette smoldering with noxious odors under a cinder; and she wrinkled her nostrils as she breathed in the dubious scent of the streets that humbly rose up to her, the idol made for invigorating aromas of the forests.

Watching the cat pounce, she murmured, stretching her limbs, "No, men are not worthy of my ardor, and I do not want to stray any further into this cesspool. I am tired … Too bad! Let it end as it will."

She told herself that if she kicked the anthill, she would never see the wild lover whom she was waiting for, and no one would ever discover sensuous torture equal to hers. Men lamented the infidelities of women, and women remained victims of the impotence of men without rebelling, without shouting at them, "Who are you to dare complain? You have neither generosity of soul, nor physical generosity!" A sort of madness, made up of melancholy vertigo, and pride came over her as she roamed her domain; she felt strong enough to fight against her ridiculous beastmaster, to get rid of him by biting him in the heart once and for all, to punish him for the audacity that he had had, that petty man, in supplying her fangs not with red meat, but with cardboard! Then, dreaming of a trip to the heavens, straddling the golden crescent like a witch, she would go and find the monstrous tomcats lurking in the attics of the heavens, the fantastic, caressing tomcats that watched her with gleaming eyes through the skylights of the stars.

One night, she threw a ribbon through the open window of the attic where the young boy was sleeping whom she had so desperately troubled the previous autumn, and it amused her to return this mischief to the one who set such beautiful cat eyes! Was she not the pretty fairy protector of sensual felines, the fairy who passed by leaving behind a subtle scent of musk, a little of her coquettish angora fur? And she slipped away, not waiting for an answer.

The next day, around eleven o'clock, she lay down in her favorite spot, in the middle of the frosted glass, more annoyed than usual, while Lion expressed his mistress's thoughts in his ferocious language, mewling over the gutters, to impossible loves. The window of the attic was lit up, and the skinny figure of its occupant could be seen anxiously pressed against the glass. With spring, the beautiful vision, the chimerical runner, had returned. How could he risk, however, returning the knot of ribbon that the breeze had tossed, the day before, into his attic? He had so often paid the price for a dangerous walk, the poor kid!

If he joins me, I will try to tame him, and he will serve my vengeance, thought the perplexed young woman, *but he has probably forgotten me, what a pity! He was a rival that Henri certainly would not have invented, this ruffian! I think he is nice! Ah! Henri will know one day what I think of him. He has to know. I want him to, because I will not prostitute myself to please him! I will give myself for my own pleasure, not for his. I cannot let myself be dismissed like a servant. Yes, I will take my revenge, it will comfort my heart and satisfy my body at the same time!*

Suddenly, the lamp over there went out; Laure perceived the sound of a window opening discreetly, a shadow wandered from chimney to chimney, and the young woman, isolated from the rest of the world, a hundred leagues from the civilized world, forgetting laws and customs only to remember that she was as free as the wind that untied her hair, stood ready to begin the romantic idyll.

"Taking some fresh air, madame?" sighed a timid voice.

Laure saw him in front of her on the sloping tiles of the neighboring roof, his two hands clasped on two roofer's spikes, his legs clamped on the gutter a few centimeters from the abyss, and so supple, so thin, that he appeared annulated like a centipede. He was dressed in a small blue canvas jacket, cinched at the back, of a laborer's workwear. His chestnut hair, frizzing on his forehead, ruffled in the raging wind, and his clear eyes, as limpid as two diamonds, reflected the moon's rays to the point of setting them on fire. As he spoke, he showed sharp teeth that a hard loaf of bread could never withstand. Half young fox, half young monkey, he was graceful with an unbearable hint of sauciness; but for the moment, he remained shy, ashamed in the presence of this mad princess who reminded him of a story whose recollection filled him with confusion.

Laure, for her part, reclining like a sphinx, molded in her black velvet robe, her hands clasped under her chin, her beautiful braid snaking over her rump, made a diabolical counterpart to him.

She replied with a mocking wink, "Yes, monsieur, I am just getting some air. I only breathe well here. Are you surprised?"

"Oh, this is your home, and there is no neighbor but your servant. Me, I am not here to deceive you, madame."

"I hope not, monsieur."

"Please do not call me 'monsieur.' My name is Auguste."

They gazed at each other in silence for a moment.

"I would still like to know where is it you go to return home. I still have not been able to sort out the place among all those panes."

"So you searched without my permission?"

"Excuse me, you did not ask permission to stick your nose in my windows!"

Laure smiled. "Monsieur Auguste, you speak too loudly. Someone's asleep down there."

She pointed to the lowered skylight, which she always kept closed so that Henri could not hear Lion's furious mewing and nocturnal frolicking.

"That is enough, I understand, it is your husband!"

She replied, fixing her dark eyes on his light ones, "No, he is not my husband."

Auguste, who went to the theater on Sundays, made a quick swooning gesture as he put his hand to his chest, and nearly fell over. He held on and pulled himself up a little closer to the young woman. Only a ridge of roof tile separated them, and Laure could see very clearly, in the indentation of his blue canvas jacket, all of the thinness of his neck, his protruding Adam's apple.

Poor emaciated cat, she thought, *does he not eat his fill?*

She added, "Are you a jewelry worker?"

"Fake jewelry, madame, at your service."

"And what do you earn?"

"It depends, sometimes four francs a day, sometimes five. I am a bronzer and a hook assembler . . ."

"I can tell!" said Laure, pointing to the clamps that he was holding tightly.

He burst out laughing. "You have a lovely eye, madame! I am sorry, I should say 'mademoiselle,' should I not?"

"Yes. Are you from Paris, Monsieur Auguste?"

"Born and bred. My mother and father died a long time ago, and my uncle apprenticed me. Good trade. I work at home when I am in a hurry. Ask for Monsieur Auguste Ternisier, the door on the left under the rafters."

"I will not ask for anything, but I will take a look at your jewels via the rooftops, if you like!"

"It is just that I am not allowed to sell them to you myself, mademoiselle, because that would cause trouble . . . and I am responsible for them."

"I will play with them without buying them."

She wants to steal, this kid! thought Auguste.

The interview languished. Despite his admiration for her, he felt a chill run down his spine. Lion came to sniff him, spat, and leaped up, and this created a diversion.

"Tell me, Auguste, would you be able to do me a great favor?" murmured Laure, approaching and brushing him with her hair.

"Oh! Mademoiselle, I have come to give you this back!"

He handed her a knot of red ribbon, which he took out, still warm, from his jacket.

"Thank you, my friend, but it would be something more difficult."

"I'll have to see the price first!" he mocked, looking down at her.

"I can give you a nice banknote if you like."

Auguste's blood rushed to his pale face. "Would you like to give me a banknote?"

"Yes, for a pair of slaps you would give to a gentleman whom I no longer love . . ."

"By thunder . . . !" The teenager stood upright on the slope of the roof, and leaped, like Lion. "You have got to be kidding me, mademoiselle! I am a simpleton, but I am not deaf . . . !"

"You think a hundred francs . . . ?"

"Do not say that again, or I will throw you over the edge."

Crossing his arms, he squared himself in the moonlight, forming a large, gesticulating shadow on the pallid roof.

"I do not know you," he continued exasperatedly. "I do not know where you are from; you caused me a lot of trouble one evening, and I looked for you on the rooftops, to the point of losing my appetite; I even think my heart was sickened . . . However, do not try my patience; oh! I know it is forbidden to joke with upper-class girls when you are poor, but I am not saying bad words to you, I did not disrespect your velvet dress . . . so I am taking back your authorization to insult me."

"Come now, my child, am I insulting you by offering to make you rich . . . ?"

Auguste, shivering, looked at her fearfully. "You think that I am a pimp!" he let out, chattering his teeth.

"A pimp," Laure repeated in bewilderment.

And she added, bursting into laughter, "Oh, my God, I had forgotten all about it."

"Do you think that is funny?"

"Do not get angry, Auguste, and above all do not shout so loudly . . . ! Come on, let us talk about something else."

"Who is bothering you? Eh?"

He lay down again in front of her, but this time with his head touching her head, eye to eye.

"I would like to teach a lesson to someone who forgets that I loved him."

"Is it possible to forget you?" stammered the teenager, his lips quivering.

Laure, flattered by this naive tribute, smiled at him. For a moment, like a double flash of livid lightning, their open mouths sparkled with the teeth of young wolves.

"Alas . . . !" sighed Laure.

"That is why you are a little mad, and why you gallop across the gutters at night?"

"Perhaps, my dear child."

"Ah! You can boast that you have astonished me, Mademoiselle Meddlesome! You smell so good! And to think that there are women like that . . . almost as many as there are candles up there!" And he pointed to the stars.

"Auguste, it is your turn to be deceived, you think that I am a girl and I am . . . a lover . . ."

He chuckled. "You're adding insult to injury."

"Do you not get it, you big kid? I love for love, not for money."

"And I, mademoiselle," said the worker in a subdued tone, "I will not serve you for money; I will obey you for love, if you like me . . ."

Laure remained pensive. She liked him.

"I am too badly dressed, eh?" sighed the young boy, trying to mock again, his throat clenched by intense emotion. "Unless," he sneered, "you would prefer I wear a nice brooch made of rhinestone."

Laure shook her head. "You are a funny little villain, Auguste."

"Anyway, I do not have any spit curls, mademoiselle!"

And, spitting into his fingers, he pretended to slick side curls behind his ears.

"Hush!"

"Let us see, let us talk little and talk well. What would you like me to do, my little bourgeoisie?"

"Listen to me, Auguste, I want this man out first."

"Bah! He is in your way!"

Laure grabbed his shoulders. "He wanted to force me to cheat on him!"

"Ah! Well, if he is one of *those*, I will punch him for free; I loathe those beasts."

"But no, on the contrary, he is a very honest man, you do not understand, he wanted to get rid of my love, which he finds cumbersome because he is getting married."

"That is quite a story. And this gentleman, you love him . . . forever."

"Oh! I love him . . . less."

"He looks after you, does he not?"

"He has been my husband for three years, but I do not need him, I can tell you that."

"And he sleeps down there . . . ?"

"Right down there."

"He lets you run around without asking questions?"

"Yes."

"Joker!" And the young worker, half smiling, half vexed, elbowed her.

Laure stretched, her eyes closed, bringing the braid of her hair around her. "Only because you think I am pretty."

Auguste Ternisier shivered, tempted to grab hold of the floating braid, and suddenly stood up. "Good grief! You have got to be kidding me! Look, I would rather not run out on you. I have got to wake up early, and you would give me bad dreams. Good night! Good night!"

He stood there for a second, staring at her, his tongue licking his lips with the air of a little boy coveting a delicacy.

"All the same, you would make me do some foolish things; only, we have got gumption, and I can see your idea."

"You are scared!"

"Me, afraid . . . ? You do not know me, mademoiselle, I go my own way and I manage. I have already slapped a few people in the face . . . Fear! Oh! There! There . . . ! Goodbye! If you ever feel like visiting my 'tinsel' again, you know the address: the door opens onto the sky. Good evening again . . ."

He tore himself away from the intoxicating pleasure that he was experiencing, brave as an old philosopher. Laure followed him with her dark eyes.

"You will be back!" she murmured.

She remembered, oh so vaguely, the child whom she had enslaved as a child herself, little Marcou Pauvinel.

Marcou was the first, will this one be the last? she mused painfully. *I feel sad to death . . . They are all such cowards.*

She and Lion returned to the yellow room.

A few days passed. Auguste was prowling. Laure stopped going up to the roof. Finally, one Sunday evening, the young woman knocked on the window of the attic. He eagerly opened the door.

"You!"

"I have come to see your shiny trinkets."

"It is madness, my God, to go through places like the courtyard fence . . . you will end up taking a dive."

He passed her a chair, helped her sit down, and spread all of the artificial jewels on the table.

"It is enough to offer to pretty women, am I right?"

For a moment, she dipped her fingers in the heap, then said cheerfully, "You know, I prefer the stars."

He was losing her completely. Now he could convince himself that she neither wished to steal from him nor to rob him by persuasion, and, even more worried, he wondered if it would not have been better to leave her moping behind the window.

"Why did you not come earlier?" he asked, packing his jewelry in its tissue paper and cotton-wool-lined box.

"It was raining."

"That is one reason. Would you not accept a little glass of sweetness—Eh! We will go down to the corner café. They do not know you there, and the concierge is a good devil."

"No, I only wore a mantilla . . . Besides this velvet dress . . ."

"Yes, that would get you noticed," he interrupted sulkily.

"Will you take me home . . . Auguste?"

"Already? I wanted to tell you some things, mademoiselle, many things . . ."

"Tell me about it on the roof."

He shrugged. "Your idea again! Oh! You are quite a character, you!"

They stepped over the window sill onto the small white terrace, hand in hand. Auguste noticed that the skylight was gaping.

"This is the entrance to my apartment. I am not a fairy, I do not vanish through the clouds," declared Laure.

They lay down side by side, because after a while, standing still could give one vertigo.

"So he is gone?" he breathed softly.

"Who?"

"The monsieur!"

She smiled mysteriously as she replied, "Not quite."

She resumed, after a long silence during which he contemplated her at his ease, brow bent, eye full with longing, "You wanted to tell me something . . . Auguste?"

"When I look at you, it produces the same effect on me as when I look at the moon for a long time, I feel like crying and I cannot find my words."

"Do I intimidate you, good comrade?"

"No, you are not a comrade! Oh! If you wore a little bonnet with long ribbons like the nannies do . . . if you had a cook's apron or a milliner's boot . . ."

"What a dream!" interjected Laure, laughing.

"We would get married and go out for stew in Suresnes, where my uncle lives!"

"If you like stew, you do not have to get married to go to Suresnes."

"He is there, the monsieur!"

Laure amused herself by striking the frosted glass with the heel of her slippers, and she laughed out loud, an evil laugh. "The man scares you, you big fool!"

"You love him."

"No, he pays me, nothing more."

"Oh!" exclaimed the young man, becoming fierce, "do not repeat that filth, I am capable of pushing you into the street . . . ! I love you, you understand, my heart is ill for you . . . ! And it has been going on for a whole winter now; no matter how much I tell myself that you are not for my damned working-class muzzle, I am still clawing for you like a fool . . . I smell you in the wind like a dog smells its master. I would like to perish, and I long to strike you! I do not know if one and one make two, so much so, you see, that if you make fun of me again, I will lose my mind. I will hit whomever is bothering you . . . But just to get you, oh! Just to get you . . . ! No, it is too bad, I told you and I did not want to . . ."

He hid his face in his arms, devastated.

"Beast . . . Can you put love in prison? It always gets out sooner or later. I forgive you."

"Tell me your name, please, and I will have it engraved here in a laurel wreath." And he pointed to the spot just below the left breast.

Laure laughed out loud, while he added, confused and sensing that he had said something disgraceful according to the judgments of the young woman's world, "It is customary and counts as one of the best oaths."

"Kiss me, it will be worth your laurel wreath, my lover."

He slid close to her, wrapping his lean, supple arms around her.

Laure had the sensation of being enveloped by a child, and he seemed fresh to touch with her lips, like a green fruit.

"My sweet, it is not very reasonable to kiss like that in the moonlight."

"Let us go back to my place!"

"No, I am inviting you. Let us go downstairs."

The young man realized what was about to happen. She was leading him, no doubt, to a slaughter, and he had let himself be led like a poor puppy for a lump of sugar. At the height of his fever, there was no turning back, he was dizzy, his head was ringing, and he could feel his knees buckling beneath him. There was no way to flee, he would have fallen into the abyss of the roofs, and no way to refuse to follow her: a thread he tried to break under his quivering fingers attached him to the cunning female. The gutter runner was dragging the male after her, because she reeked of musk! Besides, he had longed for the pretty petticoats of silk, the froufrou, in his abominable dreams, he needed to be punished.

Bibi is damned! he articulated inwardly.[1]

"Where do we go?" he stammered, clenching his nails on her black velvet dress, soft and dark like this warm spring night.

1. Bibi means "yours truly" in French slang.

"Through this hole!" she murmured, showing him the gaping opening.

He would now have passed through the "mouth of hell," according to an expression dear to Alexandre Dumas, whose dramas he knew well.

Before venturing down, they listened and leaned in.

They noticed the sound of hurried footsteps, lights came on in succession, the misty background lit up, and the splendors of the yellow room shone before the dazzled eyes of the poor boy. He descended the lower floor, still holding her dress.

Henri, awakened by the sound of those slippers pounding on the window, the noise of voices, and bursts of laughter, had thrown himself out of bed, suspecting that some scandal was brewing. Either the concierges, coming out of an attic, would brutally chastise her, or a neighbor would chase her away. Either way, it would be very annoying to argue. He got dressed, seeking above all to present himself in a correct manner, and was just finishing buttoning his cuffs when the young people fell from the sky.

Laure, very calm in appearance, her lips parted over her teeth, two teeth advancing to the right and left of her upper jaw, like two sinister little fangs, said to him simply, "Well, are you no longer sleeping?"

Suffocated by the nasty tone of the formal *vous*, he put a hand to his eyes, still puffy from sleep.

"Let us see, my dear, what all of the fuss is about, you terrified me!"

Then, turning, increasingly dumbfounded, he looked at Auguste, who was straightening up, sniffing the air like a good dog on the trail.

"Who is this joker?" he asked haughtily.

"This joker!" growled the boy, clenching his fists. "Wait a minute before you call me a joker, please! I have come to tell you that you are bothering mademoiselle, that is what! She said that I was afraid, so I jumped in to prove her wrong."

He is drunk! he thought, thinking how ridiculous he would look if he got angry right away. He grumbled, "But, my young friend, I am not accustomed to entertaining at this hour, and I would advise you to take the roof path again . . . unless you would prefer to go through the window."

The adventure was becoming so formidable for a cold-blooded man that he felt disarmed.

"Monsieur," he continued, addressing Laure, "is he a worker or a slacker?"

"He is my lover!" she replied with frightening calm.

She was so pale, so resolute, that he no longer felt like smiling: he had understood.

"This, your lover?" he exclaimed, raising his arm ready to slap her.

The teenager, both fists clenched at his chest, never took his eyes off him.

"Wretch! Oh! The wretch!" Henri repeated, livid, walking toward her.

Laure was standing in front of the large mirror in her bedroom, and as he approached her, he caught a glimpse of his distraught face over her shoulder, he did not recognize himself. It was he, this calm man about to strike a woman . . . and a wench whom he had never loved . . . Strike her because she was mad . . . It was he, this pale face, this foaming mouth! Come now! Suddenly, his anger vanished. He had sworn never to be ridiculous, and it was fitting to end this horrible farce with an act of courtesy, of fine skepticism drawn from the depths of his remarkably well-bred being.

"Congratulations, my dear!" he said in a muffled voice, looking down at Auguste, still on the defensive.

And, moving over to an armchair where his ulster, cane, and hat were laid out, he picked up these various objects with meticulous care, checked the contents of his cigar case, grabbed a cigar, then lit it on one of the candelabra candles blazing in the corner of the fireplace. "Permit me," he murmured with such good-natured ease that Auguste let his now useless fists drop.

"I am not forgetting that this is your home, Laure," added Henri, "and I am retiring . . . *altogether*. Tomorrow, I will have the honor of sending you what I feel that I owe you. Adieu."

He walked briskly to the door, opened it, turned to look curiously from the threshold at the young joker, his "replacement."

Poor thing! The singular neurotic! he thought.

And the door closed.

Laure let out a terrible scream as she fell backward.

15

She awoke, after a month, as if from a dream, and contemplating, astonished, her hands resting on the softness of her yellow blanket in the beneficent warmth of a sunbeam from the windows, she sighed, "And Lion, my dear Lion, has he left too?"

The concierge, whispering with a grave-looking old man, said, raising her voice, "She's talking about her cat, which she loves very much, monsieur."

"So much the better! So much the better!" replied the doctor in the same tone. "She is out of danger now. No more emotions, solitude, and I will not have to come back. Now, mademoiselle, could you give me your pulse?"

What did these two figureheads want with her? Laure tried to lift herself up, and it seemed to her that the tail of her hair, changed into an enormous leaden snake, was pulling her from behind; her head, so heavy, fell back on the pillow, a violent pain at the temples made her scream, then she said, exasperated, "Leave me alone, I am not ill. Where is Lion?"

"He is on the bed, my child, asleep. Oh, you do not have a fever anymore, you must do as he does; rest, rest!"

And the doctor left. Laure lowered her eyelids, dozing off in spite of herself, thinking that, as Henri had predicted, she must have crashed through the roofs into the street. Would she end up crippled with broken legs?

In front of her, she saw a series of grotesque images swimming in pink and yellow, lots of yellow. First an eighteen-year-old boy, skinny, with hairy feet like a satyr and wearing a canvas jacket and cap; he grabbed Henri by the throat, and Henri gradually faded into a grimacing chimera in the smoke of his cigar, all that remained was a curtain of very thick smoke, then the curtain tore, fled in spirals, and there appeared an immense city stretching out below a terrace. The moon approached, fabulous, all gold, and a black cat, arching its back, came to claw at it. She hovered for a moment, the images taking on the neutral hues and normal proportions of simple photographs. She found herself back in bed, leafing through an album, but as she tried to turn the pages, her arms twitched, waking her up again. She tried to remember more precisely and ended up retracing all of the scenes that had taken place a month earlier; she remembered her idea of revenge and cried. She had not fallen off a roof, only out of love.

"That is it, you have got to cry!" declared the concierge, who was moving her feather duster across the vials on a pedestal table.

Lion, for his part, came to cuddle his mistress, while the good woman added, with the cruel pity of the inferior beings of the human species, "Cry, mademoiselle, do not hold back, it feels good . . . When I was young and I held back, I used to get nosebleeds."

"He is gone forever, is he not?" murmured Laure, leaning back on her pillows to caress Lion, whose sad eyes were staring back at her.

"Well, mademoiselle, we can tell you all about it now, I do not meddle in the love affairs of my tenants, but I know that he went away angry, you could tell by the look on his face . . . I assure you, even though he did not say anything."

Laure nodded. "So be it, I wanted this."

"So, what are you complaining about! And then, my poor lady, between us, one lost, ten found."

Laure interrupted her with a brief gesture. "What do you have to tell me? Tell me everything you know."

Lion, according to his custom as a faithful beast, crept into bed, lay round in the place of the departed lover, and, his gaze still full of eternal covetousness, he tenderly licked her hair, seeming to beg her not to pursue the matter any further. Laure held him close.

"Did you take good care of him?" she said vivaciously.

"Ah! By example! I know all about beasts, such a beautiful tomcat . . . !"

The concierge sat down on the edge of the bed and continued, "I still do not know much, but you will see if it is of any use to you. The day you fell ill, I saw a little apprentice coiffed like a malcontent come down from your place early in the morning, and he shouted at me through the window of my dressing room, 'I am a watchmaker, the gentleman from Mademoiselle Laure, your tenant on the sixth floor, sent me to do the clocks, and lo and behold, while I was working, the young lady found herself indisposed; I would hate to look after a woman, could you go . . . ? I left the key in the door!' It was eight o'clock in the morning. I had not seen the apprentice go up or Monsieur

Alban come down. I said to Firmin, who was leaving to go and buy leather, 'Guard my dressing room, I have got to get up there.' I start climbing four by four. I find your cheeks like firebrands, your eyes full of water. I think that you are passing away, and I take it upon myself to fetch the doctor. What worried me most was not seeing the gentleman. The bed was not even disturbed. He had probably gone downstairs during the night, and as he was a bit stingy with his words, he had not spoken . . . (Here is one who never said a word about his business!) To finish off, you kept getting worse and worse . . . The doctor said you had an attack of hot fever, that you already had a tendency for ill health, but that you must have received a blow, an emotion, what have you!

"We stuffed you full of ice cream to your heart's content, and the potions are fifty *centimes* a spoonful. Me, I was shocked by the bill. I had the idea of rummaging through your furniture, and found money in a box with Chinese on it . . . That put my mind at rest. I have appointed a caretaker for you, oh, a good person who already looked after the tenant on the third floor during childbirth. She is like no other when she has got a glass of black coffee in her stomach! I did everything I could to make sure I would not be blamed for your death. On the third day, monsieur came to my dressing room; he said, as if he did not know anything, 'You will give this envelope to Mademoiselle Lordès, and give me a receipt,' and he said again, turning on me, 'A friend of mine will come this afternoon to take the things upstairs that belong to me: my books, my papers, and the furniture in the little salon. And off he went, stiff as a board! Well, I thought, the eel, they have parted ways, and the little one regrets it . . . ! Despite the fact that . . . well, you get the idea, mademoiselle, we have eyes to see. The movers were making a racket. 'It is that she is very downcast,' I whispered to them. He did not even know you were ill, monsieur! I was at a loss. The clearer it seemed, the more confused it got. But the best part was that the little apprentice, the boy coiffed like a malcontent, came every morning to ask about you 'on behalf of monsieur'! We cleared out the living room in no time with the movers. I stood in front of the bedroom so they could not get in. Besides, you were under the ice like a fish under the Seine. There was no danger of your moving. Monsieur's friend went away shrugging his shoulders. 'She will not die,' he said, 'and we will leave her a very chic room, a satin bed, the tools of her trade, what have you!' Young people are always joking, you understand, mademoiselle. With that, I took my leave of him, too honest by nature to reply in kind, and I never saw anyone again, except for the little poorly coiffed one with the bad hair who still comes by in the morning on behalf of monsieur, and who does not talk any more than he does. 'How is it going?' he says. 'Better,' I answer, and then he runs off..."

Laure no longer cried but remained pale, deep in her pillow, her distracted hands stroking the purring cat that blinked its soft eyes.

"Did I not call someone when I had the fever, madame?"

"No, you were just talking about cats; you were unconscious until yesterday, when I saw that the taste of bread was coming back to you. You would get down on all fours on your bed and bang your forehead against the wall, catching mice along the blanket. Your mice were something else! You found them on every side."

"Would you give me the envelope that monsieur gave you?"

"Yes, of course, I have it in my pocket. Oh, I have kept it like a blessed sacrament!"

Laure held out her hand; she was so weak that she could not see clearly. She opened it and found several blue bills, without a word of farewell or anger, nothing but the last payment for her caresses.[1] There was enough here to settle the bill of the doctor, and even that of Auguste, assuming that he ever presented his own. Henri proportioned his generosity to that of his mistress; she would have done better, perhaps, if she had allowed him to "see her" until the decisive moment that he had chosen, and even then he was really being kind; after the appearance of Auguste, he could retire without worrying about a girl who went to such extremes.

Laure murmured, distressed, "It is over, good and over . . . !"

"My goodness," breathed the concierge, "when one has their term paid for a long time!"

The day passed peacefully. The endless gossip of the concierge, with its equal mixture of contempt for irregular situations and esteem for decent young people, lulled her to sleep.

But, left alone with her Lion, who looked at her sadly, alone with the funereal night lamp replacing the sun and drawing large shadows on the fabrics and windows, she had a crisis of inexplicable despair that threw her into a fever.

The poor animal, revolutionized by this raving patient, ran from one end of the room to the other. Bouncing on the bed, bouncing on the table, climbing on the bedside table, leaning over the pillows where Laure's head rolled from right to left, as if moved by a spring, he furiously scratched the sheets, licked her hands, and let out the cries of a grieving child, cries that go through all of the tones of the scale, high or low, for minutes on

---

1. The Bank of France began printing one-hundred-franc banknotes in blue ink in January 1882 because counterfeiters used black ink in the daguerreotype process. It deprived them of legal tender in January 1923.

end, with the persistence of a gently shaken crystal bell, a hoot of an owl, a roar of a wolf in the distance. This feline, like a small being endowed with a soul, wept over his mistress's misfortune and felt his nerves twitch because there, close to him, the nerves of his adoptive mother were twitching. There was no mistaking it, he was really crying, and Laure, hearing his extraordinary mewing, listened from the depths of her pain, calmed down a little, came back to herself, without the strength to straighten up; she spotted him, around midnight, in the middle of the room, and her feverish gazes followed him in his bizarre evolutions. Sometimes he planted himself on a cushion, with the somber air of a creature gripped by an idée fixe, his russet tail ringed with jet rings beating his flanks, his brilliant eyes of phosphorus darting over the problem, always insoluble for him, the poor simpleton, of a human existence; sometimes he jumped onto the bed, came close to her lips, brushed them delicately with his whiskers. In the end, he crouched over the woman, making himself wonderfully light despite his adult weight, covering her with his robust little fawn body, clasping her in his velvety paws, adoring her, especially since he could not help her.

In the morning, Laure's last sob was a relief. She reflected, stroking Lion's fur. She no longer wanted to die. Not having died from her terrible plunge into the abyss of abandonment, into which she had been foolish enough to throw herself headlong, she had to emerge stronger, more indifferent. She owed herself to no one, she would be what she wished to be, virtuous or cowardly, and would no longer mingle so intimately the dreams of her heart with the desires of her flesh. And then she had the vision of a hydra-man—several heads on the same body—and what did it matter, after all, the dignity of these multiple heads?

She ate the lunch offered by the concierge with a fair appetite. She demanded strawberries and cakes, and found the humble act of chewing sweet things quite appealing. She was all alone! Well, good! Without shame, she would eat for two, throwing bits to Lion who would soil the carpet if it pleased him. She took stock of her resources and concluded that if she did not economize, she would live another year very comfortably. Then . . . one would see. It was brave of her to have insisted on a little more than the present moment.

Laure was soon up and about. Still very weak, she moved from her bed to the cushions arranged as a divan near the bay window, which was opened wide for her, and remained there, half-naked, for days on end, soaking up the air and light, drawing strength from what is the source of all well-being for animals, the rays of the sun, drinking from every pore this fiery liquor, the *eau-de-vie par excellence* of the creatures inhabiting the countryside.

She caressed Lion's fine, iridescent fur, and the dear beast, with a deft tongue, working like an expert chambermaid to build a ballroom *coiffure*, polished her hair.

It was June, and the skylight was left down so that the animal could get away for the night. For an hour or two, he would run up and down the gutters, then quickly return, mewing, purring, cooing, sulking, with the comical alacrity of someone apologizing for having left the patient entrusted to his care. One evening, he returned with a white object around his neck, his face furious, rolling in a ball on the carpet to get rid of the unpleasant string collar. He was carrying a letter.

Laure smiled and read the missive containing this single sentence, written in beautiful schoolboy handwriting: "I would like to see you. Is that possible?"

The boy had had the idea of using the nocturnal rendezvous of Lion to obtain a personal appointment; Laure replied by the same letter: "Yes. You know the way." The following evening, she combed her hair at length in the mirror, put on her red dress, her heart less constricted, breathing more freely, almost happy to indulge in new provocations. Jewelry worker or son of a family, a man is always "a man"! She was absolutely determined not to give in to him, and yet she did not want to make him look bad.

Around ten o'clock, Lion was moved by a rat scratch from the ceiling, then he growled, holding a grudge against the prankster who'd tied a string around his neck, and fled under the bed.

Auguste descended in a few leaps. He stopped, devouring her with his clear eyes.

"Oh, how it has changed you, all the same, this fever, Mademoiselle Laure!" he murmured, wrinkling his monkey muzzle. "You are nothing but peepers!"

She trembled nervously. These vulgar expressions, after having made her laugh on the rooftops, now displeased her in her bedroom, where Henri had once chatted in such correct, measured phrases. Her flesh and heart, softened by suffering, were ripe for the refinements of amorous poetry, and she would have liked to have been treated more gently. She felt quite dead . . . to proper men, but she had not yet given up on elegant flattery and graceful cuddling. If passion had never had a habit for her, she recognized that it had a special idiom, a kind of mysterious watchword she could not do without. When she remembered Armand de Bréville, she seemed to hear the echo of a delicious music that delighted her, even though she did not understand it, and she wished that she were still loved by a very spiritual madman.

"Auguste, my dear child, I am ill. It would be kind of you to speak to me . . . lower."

The young boy bent his spine and, crawling on the scattered cushions, huddled beside her, trembling.

"I have frightened you! Excuse me, Mademoiselle Laure! I see you hate me today! It is because I broke your doll! I am the cause of everything, am I not? It is my fault, eh, that he left? What if I complained about the role you made me play like at the Ambigu?[2] That might be a good thing!"

His eyes drowned in tears. The young woman was playing with a fan, and it brushed his cheeks.

"I admit I am wrong, my dear boy. What is finished should not interest me anymore. Tell me, why did you come 'on his behalf'?"

"Let me explain! When you fell, I thought that you were a goner, and I did not want to leave you there, all shivering. I waited until morning and told the concierges a story; supposedly, he was the one who sent me to check the clocks . . . so I came by every day as if it were "from him," so you would not be compromised. One knows how to behave toward a beautiful lady. You said, 'He is my lover, just for show.' In fact, Mademoiselle Laure, I prevented your hair from being cut! The doctor thought it was in the way of his remedies . . . The concierge said something to me about it, and I replied, 'Monsieur forbade it.' They always have to cut something, otherwise they are not happy!"

Spontaneously, Laure held out her hand, no longer worrying about the turn of phrase.

"My hair!" she murmured, making her long braid undulate with the elegant movement of her cat when he recoiled to avoid a stain.

---

2. The Théâtre de l'Ambigu-Comique (literally, the "Theater of the Comic-Ambiguity") was a Parisian theater founded in 1769 and demolished in 1966.

The young man lunged greedily for her hand, holding it in his own.

"I cannot help it, you see, it stings my eyes to find you with a face like papier-mâché. Do not mind me at all, I feel like crying, I think I am really crying."

He hid his face in the folds of her dress, sobbing, and she ran her tapered fingers through the tangles of his hair.

"I feel fine, just fine, my poor Auguste! We will go to the park together . . . I promise."

She dreamed, at once tranquil and desperate, having become a fatalist, in the manner of those beautiful oriental women who no longer love anything because they have loved too much too soon. A cat, a dog, a man, a monster, as long as she was adored the moment she wished to be adored . . . ! She lived on love as certain Indian idols live on perfumes, and she let the humblest man bring her his grain of incense. Besides, since nothing of what she had once dreamed was coming true, it was well worth reflecting: her favors, like the favors of a goddess, would fall at random.

"I love you," stammered the unfortunate child. "Oh, I love you enough to die of spite if 'the other one' comes back!"

"He is not coming back."

"You are still sweet on him, come on!"

"He has gone . . . home, to the country . . . to get married," she said, hesitating between each word.

Then, all of a sudden, she threw out very quickly, "Auguste, do me a favor! Go to Rue Racine tomorrow and find out!"

"Are you sending me to Rue Racine, to his hotel . . . ?"

"Just to know! I swear I do not love him anymore . . ."

He rested his chin, like a good submissive poodle, on the young woman's lap. "I will go," he replied. "You must not worry."

She did not love him anymore, but who is going to discover the ingenious secret of this very feminine situation: to be sure you do not love anymore, and to keep curiosity alive, to love again? Do corpses not have those muscle flexes that make you believe in a miraculous resurrection? Laure drew him close and kissed him on the brow. He remained prostrate on her breasts, drunk with grief and happiness, searching for phrases to sum up his sorrows.

"Don't you see, this will all end badly, everything is upside down," he stammered. "I do not work anymore, I do not drink anymore, I do not eat anymore . . . I have ruined mountings, the boss has been gossiping . . . and, on top of it all, my uncle came and told me that I had the face of someone who has been on his honeymoon! It is nice, my honeymoon! I ought to have strangled him. He is a busybody, my uncle, he is involved in things that do not concern him, worse than a policeman! He claims that I have got a thing for petticoats, and he is squeezing my balls by taking my savings for the sake of the kid, my cousin, whom he is going to stick me with one day."

"Is she at least nice, 'his kid'?" asked Laure familiarly, speaking as he did.

"She is flat enough to make a flounder jealous, and she looks like she has been drinking vinegar . . . I do not really want her . . ."

"You are still a kid, you have got time to think about marriage!"

"I am a scoundrel," concluded the young boy brutally.

And he looked at her, a little afraid of his own thoughts.

"You see women go by in carriages," he breathed, "who are like pretty fruit in a basket, and you must not touch them . . . ! You have neither the money nor the clothes to talk to them! Women are never free! Or they are beggars . . . ! Sometimes people fall for a little factory girl, have a baby with her and then kick themselves for the rest of their life. No, it is annoying, this kind of misery . . . The good Lord should have made separate men for work . . . men who would not be men . . . !"

He made a terrible gesture evoking socialist ideas. Laure could not help laughing.

"Let me feed you, my sweet, forget that you love me, and we will share like two brothers."

He looked at her sideways, smiling too. "While you are waiting for my new cap, here is what I am bringing you for your wake-up call!" he said, digging into his pockets.

He offered her a small cardboard box containing a rhinestone brooch, a jewel so dazzling that it could stun a person. The old redskin instincts of the young woman were reawakened, and at that minute she, queen of a wild island, would have given all of her subjects in exchange for this dazzling jewel.

"You are charming! I am so grateful. It is prettier than the real thing, and what does it matter, after all, if it is not real . . . I do not care!"

She pinned the brooch to her bodice.

"It costs a lot of money . . . I bet you are in debt, are you not?"

"But I promised it to you," he replied fatalistically. "And Auguste Ternisier does not go back on his word!"

At midnight, the young boy discreetly got up, not daring to prolong his courtship since she was still unwell. "Could I come back once in a while?" he asked, swaying from one foot to the other with a sulky expression on his face.

"Every night, if you want, and you will give me an answer tomorrow."

"Yes, you have decided, I will go over there, I will ask around! A nasty chore, Mademoiselle Laure!

"Who says I will not keep my promises?" she murmured, turning her cheek to him.

He ran away to avoid doing anything stupid.

The next evening, he arrived early, simply leaped from the roof to the bedroom floor, and, straightaway, reported back to her on the outcome of his mission. "He has moved, your Monsieur Alban, got married at home, in the provinces, I am told. Do not feel saddened, eh! Me, I have got my damn uncle, I can hardly last here."

She was in front of her mirror, braiding her hair. She replied, impatient, "I knew as much, do you need to make that funereal face?"

"Ah! Mademoiselle Laure, your eyes are shining, you are crying..."

"It is the reflection of my mirror, you beast, go away if you are in a hurry!"

"So, am I in your way?"

"You can see that I am getting dressed!"

From under his jacket, he pulled out a bunch of fifteen-cent hyacinths.

"Here, another commission from the same party . . ." he snapped, tossing his flowers onto the bed, and went whistling up his ladder, looking grim.

Laure did not see him again for eight days, but one Sunday morning, unable to bear it any longer, Auguste knocked on the skylight. "Mademoiselle Laure," he slipped through the windowpanes, "would you like to go for a walk today? I have some money left!"

The time has come to pay, she thought, *but in kind; let us go happily, it will make me dizzy!*

She shouted, "I accept, you will wait for me at the end of our street, around noon!"

Laure made a brief toilette for this picnic. She wore a pink-striped percale dress, a peignoir whose low-cut bodice she concealed under a small draped jacket, and a large straw hat adorned with a few modest shells of ribbon. With the exception of the royal train of hair, which she could not bring herself to roll up under her hat, she had the look of a beautiful, emancipated daughter of the people. Before going out, she put some gold *louis* in her purse, a vague smile on her lips. She was cheerful, or rather carefree, intent on the naive enjoyment of a beautiful day. And this rustic love gave her an appetite, she wanted to taste it in the fields, imagining that it would taste better, just as fresh milk must taste better from a wooden beaker. At home, it was too padded, too *cocotte*, and memories would have given her a fever. She left her room, humming. But as she crossed the living room, she felt a shiver of horror . . . Oh! This emptiness, these hangings torn from the nails and leaving shreds there, this window without curtains, gaping, this parquet without carpet, gray with dust . . . This was her present existence, an emptiness to be crossed perpetually, and it was necessary to do it running or accompanied by a cheerful comrade, not to fall from it in despair. She descended the stairs like a whirlwind.

Auguste was lurking on a street corner. Fortunately, he had not over-adorned himself, was wearing an ordinary suit and a correctly fitted cap, and was standing stiffly, his face scrunched up with mortal anxiety. When he caught sight of her, he turned very pale, it upset him greatly.

He repeated, his voice hushed, "Oh, how wicked you are! You look like my cousin, my word of honor!"

"The one that looks like a flounder because she is so flat?" Laure retorted, nipping at his elbow.

"Do not tease me, Mademoiselle Laure, I am moving, you know...!"

They took the boat and stopped at Point-du-Jour, where the young woman began by buying a marshmallow pastry, whose green hue delighted her. She caused a scene because the young man wanted to pay for everything himself, but she balked, declaring that they would do it by halves. Along the river, they argued nobly, and finally Laure gave in, flashing her she-wolf teeth with an ominous smile. Halfway to Meudon, they entered a ball. Couples twirled in the center of a vast arbor covered with *volubilis* leaves graying with the powder of the road. Here and there, a silvered or gilded glass globe punctuated the soiled greenery, dotting it like a little, humble planet. Girls tied handkerchiefs around their waists to keep the dancer's fingers from leaving marks, and boys, dripping with sweat, pushed their dubious hairstyles far back and wore flamboyant belts. Under other arbors shaped like chicken coops, narrow and decorated with multicolored baubles and topped with large *volubilis* flowers, the gallery drank lemonade.

Raging noises emanated from this teeming crowd as if from battle, and heel-stomping calls could be heard echoing on the planked floor, while a rustic exergue of painted letters stood out from the foliage: "At the Rendezvous of Friends!" It was banal and snide; they would exchange punches between two *contredanses*, and mothers, in a dark corner, unbuttoned to suckle their more or less well-behaved kids.

Instinctively, Auguste, not wanting to compromise a creature with flowing hair, backed off, but Laure urged him on, enthusiastic, sensing a free blossoming of young lust. There was not a man to be seen at this ball; they were all kids between sixteen and eighteen, some with childlike faces, pure eyes above faded mouths, and the women were all gracefully swaying, with hardly any bosom, and the supple waists of snake-like girls. Laure inhaled this heavy atmosphere, burned by a coppery sun, a deceitful sun haloed by unhealthy vapors, by the fire of stoves, fried foods, and secondhand tobacco smoke, and declared herself very happy. The devil got into her nerves. She had already dreamed of those interlopers where one finds almost naked rowers, displaying their tender, tasty flesh in the light of the heavens. Henri, who did not share her tastes, had naturally kept her away from them. He preferred the Eden-Théâtre, where it sometimes smells worse because it smells so good! Laure tightened her fine nails on Auguste's wrist, pulling him along. They sat down under one of the chicken coops, opposite a spotless table. Laure ordered a bottle of champagne.

"You are going to get us kicked out!" he stammered, speaking to her casually because he was so terrified. "Do they serve that here?"

"You wanted to treat me, my dear simpleton, well, treat me! I do not like lemonade. Do not worry, we will find us some champagne, mark my words."

Indeed, they had a bottle of some kind of detonating mixture that foamed remarkably, and Laure, unable to swallow it, sprinkled it over the purple wreath plants. Auguste, believing he was approaching his final hour, closed his eyes.

"Why do we not go somewhere else and you can dance there?"

"Why? Do I look more decent than these women?"

"Please, no jokes, you are mad!"

"You know how to waltz, do you not?"

He was forced to waltz. At first sorry at the turn their escapade had taken, he swayed indecisively, thinking of saving himself by taking her with him, and little by little, intoxicated by the rhythm of the waltz he loved wildly, he forgot the expense, grabbed his beautiful dance partner with both hands, breathing her scent through the neckline of her tight little jacket. Laure had never been to the ball; she had waltzed once, at Bullier, despite Henri's mocking reprimands.[3] She was having the time of her life. Auguste could not take it anymore; like the others, he put his cap back on, mopped his brow, laughed—also enraptured to see her so pretty, so mischievous—and drank the rest of the bottle, so as not to waste any drops. Eventually, he collapsed on the arbor bench, begging for mercy. Laure accepted an invitation from a tall buffoon, their neighbor, a pallid figure dazzled by her chic style.

"No," exclaimed Auguste, darkening, "I forbid you to move."

"What's that?" said the tall, funny man, sizing up the young rooster with his eyes. "And if it pleases madame?"

Laure had an intuition that a scene was brewing. She separated them with a gesture, saying she wanted to rest, and she opened her garment, fanning herself with her handkerchief.

"Listen, monsieur, I am positively swimming right now! He is right."

She had put on her rhinestone brooch; for a second the buffoon marveled. "Well," he replied, "as long as madame is with her little brother..."

And he turned on his heel.

Auguste wanted to punch something. His palms itched.

---

3. Bal Bullier was a ballroom in Paris created by François Bullier (1796–1869) in the mid 1800s. It closed its doors in 1940.

"But keep this hidden, you look like a harlot!" he breathed, irritated as much by the softness of her skin as by the brutality of this false splendor.

When it came time to pay for the champagne, Auguste realized that there would only be enough to pay for the stew. He had brought his entire fortune with him: twenty francs, assuming that would be enough. He complied, distraught, and they fled.

"Mademoiselle Laure," he said seriously, as they entered the restaurant in Meudon, after running through the woods, "you have to be reasonable, it is too expensive here!"

Laure was silent, her eyes mocking. She asked for a booth on the river.

"I am leaving you," he growled in exasperation, for he had not stolen a single kiss.

She put such real zeal into her flights of fancy that she no longer thought about him.

"Try it . . . !" she shouted at him, climbing the stairs to the booth and lifting up her lace skirts. He sheepishly joined her. She chose the finest dishes, a filet Madeira, a matelote, and obtained genuine champagne, flanked by its respectable bucket of ice.

The whole sky came in through the open window; a fresh smell of swirling water, of trodden grass, mingled with the warm, peppery odors of the meal.

"Is it not good, sweetie?" she asked.

He buried his burning head in her pink blouse. "But I will die of shame!"

"Bah!" she said, with a smile whose bitterness he could not see. "Nothing kills love!"

They dined side by side, doing the thousand and one extravagances that crossed their minds. Auguste, a little drunk, his heart ready to burst, drew the money from where she ordered him to draw it, there, between her dress and her petticoat, so loose, so light, this petticoat that brushed the exquisite roundness of her thigh . . . (Women have the singular habit of stuffing their pockets under a pile of folds!)

She had to take him back, at night, the gourmand. He wanted to sleep in Meudon. They strayed from the towpath, lost their way, and trudged on for hours. At last they found each other, after passing a number of brothels, at the foot of the fortifications.

"A mountain!" cried Laure.

And the young people climbed back up the grassy knoll bouncing again. On the deserted plateau, a wild breeze, the breath, it seemed, of the burning city, whipped their cheeks. Paris stretched out before them, spangled with its streetlamps, and the sky, filled with stars, covered them with its subtle light.

Down below, the vain glitter of rhinestones, up above, the pure, sad gleams of solemn diamonds as if veiled in tears.

"Oh!" he begged. "It would be good here, if I dared . . ."

"Dare!" she replied, throwing her arms around his neck.

16

And he left one fine evening, having borrowed her last banknote, saying to her with a grim air, as if at the Ambigu, "You know! Me, I do not eat that kind of bread! All my uncle would have to do is ask me to come back here . . . I would rather get out of here before he finds out."

For these young, skinny gutter cats are even more capricious than they are greedy.

The next day, no matter how hard she counted and recounted the few louis lying at the bottom of the Chinese box, she could see that misery was close at hand. She would have to create new sources of income, but luxury pets do not work, and Laure thought with a shudder about the only profession permitted for pretty females, prostitution. She examined her modest jewels, gifts from Henri Alban, a bracelet, a ring, and told herself that by taking them to the *Mont-de-Piété*, she would pay a term, earn the spring; then, in her nerves, she threw a lot of logs into the fireplace, because it seemed to her that she was already cold, and that she could already see herself begging a man under a lamppost.[1]

---

1. A *Mont-de-Piété* ("Mount of Piety") is a charitable pawnbroker for European citizens begun in the Renaissance and still running today.

It was during this dark winter that, living in perpetual *tête-à-tête* with her cat, she discovered a passion that she had never tasted before; Laure *sensed* that Lion was in love with her, this wasn't too much of a surprise, her neurosis accommodating any ridiculous situation. The beast's love for her was obvious, and she should have been moved by it sooner; the poor boy must have suffered from jealousy. Hours passed in mutual contemplation, and the animal, gravely tender, spoke to her in the eloquent language of the eyes. Huddled by the hearth after their sad meal, when she had stuffed herself with bread and sacrificed half her meat to the voracity of the cute beast so that he could have his regular ration, they lay limply on the cushions. Laure, gradually hypnotizing herself, searching for thoughts in these holes of light reflecting the ardor of the embers, thought she was plunging into an abyss of mystical pleasure, and the phosphorescent sparks, sometimes green, sometimes red, kindled a delicate fire within her. There were unknown horizons there, a whole world opening up to her through those mysterious little slits. When he ran across the rooftops to rub up against the stars, did this cat not bring back a divine essence of love? This essence made his coat glow with all of the shades of the rainbow, it impregnated his eyes with an ecstatic flame, it sharpened his teeth, making them both cruel and gentle, it gave his pink tongue alternately the fine asperity that irritates and the sweetness that comforts, and this being, born exclusively for caresses, lived only for his pleasure!

In the narrowness of their existence, where the love of a man could no longer find a place, she delighted in her cat and truly enjoyed a most exquisite animal bliss. These two simple creatures, so naturally complicated, got along wonderfully, and shared the same troubles, the same impatience, the same joys.

When Laure had a headache, Lion was restless, whipping his tail on his flanks, mewing, raising his nose as if to rid himself of a weight on his skull, and seemed to be suffering from the same ailment. When Laure was cold, at night, in her big yellow bed, Lion would sneak under the covers, press himself against her, and, exasperated by the same cold, purr breathlessly in an attempt to react. When Laure sulked, regretted the time that had passed, thought of her other, more practical lovers, Lion curled up in a ball of bad temper, closed his eyes, dried up his outpourings of radiant tenderness, and gave no sign of life; and when Laure, happy under a pale ray of sunshine, finally deigned to resume the games with joyful cunning gestures, Lion leaped up, displayed his graces, and seemed to enjoy himself just to distract her, his queen!

Sometimes, lying in the cradle of her lap, he would place his paw, with reflex movements, on her hand, and, a mischievous smile floating in his old philosopher's white whiskers, his two little fangs protruding, the tip of his tongue barely drawn out, curved like a dahlia petal, he looked as if he were saying to her, "No, I am not one of them, but in terms of loyalty, I am worth all of them."

Sometimes, in an extraordinary delirium, the beast would leap at her from the height of a piece of furniture, sneak up on her from behind, clutch at her shoulders as though trying to knock her over, nip at the back of her neck with wild cries bursting with all of the imprecations of a rebellious, respectful love; And Laure would run off, carrying him to her bed, worried to find him so powerful, rolling him in the satin and fanning him, because she had suddenly been terrified of him, had seen herself at his mercy and felt her sex fluster at these heartrending calls of another sex.

He would also smell her more tenaciously at the times of her monthly returns, on days when she smelled more like a woman, closer to the female.

As if exultant, he followed her step by step, with passionate gait, sniffing dubious petticoats, scratching cloths trailing in dark corners, tearing cloths to shreds, and then coming back on her heels, half-open-mouthed, fierce-eyed, comical by dint of being enamored of an impossible thing, crying in the heartbreaking tone of an idiotic beggar whom nothing will ever satisfy.

He tyrannized Laure with selfish habits, making her stand with her arms outstretched for days on end, not allowing her to eat, demanding that she cut his meat in imperceptible scraps that he deigned, every quarter of an hour, to chew reticently. He would then remain there for his digestion, his head resting limply on the young woman's breast, his paws gathered in a bunch, or suddenly relaxed like springs, throwing out mewing syllables, implicit whispers to distract her when he saw her ready to let him go.

"Just the two of us!" he seemed to say, savoring his intimate jubilation, so intimate that he did not even let on a tremor, and ended up pretending to be asleep.

An electric bond united them. Lion understood at a gesture that Laure was about to open the door and go out to fetch their dinner. He would hurry around her, wanting to show her his pleasure and his sorrow: pleasure to soon be eating a treat, sorrow that she would be cold outside, all alone. Often, sitting on the landing, he would watch for her to come home, already prone to jealous scenes because he had waited too long.

"How will we manage," said the young woman naively, "when there are three of us?"

The deeper their intimacy, the more the animal seemed to rise to the dignity of a man, greedy for his flesh, imperious in his caresses, and above all willful in his capricious fantasies.

At Christmas, when he stole the meager piece of pâté that she had bought for Christmas Eve right in front of her, she scolded him; she seized the little ash broom, threatened him, pursued him, but the cynical animal turned around, his eyes blazing, and with a huge leap jumped in her face, and she thought he was going to bite her, plow her cheeks with his claws; she screamed in fear in spite of herself, but he, holding her by the neck with his two nervous paws, contented himself with licking her eyelids, which she had immediately closed. It was as if he had first wanted to slaughter her, but then thought that she was his mistress after all, and that he had deigned to spare her for that day, just to prove his strength. Laure was so moved that she wept. From then on, whenever she wanted to scold him, he used the same means, rushing at her and begging forgiveness, making her arms fall in grateful admiration.

Maddened by the contact of this fur, which she galvanized with her warm humanity, into which she introduced her cerebral essence, she lost herself, sinking her mind in the contemplation of the impossible. She was equally frightened and attracted by it, as if, through those small luminous slits where the sparks of a diabolical fire shone, an emptiness was breathing her in, drinking her in. *Someone, something*, perhaps the soul of the beast itself (did we mention all of the mysteries of this walled-up world?) was casting a spell on her behind this undulating ghost of a cat, bewitching her, and she meekly let herself be subjugated, content to lose in intelligence what Lion returned to her in caresses. An old maid by a certain mania for order, because of certain provincial ideas that remained with her, she must surely fulfill the dream that this cat might have formed of a companion.

Careful of his person, Lion preened himself all afternoon; Laure could darn her dress; both gourmands as much as the other, they were ecstatic about good food, and everything in their shared dwelling was as correct as it was extravagant. They slept by day, roamed the rooftops by night, enjoyed the same fantasies, and passed out in the same bouts of idleness.

At carnival, the unfortunate girl, having almost no money left, had to give up feeding him meat. She soaked their bread in a penny of milk for the two of them, and Lion withered away. Moreover, a kind of languor had already taken hold of the beautiful beast, who became sullen, disdained all games, and stretched out in hysterical poses with mad yawns. The heating was bad, Laure had put her last jewels in the pawnshop and was now in debt to her purveyors. They lay in bed for days, shivering, clutching each other tighter and tighter, both having who-knows-what ominous twinges. He contemplated her desperately, instinctively guessing at the horrible things brewing in the murky atmosphere, and Laure, ever the fatalist, smiled at him, still enjoying him despite the hunger that tortured her, the cold that veiled her future in a white shroud. Once, as he rolled around in her hand, with a vague desire to scratch her, growling dully, she dared to play with the cute coral horn rising up among the russet silks of his belly, and with a mocking gesture, turned it against their misfortune, *la jettatura!*[2]

On the evening of that day, Lion, perhaps offended and looking glum, painfully climbed the ladder to the roof. She opened the skylight, and he looked up at the moon, suddenly mewed,

---

2. *La jettatura* is the Italian name for the evil eye. Magicians claimed that to guard against it, a gesture of horns must be made with the fingers.

jumped up with bristling fur, then ran off with a sinister howl, one of those strange cries that make you think that there has been a massacre.

Laure waited for him the next day for lunch. He did not come. She waited a whole week.

He will have found a nice pussycat! she thought indulgently.

17

Shyly, Laure asked, "Have you not seen Lion, madame? Funny, he never stays out that long . . ."

The concierge replied, shrugging her shoulders, "It is your cat! Feed him better and he will keep to the house!" She added roguishly, "At any rate, mademoiselle, you must have some protection; so you will have to use it, now is the time . . . !"

And, turning her back, pressing her feet hard, jostling the cushions, the concierge withdrew, taking the rent receipt with her.

Laure fell back onto her bed, her brow moist. What was the point of delaying the supreme fall? She was not in the category of people who had the right not to pay their term. She lay prostrate for an hour, no longer thinking, no longer seeing. Work? Where was the work for panthers, apart from their normal occupation of crushing men! And now she would give love in exchange for money, and she would always be a dupe in these shameful deals, one lavishing the art of life, the other procuring only life! She had already been fooled by being loved, now she would no longer be loved, she would have to give up pleasure for herself. The last misery of misery! Once again, "the stranger" would enter her home, and instead of imposing himself on her, she would have to endure him!

She got up and walked around the apartment. Nothing to sell but silky fabrics of zero value at the Mont-de-Piété; she had no jewels, no lace, no linen; her only beautiful suit, she could not get rid of, for it was going to be useful for earning her bread, and auctioning it there meant barely eating for another week! She smiled painfully.

"Of course! Mimi left because he was starving! See! I must choose: run myself over in the street by falling off the roof, or look for a man. It is clear that this cat cannot give me an income!"

She opened the closets, spread out her muslin undergarments, hastily mended torn Valenciennes, reattached ribbon bows, and shook out her dress and coat.[1] The dress, a sheath of brown plush threadbare from use, was carefully inspected at the seams; it was a mid-winter costume, but the very rainy month of May allowed for plush, and her ample otter coat lined with white satin would protect her from the night chill if she *had* to go far.

Dressed like this, her head topped with a little beaver hat, all molded in plain fur, as if in her own monster skin, her fur like that of a furious beast, with no other jewel than the flash of her eyes glittering under the veil and the bluish reflection of her formidable braid of hair, she looked fearsome, and when she unclasped her cloak, one caught a glimpse of that white satin, a soft swan's whiteness, evoking the lascivious idea of a female belly, inviting sudden pleasures, like the down of a nest. She could not find any gloves. They were all very dirty. She simply hid her hands under her sleeves, after rubbing them with a drop

---

1. Valenciennes is a type of lace named eponymously for a commune in France where it originated.

of perfume discovered at the bottom of a vial. Then, standing in front of her mirror, she examined herself and nodded.

It was good. Her lips curled up and she licked them quickly. She prepared a lamp and pulled down the blinds, remembering to leave the skylight ajar in the unlikely event that Lion came home before she did, then looked at the bed, made a gesture of rage, and left.

In the streets, she walked fast, heading for the "other side" of the water, attracted, like all of them, by the blazing line of the grand boulevards, and she had, every minute, instinctively, a fear of the police, imagining that, if she made herself stand up like a mere strumpet, they would seize her, right away by her heavy tail of hair that beat her rump and looked far bolder than any decolletage. She would have liked to take a carriage, but she was piously saving her fifty sous, her entire fortune, for the night's eventualities. Arriving on Boulevard des Italiens, she entered the first café that she came across, childishly afraid of an imaginary police officer and serenely committing a major breach of the laws governing girls' society. She did not know that certain cafés were forbidden to consumers of her kind.

Instead of serving her, a waiter leaned over and glared at her. "Are you looking for someone?"

"No, I do not know anyone, I just came to . . . sit."

The voice exhaled through clenched teeth. "You've got to be kidding me," said the waiter, wrinkling his nostrils in a disgusted grimace that was meant to be friendly. "There's no loitering here."

Laure was furious, and the thought occurred to her to pick up one of those polished wooden tables and throw it at the server's bald head.

"So be it!" she said haughtily, "but you are mistaken."

She said this with such conviction that the boy himself, despite the long otter coat worn by all of the "little pussycats" that year, was ashamed at having bullied her.

"There are those women of the world who look so much like hussies, do they not, monsieur?" he declared to a familiar man sucking on the straw of a soda.

Laure wandered along the boulevard, her soul terribly tormented, wondering how she could sit down, already so weary. She thought of lying across the street, shouting to them, "Take me, pass me all over the body, men and horses, I have had enough before I have even started...!"

When she looked at a clock, she saw that it was late; this wet spring must have frightened the rich night owls, and the whims of jaded carousers probably could not resist the cool air on evenings of amorous need. Besides, men had a thousand other opportunities in places that were off-limits to her. Fifty cents! What if she went home? But tomorrow, she would have to eat, drink, listen to the concierge carrying on about the state of morality of a person who receives procurers and does not know how to procure...

Finally, to go home without a man, when she had formally decided to sell herself, was almost a disgrace, an affront! She wanted a man, and she would hunt her game bravely until daybreak...! Walking through the feverish boulevards, in this humid weather, emanating violent odors from all of the perfume stores and flower stalls, she was whipped by violent desires; brushing up against the men coming out of furnace-like restaurants, cigars in their mouths, as if they themselves were embers beginning to glow, and the elegant girls all worked up—some by lust for fine clothes, others by recent indulgences—she took on a wild appetite. Why should there not be glory in fighting this battle for hunger? And wolves and lions are not dishonored because they want to eat man!

In front of L'Américain, she recalled a phrase of Henri Alban's, who once claimed that this café no longer became affordable at one o'clock in the morning, and saw that it was late enough to enter, to wait for the moment.

Resolutely, as she was feeling faint, her mouth distended by a funny urge to yawn aloud, not having had dinner, she asked for a *menthe.* Behind her, in the embrasure of a multicolored skylight linking two columns of faux marble, a bench seat happened to be unoccupied. This half-dark, half-lit seat appealed to her, and perhaps the shimmer of the stained glass attracted her. She huddled, trembling, fearing another refusal, her eyes fierce. With an indifferent gesture, the waiter pushed aside a table, poured the *menthe* and left. More reassured now, Laure stirred her spoon in the green liquid, spying curiously on "her fellows." At this hour they were few, some brought by their lovers from an act at the *Nouveautés,* others waiting for an acquaintance, spyglass and fan in hand.[2] The boys served the ladies with debonair faces, looking as if they did not believe in bad behavior at all. One sumptuously dressed girl, thinking that she recognized a friend, threw herself at Laure, calling her "my dear," then apologetically murmured a very gracious, "Pardon, madame."

So she was a special kind of girl, called madame with that gesture of astonishment, and even in this café, where naughty creatures came, they did not sanction her presence with equivocal glances; would she, my God, have trouble selling herself, the giver of love, lost among the sellers of flesh?

---

2. The name Théâtre des Nouveautés ("Theater of the New") has been used by several Parisian theater companies, beginning in 1827.

She stayed there for several hours, sipping her *menthe*, her heart pounding, not daring to wave or start a conversation, terrified that once she had finished her drink, she would have to consume something else, finally getting drunk on an empty stomach, as the slightest stimulant would set her on fire! The men did not see her in her corner, and she did not risk a smile to catch their attention. For a moment, she even realized that her instincts of freedom were getting the better of her, and that she was amused by following the eyes of a salesman handing out advertisements, because he looked better than the men sitting next to her . . .

At the end of her last hour of waiting, she asked for a second drink, the least exhilarating of all, a glass of sugar water. She was looking for a supreme way to be seen, was about to spread the flaps of her coat, the inside of which dazzled like an emblem, when a man, crossing the crowds and carrying papers, sat down next to her.

He seemed to know this corner well, and under the soft light of the stained glass window, he organized himself a sort of traveling desk, jostling the table where the young woman was placing her glass.

Darkly dressed, but not in mourning as he wore no crepe, he appeared soaked from head to toe in thick ink. Quite tall, with slightly hunched shoulders, well set at the waist, and long, slender legs, he was neither the fashionable man, nor the rich man, but someone eccentric, yet still a proper person. He had a searching gaze, a particular piercing gaze, not counting on nuance, but all depth, eyes that, not stopping on you, had already seen everything and seemed to come back to you from afar.

His mustache, a little bristly, reddish, very sappy from the smoke of oriental cigarettes that give it a citrine tint, turned up over his mouth, leaving it naked, shamelessly sensual, hollowed out at the corners with a smile that was half benevolent, half skeptical—the smile of a good resigned person who should not be teased without a reason.

His head, with its short, graying hair, lent gravity to the youthfulness of his thirty-year-old body; his brow widened at the temples, and his broad jaws intimidated. This man could, in a pinch, have come out of an ice cube; his cheeks shone with a pale varnish such as one finds along the cheeks of the dead at the morgue, but beneath this varnish the blood was rising, surging, plastering the thin skin with pink and yellow blotches, extravagating in rapid waves, boiling underneath like a lava boils under its layer of vitrified ashes. Nervous and strong, to be sure, a violent man who, in civilized life, holds his own against the onlookers of the street, the ridicules of the salons, or the injustices of the temples. Just by observing the way he occasionally kneaded his quill and the polished jerkiness of his gestures, one sensed that he was stirred by a perpetual feverishness and yet knew how to subdue himself, jealous of a fine reputation for courtesy.

The man unfurled a sheet of printed paper and scribbled small hieroglyphics on it, crossing out, rereading, one hand resting on his right ear and the other tormenting the pen with astonishing hesitation. This work must have been the counterpart of his character, sometimes restive, sometimes gnawing on his bit, a shady horse that needs a lot of grooming. One minute he laughed, inwardly cheered by a discovery, a truncated word or an illegible line, and showed his sharp teeth with two protruding canines on both sides of the upper jaw, two small fangs.

Laure twitched and drew her powder case adorned with a tiny mirror from her pocket, realizing that this slight defect of the teeth was common to both of them. She took back her glass, and the man, very annoyed with the neighborhood, called a waiter, asked for a grog, and pointed to another table.

"Monsieur is not back in his usual place," said the waiter obsequiously. "If monsieur would like to come in . . . ?"

"No, thank you, it is stuffy in there," he replied briefly.

He got up and picked up his papers, chewing on a discreet "good Lord."

Then she murmured, suddenly seized by a great melancholy, "I am going to leave, since I am in your way!"

She was too disgusted with them all; she was offering them beautiful, healthy merchandise, and they preferred rotten creatures, too bad! She would not put up any more of a fight; she would rather throw herself off a bridge! Upright and serious, her face calm, invaded by thoughts of suicide, she waited for him to step aside and let her go.

"But you are not in my way, child," he replied, stopping his shadow-searching eyes on her and sitting back down.

Something rang in Laure's chest. She sat down, beaming, believing herself saved without knowing why. He folded up his sheet of paper, tucked it solicitously into a pocket of his jacket, and stared for a moment, his eyes half-hidden beneath the blinking eyelid, examining the young woman without smiling, his lips bitten by his two protruding teeth, the physiognomy of the hesitant man who has sometimes been pinched at these nasty games of chance.

He began with a banal, almost traditional phrase: "Are you expecting someone?"

"No, I am not waiting for anyone," replied Laure, whose words struggled to emerge from her anguished throat.

"A beautiful evening. Do you like pure water?"

"Yes, monsieur."

Confused, she shook her little spoon and poured more water over very little sugar.

He said dazedly, "Would you not prefer my grog? You can pass me your carafe, for I am dying of thirst."

She murmured, "Thank you, monsieur," not knowing whether to accept to be polite.

"Champagne, then, or ice cream?"

"I . . . I . . . do not want . . ."

She felt excruciatingly intimidated, so bold in her whims, and a crimson flush spread across her cheeks. Looking under the table from time to time, she told herself that someone was probably going to press her knees, take her foot or tickle her ankle with the end of a cane, and she thought that from this man a silly provocation would destroy her.

"Let us see, madame," he said, crossing his leg and leaning in with a cordial smile. "Am I mistaken?"

Her hair, in a quick movement, fell from her shoulders onto the man's thigh, and he gasped.

"And you come here with your hair done, or rather undone like that?"

Laure endeavored to plait her braid and fasten it with the pin of her veil; in turn, the veil slipped. This docility cheered the man up.

"I understand! It is not your fault that it is so long! But we could go to a hairdresser."

Scoffing, she added, "In the Bois de Boulogne, for example!"[3]

---

3. The Bois de Boulogne was conceived by Napoleon III in 1852 and executed as part of Baron Georges-Eugène Haussmann's urban development plan. By 1867, the *Baedeker Guide* included it in its pages, and it became a model for later urban parks.

Not listening to her answer, he called a waiter, paid, and asked for a car.

When the car arrived, he stood up, stepped aside. "Hurry up, you are being watched!" he said briefly, striking her imperiously with short strokes of his cane. Murmurs followed this departure, or rather this abduction: other men regretted this splendid hair which did not belong to a regular.

A dandy, cinched into a gray jacket, came to shake hands with the happy mortal, saying, in a familiar yet respectful manner, "My compliments, you are a lucky man, my dear!"

Laure remained dumbfounded. They knew him, this man whom she did not know!

"Madame has lost her way, good evening!" the blissful man retorted harshly.

With a leap, he joined Laure, who, moved and teary-eyed, was putting her veil back on. As soon as the carriage had passed La Madeleine, running toward Le Buis, the man, who had remained silent, took her arm and gave it a gentle caress.

"Do not tell me anything. You are crying, I do not want to know why! We are going to breathe cleaner air, like good old friends, and then we will have supper, or not supper, depending on your state of mind. Act, my dear child, as if I were far away, behind that car."

"Oh! Monsieur!" she sobbed. "I cannot help it. I cannot help myself..."

"Hush!"

And they fell silent. Lulled by the gentle undulations of the carriage as it rolled noiselessly along the lanes, Laure gradually calmed down and gave herself over to the pleasure of breathing, still free in herself, convinced that she could get out of this adventure whenever she felt like it. Near the lake, a clearing in the sky allowed them to see each other, and Laure smiled at him, opened her mouth to speak, closed it again, finding nothing to say.

"You have given up telling me a true story that might be a lie. You are very pretty, madame, and you must have frightened a lot of people during your life. You have the eyes of an Egyptian!"

"I am not a madame!" sighed Laure softly.

"And you are not a *demoiselle*, either!"

He stopped, got out, and offered her his hand with a gesture so kind that the young woman felt absolute trust in him. She let go of his hand and they walked side by side.

"Do you not love, after pure water, tall trees and starry nights, the warm summer nights when you swoon when a breeze touches you!" he murmured, as if continuing a conversation long begun.

She replied, shaking, "Yes, monsieur."

"And in winter, you will love the soft, deep furs, where you can lie back and see nothing, say nothing, stifling lazy yawns."

"Yes! Yes . . ."

"And you would also love, in any season, those who would love you."

She exclaimed, "My God, you are a wizard!"

He laughed and wrapped his arm around her waist. "Where do you live, my child? I confess I do not know."

She trembled.

"My poor lost one," he continued after a long silence, "I will not bother you with this question again. You are as free as the air we breathe here, and I can even take you back to where I found you, if you are so inclined."

She shrieked and threw herself on his chest. "Never! Never . . . I never want to go back."

"Indeed, the picture is not tempting," he said, gently pushing her away. "Over there, the men are even more repulsive than the girls . . . But, let us see, my dear, supposing we both went back to town, we would have to arrange things; you frighten me with your hair—one can get scalped in Paris!"

Half fearful, half laughing, she replied, "I have always worn my hair on my shoulders. I have kept my little-girl hairstyle, because I do not know how to comb it any other way."

"You were a little girl a long time ago."

"You must know. Guess!" She threw out these words with simplicity, without any coquetry, convinced that he would know.

"You are twenty-three, a little older, and you are not from Paris, eh?"

She clapped her hands. "Correct . . . !"

They sat on a rock on the rise to the waterfall, and he drew her against him with a slow, possessive movement. He held her under his gaze, smoothing her braid, his fingers shivering. There, in the midst of the semidarkness of that warm night, whose moist wind caressed her cheek like a kiss, between the muffled sound of water gushing over the lake and the vague glow of stars piercing the mist, the mournful glow of sorrow, they measured each other with their eyes. Laure was suffocating. She pushed aside her coat, and the white salina of the lining appeared as livid as a shroud around the woman's dark silhouette, which not a jewel illuminated.

"You are poor!" he said, his tone sharp and to the point.

"Yes, I mean, no . . . I have a bed!" stammered Laure, lowering her eyelids.

"Have you eaten?"

"Not much for two days. But I could sell this coat. I was wrong to hesitate, monsieur."

"I am not accusing you . . . since you kept it to come and find me."

She was seized with a superstitious fright. She had the absurd idea that this stranger would kill her. It was said that men of sinister passions often entered the homes of girls in the hope of a bloody orgy. And she would no longer escape the fascination that he already exerted over her, for she felt ready to follow him anywhere.

"Have your lovers abandoned you?"

"Yes, the one whom I loved did not love me; the others, I gave them grief. They said that I was very mean."

"Naturally!"

Hypnotized, it seemed, by this strange man, she responded with a sound of the timid, submissive voices of sleepwalkers.

"If I wanted something, would you give it to me?"

"Oh, monsieur!" She clasped her hands together. "I would do anything to please you! The only thing is . . ." She stopped, ready to tell him: "Just do not ask me to prostitute myself now . . . that would be horrible!"

"Give me a kiss!"

And in this order there was a tenderness, a pity, as if he had tried to tempt a little child.

She moved away from him.

"I cannot," she said, frightened again, rebelling.

"Come now, that is fine!" he murmured quietly, without resentment.

They went back down the rocky stairs, looking for their carriage. When they got in, he said to her in an affectionate accent, though no longer on familiar terms, "Where would you like me to take you?"

"I want to eat, my head is spinning, you understand."

He gave the coachman an address, and she heard him name the Café Anglais. In front of the restaurant, he avoided the groups on the sidewalk, still pushing her with ill-concealed impatience.

She sighed, wasting neither time nor mouthfuls thanking him for his alms. She did not play the coquette, did not pass her powdered rice puff while looking at herself in the mirror, did not upset the fruit compotes, did not waste her pieces of bread, and refused to sit on the sofa. When she had finished, he, who had been studying her the whole time without speaking, took hold of her hand, contemplating it in his palm.

"You must be a rare lover," he declared, thinking aloud.

She blushed. "It is possible!"

He picked a flower from a basket and graciously helped her put her coat back on. On the threshold of the café, he hailed a car, but did not get in beside it. He handed her the flower, which he had just twisted with tissue paper.

"And you?" she shouted, seeing that he stayed back and now imagining that she would die if he separated from her.

"Me," he replied gravely, "I have saved you tonight, it's up to others to save you tomorrow!"

And he placed the flower, a red camellia wrapped in a banknote, on her lap.

"Oh! Come here!" she stammered, bending over in despair. "Do not leave me! I do not want your money, I want you . . ."

"You want to do this job to the bitter end," he scoffed, laughing coldly, "but the adventure itself is not enough for you?"

She repeated, madly, clinging to him, "I think I am afraid . . . Oh! I think I love you!"

And she dug her fingernails into his clothes to make sure to hold him. Then he joined her, with the gesture of a man who says to himself, "After all, I would be a fool . . ."

At home, as she climbed the stairs, she was dazzled and staggered, thinking of that vixen, her concierge, who was watching for her last fall to come and show her the rent receipt. He stopped.

"Are you thinking?" he quipped. "By the way, let me give you a piece of advice, you should not live so high up when you must bring back nice gentlemen. It is enough to discourage them and prevent them from being generous."

She placed her hand over his mouth. "You do not want to laugh any more than I do, monsieur. Be quiet!"

In her room, she turned on the lamp and called Lion after taking off her coat and mussing her hair. Remorse gripped her. She had eaten there without even saving a cake for him, a crumb of all those expensive sweets.

"You own a cat," he exclaimed, this time laughing harder. "You are ridiculous and too old-fashioned. One should have a Havanese or a griffon, madame."

One could tell that he was joking, in fact, to defend himself from emotion. She sat him down on the cushions, in the luxurious sparseness of this silk-upholstered room, where there was not a single armchair to be seen.

"Yes, I have not been feeding him enough lately, and he has run away. I loved him like a son, and to think that he is unfaithful gives me great grief. Mock if you like . . . When you live in complete solitude, you get strange ideas . . . I loved him, because he was a little heart without a body, wandering around me. He left a bit sick . . . I hope that he did not die in the gutter!"

"What a creature!" murmured the man, touched by this mixture of cynicism and naivety.

Then, stiffening against his tenderness, still troubled by a skeptical thought, he tossed the banknote into a crystal cup on the mantelpiece.

She roared with anger at his action, jumped up, grabbed the paper, lit a candle, and set it alight in front of him. "You gave it to me, so I have the right to do what I want with it!"

"Come, my darling," he said, "do you intend to prostitute yourself for pleasure?"

"Well, yes! Just for fun! It will be the last time! The last time!" she repeated in exasperation. "And then I will kill myself, because I cannot live alone!"

He stared at her. "Are you not ashamed?"

"No, not anymore! Pleasure is my religion . . . !"

She bowed toward him, smiling through her tears, offering him a kiss.

No sooner had their lips touched than he carried her off to the big yellow bed, and from then on they never spoke another word, so closely united that they did not even think of asking each other their names.

18

At dawn, the man got up, dressed hastily and, in spite of himself, returned to contemplate this woman before fleeing from her. He could not pay her. He could not stay there if there was another lover, and he felt an irresistible tenderness for this madwoman. If he let her smile at him again, he would not want to abandon her. Oh, it was above all that sullen voice, the voice of a creature both proud and submissive, that captivated and disarmed him. No! He would not leave without waking her up, telling her that she was beautiful and that he would never forget her!

Laure opened her eyes and, with a gesture of extraordinary modesty after such a night, pulled the sheets up over her bare breasts.

"Are you leaving?" she asked anxiously.

"Will you tell me your name?" he begged fiercely.

"What is the point? I am not asking for yours."

"Are you sad?"

"I know that it is over, and I am sure that I love you."

She leaned her head against the distraught heart of this man who was kissing her hands, and, in a delicious annihilation of her whole being, she murmured, "Would you not even want me for your servant?"

"Oh! Hush! Come on! We would be foolish to separate, since *we are meeting again*. Tell me, my darling, would you follow me to the devil if I wanted to take you with me? I am obliged to leave for an ugly burning country where your sisters, the lionesses, roar! Would you like to go to Africa with me?"

"In a desert, with you . . . ? With you . . . ! It would be too charming a dream, and I am no longer worthy of any love."

"You are free, absolutely free, are you not?"

"Yes, but you will regret it . . . ! We are very far apart, I can tell, and I am such an ill-bred girl."

She had smiled, she had spoken, then she had wept with joy, wrapping her pale arms around him, downy with a silky brown fuzz like a shadow of fur.

"I adore you!" he said, defeated, kneeling before the large courtesan bed, all gilded, all shimmering, and yet so poor in its elegance—that of a princess of the streets.

"Thank you!" replied an intoxicated Laure. "I must not die . . . No, no! I do not want to die . . ."

She put on a peignoir, making herself chaste, no longer wanting to show him her body where he had, that night, infused new life. She ran to get the two keys to her apartment.

"Behold!" she said simply, "I give you my complete freedom!" And she added, as if in spite of herself, "With my life, if you ever have need of it."

"I accept! I will come back later today to pick you up and make our departure arrangements. I want us to be on our way this evening, my darling, the air is too heavy in Paris . . . it is like breathing mud . . . ! When I deliver you, my beautiful madwoman, I will have to find you all ready, and I forbid you to take anything with you . . . you hear me? Leave these things with your memories at the bottom of the abyss. We are heading for a shining sky that will give you the halo of a pure lover. I am jealous, I warn you; do not explain the past to me, do not remind me that you were cold, hungry, and begging for pleasure. I know your story better than you do. We were supposed to love each other, were we not? I imagine I have known you since I was born."

Laure, her forehead on his shoulder, could not bring herself to see him leave. He lingered, sitting on the edge of the bed, pressing her in his arms, breathing in the scent of her hair and skin, covering her with feverish caresses.

"Why are you crying?" he asked abruptly, frowning.

"I do not know! I am not sure."

"Because of me?"

"No, my happiness! It comes from infamy, and one has not the right to be happy when one is vile. Last night you were offering me money; this morning you are offering me love . . . How do you expect me not to be terrified?"

"Oh!" he cried, clenching his fists. "Do not think! I am already thinking too much for you . . . ! You are simple, keep it simple! And may my complications of mind, my cerebral tortures never reach you. We love each other. Outside of that, there is no salvation. We have not wasted our hours of love on grotesque preambles and unhealthy hypocrisies, that is all, I take responsibility for your crime. The true woman, according to nature, is you, without the prejudices, without the detours of our modern societies, without the stupid fear of appearing as something other than the beautiful creature you are! You have suffered, so you are ripe for lasting passion! And besides, if I am wrong, if you betray me, I can always put a bullet in your head, as one would do to defend oneself from a beast turned cruel by caresses. But it is quite logical, my friend, to become mean under friction or injustice . . . Were those you deceived even worthy of you? As for me, I had given up hoping to meet a woman who was not either a doll stuffed with sound or a female stuffed with principles! I have finally found the beautiful, intelligent beast I consider to represent the desirable woman, and I do not care about the subtleties of our upbringings. I am taking you out of this world. They will regret it more than I! I do not think that it is given for a fool to measure up to a tiger. But a fool is a man, and a tiger an animal! If you have only known the naive or the stupid, my poor little tigress, it is not your fault. I absolve you."

Laure admired this new language, without quite grasping the reason for this sudden outburst of paradoxical anger; she wondered if, by chance, he might not be one of those deranged artists whom Henri Alban once spoke of with contempt!

She replied, kissing him, "You can knead me any way you like, my beloved! I am not vain, I feel I am inferior in everything, but if you want to love me as I will love you . . . I will still be the more learned of the two of us . . . !"

As she blossomed in exquisite generosity, she vowed, at that dawn of resurrection, to live only for this man, and she gave herself up, it seemed to him, for eternity.

"I will be waiting for you, counting the hours!" she sighed as he headed for the door. "Do not forget my keys!"

He turned, smiling, showing them to her in the air.

"Oh, the cunning one, who wants to make it impossible for me not to come back, as if I did not leave her something better to pawn!"

She smiled too, blowing him a kiss. "I will sleep, then, until you come back, and I will have no more doubts. Adieu! Adieu!"

"Au revoir!"

The key made a slight creak. He withdrew it, and Laure remained a prisoner.

She went back to bed, quivering with wild joy, and rolled around in the warm place that he had just left, transported with pleasure. At last she had him, her male, her master and her devotee . . . !

An amusing idea crossed her mind: *We still have not told each other our names!*

She laughed heartily.

But there would be plenty of time. They would start at the end, and they would work their way back down the sweet path of passion to pick, one by one, all of the flowers that they had disdained so quickly. In the midst of her frenzy, Laure could see a more delicate sentiment blossoming. She would be able to love chastely if necessary.

Secret worries gripped her, much like remorse. Like a fine corolla blossoming in a black ruin, her burnt heart bore the pale rose of the repentance of love, and, rotted a little by lust, her imagination created phantoms and humbled her with pious acts of contrition. Her state of mind would have aroused the envy of an honest woman. She wished to atone for things, to confess all of her sins, to obtain, after the details and circumstances that had been explained, the balm of sincere forgiveness; for she was so pretty, was she not, that she could trust the absolution of her lover . . . ?

She glanced from afar at the large mirror placed opposite the bed at the other end of the room and sent herself another smile; then, weary as she was, dreaming of the man for whom she was waiting, she fell asleep naked, arms crossed above her radiant head, drowned in the dark flow of her undone hair.

She was fast asleep when a frightening noise, the guttural cry of a beast, startled her awake. She trembled, and her insides were stirred by the wrenching cry, as by the death rattle of a child whose throat is slit. She guessed that Lion, her "son," had just come home, starving or wounded perhaps, and sat up with sweat on her brow and arms outstretched.

"Mimi!" she exclaimed. "My poor, forgotten Mimi! What can I do? Can I suggest to a man who is going to the land of real lions that he take a cat with him? He would laugh at me . . . And yet, to abandon Mimi . . . Oh! Never . . . !"

She searched the room with her gaze, shielding her eyes with her hand because of the sun now blazing through the windows, noticed him standing in the cushions, and was petrified: what she was seeing was strangely terrible.

Lion, unrecognizable, his fur soiled, his eyelids bloody, his muzzle drooling, so skinny that he seemed to have grown by the fantastic slenderness of his body, stared at her while chewing on nothing. He moved his fangs in a slow, mechanical swallowing motion, the tic of a mad animal devouring invisible prey, and his tail lashed its hollowed flanks in furious strokes, twisting with the violence of an irritated snake, a long black and yellow snake. His ears, folded back, gave his head a frightful expression of bestial lust, and his eyes seemed to burst from their sockets, sometimes ruby colored, shooting jets of fire, sometimes emerald colored, gleaming like the reflection of phosphorated water, so brilliant and treacherous, in their moiré-like undulation, that Laure, fascinated, remained motionless, bathed in perspiration, instinctively afraid of losing sight of them.

"Mimi! My dear Mimi! Do you not recognize me? I do not dare recognize you either! What is the matter with you? Are you ill? Has someone hurt you? Were you chased, eh?"

Lion mewed a second time. He roared in a hoarse, strident voice, exhaled in a sort of convulsive sob, chewed again, revealing his teeth covered in drool, and Laure understood finally that something abnormal was happening. The cat was not hurt, he had not been beaten or chased, he was not crying out of hunger or love, he was crying with rabies!

The flesh of the young woman froze, she huddled at the bottom of the bed, pulling the covers to herself, not wanting to see him anymore, fleeing from those monster's eyes, that demonic gaze terrorizing her; she, a human being, like a poor little bird frozen with fear.

But no, it is not possible! she thought as soon as she could no longer see the hideous beast. *No! No! I will never believe it! Lion, my dear rabid Lion! Him, so gentle, so kind . . . who loves me so much! I am mistaken . . . It is dogs that become rabid! He is ill, that is all . . .*

With an abrupt gesture, she pushed back the sheets, wanting to look at him again; it was stupid to be afraid of an unfortunate mewing cat . . . The animal, with painful, jerky steps, circled the bed, prowling around, his fur bristling on his back like a mane. Just as Laure ventured out of the sheets, he regained all of his elasticity, leaped onto the chest of his mistress, and before she could think of saving herself, he leaped at her, digging his four paws armed with powerful claws into her breasts, his fangs into her throat.

The bite was so swift and so painful that the young woman did not even have the presence of mind to try to grab him by the scruff of the neck, she could only grab hold of his long, whipping tail, and Lion, made more furious, began to lacerate her cheeks, nose, mouth, with his claws and fangs, plowing into her shoulders, arms, tearing off shreds of yellow satin when he could no longer find shreds of flesh. The cat and the woman rolled on the carpet, tumbling off the ravaged bed, howling, yelping, struggling, as if both possessed by a supreme rage of despair.

Instead of fleeing at once, even if it meant carrying him embedded in her own wounds, Laure, distraught, wanted to soften him, begging him, imploring him with tears; then, exasperated by the stinging pain of the horrible wounds he was inflicting on her, she tried to remove him by pulling frantically on the snake that wrapped itself around her naked limbs, biting him in turn, digging her fingers into his hollow flanks, turning on him to crush him, trying to break his loins under the weight of her loins, and still the cat held her between his steel claws, from which spurted thin streams of blood.

For a moment, her brow raised in the direction of the roofs, toward the skylight, she uttered sharp cries of "help"; and then she remembered that she was locked in, a prisoner of this unknown man who would return too late, perhaps never to return . . . ! The cat stifled her cries by devouring her wide-open mouth; it irritated him to hear her complain; he split her lower lip, pierced the charming dimple of her chin even more, spat his poisonous drool with a fetid musk odor on her white teeth, her pink gums, her crimson tongue. Like a ball bristling with stingers, the beast struck everywhere at once, just by spinning around. After her lips, it was her left breast, of which he removed one end, the flower in bud, it was her belly, which he covered with grooves capriciously entangled like a pattern of garnet embroidery in a milky shade of satin; he tore off one of her eyelids, and almost at the same second slashed her thigh with a formidable claw stroke.

She dragged herself among the cushions, often on all fours herself, carrying him on her rump in the pose of a defeated beast, overpowered by its stronger foe, devoured alive, writhing under new attacks, and straightening up to fight, raising her clenched hands with fierce energy, shaking the cat stuck to her wounds, splattering the carpets, the windows, the big golden bed, with red stains. Then, seized with bleak despair, she fell back with her hands clasped, offering her body of an unfortunate girl, naked as an offering to be consumed by this burning fury.

Lion really seemed to be out for revenge. He went after everything that was beautiful, graceful, sweet. He wanted to gouge out her eyes, those Egyptian eyes, those tear-filled eyes, already darkened by a thought of death; he wanted to eat her mouth, still so fresh from the appalling rictus that he had imposed on her; he wanted to kill the grace of that round, firm bosom, to kill her breasts that pointed their exquisite Bengal rosebuds toward him; and he seemed to regard all of these marvels of womanhood as other beasts whose lustful rages had once cruelly offended him. He had to destroy everything, desecrate everything, mark everything with his seal, that is, with his claw and his poison-soaked teeth.

Dragging herself up, Laure made her way to where the mirror was; she had a vague idea that, if the cat gave her a single moment of respite, she could climb to the bottom of the ladder and escape through the roofs, but her strength was waning more and more; she now imagined that a garment of embers enveloped her, her veins inflamed, vertigo gripping her brain. The persistent idea that she would get rabies and die of it, if that cat did not manage to finish her off, was beginning to drive her truly mad. A strange delirium made her see oceans of green and ruby flames in which her bruised body swam as she received stab wounds; she saw eyes in a heap, eyes of carbuncles, and she rushed into the stream of precious stones, into all of those cat eyes that accumulated around her, dazzling against her crude nudity, casting jets of sparks at her.

The cats' eyes penetrated the back of her head, slid into her empty sockets; they settled into her skull as if it were their own; it was she who had phosphorescent eyes, and she could see with a blurred gaze, and objects gradually changed shape!

In the depths of her hallucination, a single *human* thought remained . . . She perceived a muffled voice moaning, "The name! The name! I will not know the name of the man . . . !"

But she no longer understood what her "thoughts" wanted to tell her! When she could raise her head, the animal had stepped back to bite her hair instead of her flesh, probably tempted by the soft undulations of that superb tail; she saw, in front of her, ready to pounce, a diabolical feline, an unknown, frightful monster . . . A beast, its muzzle gnawed to the teeth, its nose cut off, camel-like, showing off two blackish ovals, a beast without eyelids, its eyes the color of rubies, a beast with pendulous, split teats, with large, red, webbed paws, its spine flattened under a splendid fleece, a brown fur that the cat extended and ended in a yellow tail ringed with velvet.

Through her veil of blood, Laure had seen herself in the mirror.

She approached the ladder, and, climbing with incredible effort, crawling on her feet, stomach and hands, she reached the roof.

At the top of the ladder, uttering a quavering clamor, like a howled mewling complaint, she stopped herself, weeping for her lost beauty; and the woman metamorphosed into a beast, still crawling through the opening of the skylight, leaving bits of her slashed skin between the iron and the glass, but still carrying her ferocious male clutching the nape of her neck.

Together, the two rabid beasts rolled along the crystal roof; both suddenly standing upright in the azure, haloed by the spring sun and dripping with crimson, they wrestled one last time to the edge of the gutter, then with the same momentum leaped into the abyss.

As the body of the woman crashed to the pavement of the street, the man, with infinite precautions to wake her more gently, turned the key in the lock ...

THE END

Acknowledgments

The publication of this book was possible with the support of many. Foremost acknowledgment goes to decadence scholars Brendan Connell, Jane Desmarais, Brendan King, Melanie C. Hawthorne, Conner Moore, Claire Nettleton, and David Weir, who deserve kudos for their generosity with this project. San Francisco friends Marian Wallace and V. Vale of RE/Search Publications merit recognition for their enduring influence. In addition, it is impossible to express enough gratitude for copy editor Lore Alexander—who edited the translation—for their patience and expertise. Immense thanks to consultants Christine Vogt, Mark H. Wittow, Mark Warnick, and DeepL translation support. Warm tribute goes to friends Jane Ainbinder, Jean-Loup Baer, Ben Johns, Will Murray, Donna Polehn, and Amy Stafford for their interest. And finally, deep appreciation goes to Ross Cottrell.

This project was also created with a grant from 4Culture, the cultural funding agency for King County, Washington; with free services from Washington Lawyers for the Arts; and with the free programs of Hugo House, Seattle's non-profit literary arts center.

ABOUT THE AUTHOR

RACHILDE (1860–1953), born Marguerite Eymery, was a French novelist, journalist, and playwright who was a prominent figure of the decadent movement in France. In addition to *The Animal* (*L'animale*, 1893), she also wrote the succès de scandale entitled *Monsieur Vénus* (1884), which launched her career at twenty-four. She was a creative advisor and book reviewer at the *Mercure de France*, and a *salonnière* of a weekly literary salon that ran for more than fifty years.

LAUREN FISCHER is an American editor and translator from the French.

ABOUT THE TYPE

THE PRINCIPAL TEXT of this Rachilde & Co. edition was set in Chronicle Text, a typeface that was designed by Jonathan Hoefler in 2002. Chronicle is an update to the "scotch" genre of typefaces—which emerged at the end of the eighteenth century and remains one of typography's most enduring and serviceable styles of letter.